S.B. ALEXANDER

COPYRIGHT

This is a work of fiction. Names, characters, places and incidents either are the product of the author's imagination or are used fictitiously, and any resemblance to locales, events, business establishments, or actual persons-living or dead is entirely coincidental.

Cover designed by Hang Le
Cover copyright © 2023 by S.B. Alexander
Visit: https://sbalexander.com

First Edition: April 2023
The Prophecy
Book Six: Vampire Navy SEAL – Sam and Layla Series

E-book ISBN — 13: 978-1-954888-39-5
Paperback Print ISBN — 13: 978-1-954888-40-1
Large Print ISBN — 13: 978-1-954888-41-8
Audiobook ISBN — 13: 978-1-954888-43-2

BOOKS IN THIS SERIES

Books in this series should be read in order for a better reading experience.

1. The Hunted
2. The Predator
3. The Union
4. The Dawning
5. The Prodigies
6. The Prophecy
7. The Rebirth

ALSO BY S.B. ALEXANDER

PARANORMAL ROMANCE

The Vampire Navy SEAL series: Jo & Webb

The Vampire Navy SEAL: Sam & Layla

NEW ADULT ROMANCE

The Maxwell Series

The Hart Series

Standalone Romances

SWEET ROMANCE

The Maxwell Family Saga Series

AUDIOBOOKS

Visit https://sbalexander.com/all-books/ to learn more about S.B. Alexander books and future releases. Please note release dates are subject to change based on reader demand and the author's schedule. Subscribing to the author's NEWSLETTER: http://sbalexander.com/newsletter or following her on Facebook is the best way to stay updated with planned new releases.

1

SAM

I pushed the door in at the sheriff's station and marched past Grace, the sheriff's administrative assistant, who watched me intently from behind the glass window that separated her from the lobby area.

Her pulse was beating fast, and her brown eyes were wide as fear crackled in the air. "Sam, you can't go back there without Stan's approval."

I was a man on a mission, and the sheriff could fight me, shoot me, or knock me out, but I was getting answers if I had to crush Norman Collier's skull, which I should've done last night when I found the vampire guardian in my children's nursery.

Eight hours had passed since whoever had been with Collier had taken Orion and Luna from my sister's house in coastal Maine, where I thought we would be safe. No fucking luck.

I wasn't sure what was up or down or if I was even breathing. My lungs burned like a motherfucker, and my black heart was ready to stop beating every time I thought about my kids in the hands of strangers.

My wife had been beside herself, crying, mumbling, and running around town with me, the deputies, Tripp, Sheriff Stan, Conrad, George, and the townsfolk. She was ready to murder someone too. Together, she and I could leave bodies like roadkill in our wake. As it stood, she was in the car on the phone, talking to her sister Jordyn, checking to make sure Ellie and Rorie were okay. We had an army of townsfolk at the house, including Tripp, Conrad, and George. So, I didn't see anyone getting through this time.

Layla and I had snuck off to confront Norman Collier and her deranged sister Rianne. Both of them were locked up behind three layers of protection—a metal door, a glass barricade, and steel bars. I was counting the minutes before the sheriff realized where I was. He knew I could do some damage, but even as powerful as I was, it would take a large amount of my energy to shatter a two-foot glass door. Like I gave a fuck. Nothing was about to stop me from getting answers from Collier. He hadn't cooperated with me last night, but I wasn't giving up.

We'd torn up every place in Dewsbury, Maine, including businesses, homes, backyards—every nook and hidey-hole there was in this town. Even Rebekah had shifted into wolf form and searched all the wooded areas nearby. Nothing. She couldn't even detect Orion's or Luna's scents. The kidnappers probably sped off in a vehicle or a boat. I couldn't wrap my head around the latter. I would've heard the engine since Layla and I had been on the beach with Rorie.

I tore the handle off the locked door that led from the lobby into the large space filled with desks, filing cabinets, Stan's office, and the entrance to the basement where the vampire cells were located.

Grace, a petite vampire, squealed. "Sam Mason, you know you can't get into the cellblock. Wait for the sheriff."

Like hell I was waiting for anyone.

Patience wasn't my strong suit, especially now that two of my quadruplets were gone. I itched to pull out every strand of my hair one by one. Guilt was riding me hard. I should've sensed danger—heard it, smelled it, even. I was a vampire, for fuck's sake.

But so were George, Conrad, and the three deputies, and they hadn't heard or seen a fucking thing. It was as if the kidnappers were invisible. Everyone was scratching their heads, replaying the moments leading up to when they'd been struck with tranquilizer darts seemingly at the same time. If they had been, it meant that there were at least five assholes hiding on top of the rocky embankment across from the house. The only odd thing that they remembered was a distinct odor of eucalyptus right before they went down.

Grace continued to call my name as I trudged into the empty room. If the deputies weren't at the house, they were interviewing residents and hunting for my kids. We just needed someone to give us a description of any strangers that they might've seen. The problem was that most residents had been asleep during the abduction.

I stomped around a table and a desk, my attention on the door that read "Personnel Only."

Collier would talk, or else I would kill the fucker. The only reason I hadn't last night was I'd thought that the sheriff or Tripp might be successful. But no such fucking luck. It was time for torture tactics, as in my elemental powers. In particular, my fire element, which was pulsing down my arms and heating up my palms.

Reading his mind would have been an option if my twin sister Jo and my old man were here. Even still, guardians lived on mind-blocking potions. Eventually the drug would wear off, but it would take months or weeks, and we didn't have that amount of time.

Heavy footsteps pounded on the floor behind me. "Sam Mason, don't you dare go down that basement without my permission," the sheriff warned in a tone that would be lethal to anyone other than me.

It didn't take long for Stan to realize Layla and I were missing from the house or to figure out where we'd run off to. Still, I dug deep for the restraint not to tear off Stan's head. He was trying to help, but he was also the law and followed the vampire government's orders to a T.

On an inhale, I spun around. "I have to talk to Collier again." Or rather, somehow force him to spill his guts.

According to Jordyn, she'd faintly heard a female voice in the nursery while on the edge of dropping into a deep sleep. But when she woke, she didn't see anyone but Collier. We needed to know who that woman was.

Stan, tall, lanky, and sporting fangs, marched past a table covered with stacks of papers and folders. "The asshole isn't talking. All of us tried, Sam."

I fisted my hands at my sides. "I have to give it one last shot."

The sheriff skirted past me and blocked the door leading into the cellblock, the gold badge pinned to his uniform glinting beneath the overhead lights. "The last thing I need is a dead vampire. The council would have my ass on a platter."

My face twisted in all directions, my nostrils flaring. "Fuck the council." My voice boomed, shaking items on desks. "Why are you worried about your ass? My babies are missing. They're newborns, for fuck's sake. They'll be a month old next week. *A month old*." I emphasized the last statement.

I seriously was ready to strangle the law enforcement vampire. This was one instance when laws and rules and asking nicely went out the window.

He crossed his arms over his chest. "I can't say I understand what you're going through because I don't have children. I'm helping in any way I can. But killing Collier will not further our efforts."

But it sure as fuck will make me feel better.

"Sam." The sheriff lost the tension in his voice. "Your tech guy, Sawyer, is looking into Collier's background. We'll find something there."

I shoved shaky fingers through my hair. "That might take forever, and that's time my kids don't have."

"Think about your ass for a second," the sheriff said. "If you kill him, you can kiss any freedom you have goodbye. That doesn't help your situation."

I paced in a small aisle between desks, hating that he was right. Up until two days ago, I had a so-called warrant out for my arrest. Or rather, the elders wanted to use me as a scapegoat—bring me in and show their human government counterparts they were willing to punish vampires. All because I'd accidentally shown my vampire side to a parking lot full of humans, and since then, my ugly mug had gone viral nationwide.

Thankfully, that warrant was put on hold while my father forced the council and heads of state to vote on whether or not to keep our existence a secret or launch a full-blown campaign that would announce our existence to the world. If the former was decided on, I would be hunted and brought in to face the council.

I came to an abrupt halt and threw up my hands. "Then what the fuck can we do?"

"Sam!" Layla shouted from the lobby. "I want to talk to my sister."

The sheriff tensed.

"You think *I'm* trouble?" My wife was a tornado about to wreak havoc if she didn't get her way. Then an idea hit me. "Let Layla question Collier."

My huntress rushed in. Her auburn hair was windblown, her face blotchy as if her blood pressure had soared to new heights, and she was gasping for breath.

She held her chest, gulped in air, and regarded me with fire in her blue eyes. To say she was pissed, upset, worried, and ready to pluck someone's heart out was an understatement. "We need to know where my grandmother is. I'm certain she's the leader. She's working with Norman. She has to be. It's too coincidental for Rianne to breeze into town at the same time as Norman."

I wrapped her in my arms, her cherry scent calming me for a brief second. "Baby doll, breathe for me, please."

She obeyed as a second of silence glued us together. Then she shrugged out of my hold and fixated on the sheriff. "I want to talk to my sister again."

The sheriff's dark eyes were shifting back and forth as he stared at her. "How about you question Collier? It seems Tripp, Sam, and I didn't have any luck. Maybe you will."

"Thank you, man," I said to him. I knew it would take more than talking to Collier. We needed to inflict pain on the asshole if we wanted answers. But maybe, just maybe, Layla could get him to open up with one tiny clue. "Baby doll, you might be able to pull something out of him. And I'll question Rianne. If she doesn't cooperate, then I'll compel her." Maybe the bitch would sing like a canary at that threat. "You know how much she hated when I put her into a coma-like state. But, Stan, that means I have to go into her cell."

The sheriff reared back. "No way. You'll kill her."

I scraped a hand over my unshaven jaw. "You know I have to be close to her to compel her. More importantly, Rianne feels the only way to fight me is to be like me. What if we give her the opportunity to confront me face-to-face? She can even take a shot at me if that gets her talking. If she doesn't, then I'll compel her. I promise that's all I'll do." As much as it pained me to keep my fists to myself and not tear off her head, I wanted answers more than anything.

Stan rubbed his temples, still blocking the door.

Layla chewed on a fingernail, her eyes brightening. "I like the idea of me talking to Norman and Sam questioning my sister. She hated when Sam compelled her. I'm sure she'll talk if we use that as a threat."

Stan bobbed his head, finally warming up to the idea. "Sam's technique could work, because I tried to compel her the normal way last night with no luck. But I'm not thrilled about Sam entering her cell. Still, she's not exactly a vampire governed by our laws." Now he was talking.

"Who cares about laws?" Layla fired back. "Our babies are

gone, Stan. Orion won't survive without Sam's blood. I'm—" She bent over, sucking in air as she held her stomach.

I grabbed her arms. "What is it?" I helped her into a desk chair.

"I don't know. I'm dizzy all of a sudden." She rubbed her legs. "I have this weird tingling sensation radiating in my thighs too. What's happening?"

"I'll get some water." Stan hurried off.

"Maybe you need blood." I felt her forehead. "You're warm. When was the last time you had anything to drink or eat?" We'd been so consumed for the last several hours that we hadn't had time to grab food, and at some point, I had to quench my bloodthirst or I might pass out. "Your face is red, baby doll." My guess—she was about to have a nervous breakdown. "Your heart rate is off the charts as well."

She blew out a breath. "My throat isn't burning, but I haven't had blood since two nights ago, which isn't unusual. I only have it when I feel that scratchiness that comes with bloodthirst."

A boulder dropped into the pit of my stomach as worry coursed through my veins. "You need to rest."

She narrowed her eyes. "Don't treat me like I'm fragile, vampire, or I'll twist off your balls. Our children's lives are at stake."

My anger rose even though I loved her stubborn and feisty side. Those attributes had drawn me to her. "Layla Mason, you won't be any help if you're laid up in the hospital like your uncle Jack. Remember, heart attacks run in the Aberdeen family."

The man had worked himself into a breakdown after he'd seen his son Noah, who'd been the first victim to take the serum. The sight of Noah's animallike features had sent Jack to our infirmary. Regardless, as of three weeks ago, Noah had been in our prison on the naval base in Massachusetts.

She shuddered as I helped her to a desk chair. "I know. I'm so out of my mind, Sam. What will happen when Orion doesn't get your blood? Plus, Ellie and Rorie aren't safe here. That woman with Norman in the nursery said they needed all four of our children.

Why? Is the answer related to my mom's message from the dead about the prophecy? Which I can't stop thinking about, and Kendra comes to mind."

Squatting down in front of her, I gripped her calves, growling for nothing more than to quiet the beast within as I felt every emotion bottled up inside her.

"My mom told me to find Kendra," she said.

"She probably wants Kendra to explain to you what she knows about your mom's family. After all, Kendra grew up with your mom."

We'd learned recently that Kendra knew Layla's mom, Meredith Drake, and Meredith's sister, Vanessa.

Layla sat forward. "Maybe, but there's more to my mom's message about one of our children being prophesied to change the course of humankind. I mean, after she told me that, I asked her which of our children she was talking about. Her immediate answer was to find Kendra."

I rubbed her legs. "We'll connect with Kendra, but right now, we need to focus on what's in front of us, which is you and your health."

If anything happened to Layla, I would be toast. I needed her more than she would ever know.

2

LAYLA

Insanity skirted the edges of my mental periphery. I felt like someone had ripped Orion and Luna from my womb. I swore I could feel them somehow. Maybe that was the reason I was suddenly feeling dizzy and ready to keel over. Maybe Orion was trying to tell me he needed blood.

Closing my eyes, I rubbed my chest, feeling as though my lungs were one size too small. "I'll call Kendra as soon as we're done here."

She and I had exchanged text messages not long before I gave birth. Her message indicated she was out of the country for a few weeks. Well, it had now been that long, so I prayed she was reachable. I was sure she was the key to learning more about the prophecy. Which prompted a burning question. Was my mom's prediction related to why Orion and Luna had been taken? If so, how? I couldn't wrap my foggy brain around that, but I believed my grandmother was involved somehow. Yet, the lines of what, who, and why blurred together. We had so many enemies that any one of them could be complicit.

Sam's fangs clicked into place before he bit his wrist, then extended his arm to me. "Drink."

The aroma of the sticky red stuff had me licking my lips. I wasted no time in suctioning them to Sam's wrist. As many times as I'd drunk from him, it was still weird that I, a human, was drinking blood. But the moment it slithered down my throat, I let out a moan as a tear leaked out.

He smoothed a hand over my hair. "We will find our babies. I swear, if anyone gets in our way, they're dead."

I cried as I continued to drink like a starving animal while the sounds in the room, including those from Sam's, faded.

Suddenly, I was standing in the middle of tall trees that climbed seemingly to the night sky. The full moon was large, luminescent, and had a red tint to it. I spun around and searched far and wide, my legs trembling and my breathing labored as if I'd run a fifty-yard dash. In a blink, I spotted a woman coming toward me, wearing black leggings and a white top that shimmered beneath the moonlight. But what had me edging away from her was her eyes—fiery orange, which reminded me of a blazing inferno. The faster I moved away, the more she began to disappear and the louder a husky voice resounded in my head.

"Layla. Layla." Sam's panicked tone drew me out of the vision.

I flew back in the chair, breathing heavily as sweat slid down my temples.

Fear swam in his green eyes. "Baby doll, you're white as a ghost. Did you have a vision?"

I brushed a shaky hand over the side of my head, nodding. "The last time I had one while drinking your blood was when I first met you." At the time, I thought I'd been hallucinating and that Sam had done something to me. Of course, that was well before I knew I had supernatural ancestors, including witches, and before I'd died and seen my mom, who admitted she'd had recurring dreams and visions herself.

The sheriff, concern etched in his dark eyes, stalked over and handed me a cup of water. "Here."

I downed the contents as if my mouth was parched from trekking through the Sahara Desert for days.

"What did you see?" Sam unfolded his body from the crouched position.

I set the empty paper cup on the desk. "Just a woman with white hair and orange eyes. I can't be sure if she's the same one from my recurring dream." I was slightly relieved the mystery woman wasn't Rianne or my grandmother, but that didn't mean they weren't on the list of suspects. "Maybe she's also the same person who was with Norman in the nursery." Now I was more than ready to talk to that creepy asshole.

Sam extended his hand to me. "Are you ready?"

The second I was on my feet, I swayed. "I'm okay," I was quick to say, knowing my husband would insist that I rest, and I couldn't right now. "I promise, once we're finished here, I'll eat something."

Sam hugged me, his body slightly trembling. We were both a mess. From his tense muscles to the sadness in his eyes, he was barely holding it together. He was doing better than I was, though—exuding confidence he didn't have. But I was glad he was masking some of his emotions because if Sam allowed himself to fully feel the impact of his son and daughter in the hands of an enemy, he would bring down the world. Then I would follow suit. One of us had to be sane enough to keep the other in check.

"Follow me." The sheriff headed toward the basement door. "Layla will question Norman first. Sam, I'll allow you to enter Rianne's cell, but if you kill her, I will lock you up. Your fate will be in the hands of our government. Agreed, Mason?"

As much as I didn't care about Rianne's life, I certainly was concerned about my husband's. I couldn't afford to have him behind bars. I was a strong individual, and I would like to think I could handle mostly anything that was thrown at me. But the supernatural world was a different animal despite my vampire-hunting expertise. Above that, our children needed their father, and I needed my husband.

"Yes, sir," Sam said as if he were talking to his superior.

"Good," the sheriff replied. "Now we need answers. I'm hoping we pull something out of both of them."

I liked the sheriff. He seemed to go above and beyond to help people in need. Much like my dad, who had always gone out of his way to do the same.

My stomach began to pitch and roll with every step I took. I was the same ball of nerves I'd been yesterday when I was about to talk to my sister, except today, I was in freak-out mode, which only enhanced that nauseous feeling. Though anger was displacing it as I thought about Norman standing in the nursery last night with his grubby hands on Ellie, about to kidnap her as well.

That's it, girl. Bring up that rage. Use it on him in some way. I wished I could enter his cell and chop off his dick. That might force him to talk.

"Your heart rate is high, Layla. Grab on to the railing, please," Sam ordered from behind me.

I did as he commanded only because I was feeling light-headed. Once we were grouped near the computer—the key to unlocking cell doors—I felt less shaky, but that was because my mind was scrambling on a questioning technique. I wasn't stupid enough to believe I would be successful with Norman. It was clear from those who had tried before me that the jerk-face wasn't opening his mouth. Nevertheless, I had to try.

The sheriff began tapping on keys.

Sam moved hair off my face. "Are you sure you're okay, baby doll? Any dizziness?"

I rose up on my toes and ghosted my lips over his. "I'm fine. The blood helped. Hey, Stan. What will happen to Norman?" Maybe I could make a deal with him.

Stan hit the last key, and the screen that was tacked to the wall above the desk turned on. "We send our vampire criminals to Boston. The Council of Eternal Affairs handles them there. Norman will be appointed a lawyer and go before the elders. Given the state of the council, Collier could be here longer than usual or at least until the vote is settled."

If the majority voted to keep vampires hidden, I worried that the elders would resume their efforts in making Sam a scapegoat. Take the beating heart out of the matter, then human chaos would die—at least, that was what the ancient elders believed.

I filed away vampire politics. "Does the same go for Rianne?"

"Given she's not a true vampire," the sheriff said, "I'm not sure. Dr. Vieira and the Boston medical group can petition to have her brought in for studying, which brings me to the two syringes Rianne had with her. Those will be sent directly to Dr. Vieira."

"Good," Sam said. "Maybe Doc can develop a preventive measure against the serum."

I gnawed on a fingernail. "Or a way to reverse the effects— change someone like Rianne back to human."

My emotional state with my nutso sister was up, down, and sideways. One minute, I wanted to save her. Next, I wanted to kill her. In the end, I would like to see her redeem herself. If Doc could reverse the effects, it would help more people than just Rianne.

Stan glanced at his watch. "I'm pressed for time. A lawyer is coming in today to post bail for Tim Cox."

I hadn't forgotten about the journalist. My plan was to pick his brain. How did he meet Rianne? Did he know anything about our grandmother?

Then something hit me, causing a smile to break free. "I think it's time we make a plea to the nation."

Sam reared back, and I couldn't tell if he agreed with me or not. Originally, I'd suggested the SEALs or the council should control the narrative with a show-and-tell. For example, we would use my cousin-in-law Carly or Noah as proof that Intech's prototype program—genetically engineering humans into supernatural soldiers—wouldn't work. Then, Sam thought the idea could backfire, including disrupting Steven's efforts to garner the majority vote.

This wasn't about anyone but our children, and I had one thing on my side—humans. A large group of them had been picketing, not only outside the naval base but around the country with signs that said Free Layla.

"Humans want to know that I'm okay, right?" I started. "We can let them know I'm alive and well, then plead with them to help us find Orion and Luna. We can even add a monetary reward."

I'd never wanted to publicize my life and family, but that choice had been taken from me when Rianne announced to the nation that I'd been compelled to fall in love with Sam and have his babies.

Sam held his chin between two fingers. "I don't know."

The sheriff swung his gaze to Sam. "It could work. When children go missing, parents engage the public for their help. Children have been found that way. And it's not like humans don't know you two, and they're aware of vampires now. The elders might shit their pants, but I would suggest that only Layla pleads to the public. That way, it keeps you out of the elders' spotlight."

"That, and humans think I'm an evil monster who eats kids for breakfast," Sam said. "So I wouldn't help our cause. But I would suggest we stick to you, your well-being, and our kids."

A relieved sigh escaped me, knowing I had Sam's support. "Is Tim leaving today?" I asked Stan. "We'll need to snag him before he does. Plus, he has his cameraman with him. He can tape the segment." I was talking like I'd been a reporter previously.

The sheriff waved a hand at the ominous-looking lighted cellblock. "We'll address that issue afterward. Collier's cell door is open, and the glass barricade is in place. Same protocol as when you spoke to your sister yesterday. Speaker is on the wall. I'll engage it when you're standing outside his cell, which is the second one on the right."

Sam gave me a good-luck kiss. "You got this, baby doll."

Determination and vengeance brewed as I stomped down the hall, blood rushing to my ears, chest tight, hands balled into fists, and my adrenaline biding time beneath it all.

The vampire guardian was lying on his cot, his dark gaze pinned to the doorway, when I settled outside the two-foot glass barricade.

"You think you can get answers out of me." He roared with laughter.

Destroy, kill, gouge his eyes out, cut off his pointy nose, yank off his balls, then shove them in his mouth. Visions of his death danced in my head.

Gritting my teeth, I cupped my hands in front of me as I swallowed down the thoughts of every way I could slaughter him. "We found the lady you were with." The lie spilled out easily.

He stomped over to the steel bars, piercing me with his soulless, dark eyes. "Bullshit."

I cocked an eyebrow as flutters of excitement swirled inside me at the idea that I might have hit a nerve. "We have her in our custody."

He considered me with a calculating glare.

"The vampire council will release her if you tell me where my babies are." I dug a nail into my palm simply to feel any sensation that would keep me grounded.

"You're lying."

"Okay, I'll give Steven Mason the thumbs-up to do as he pleases with her." I started to walk away on shaky legs, not sure if that was enough to scare him. After all, he knew Steven Mason was powerful and lethal. The Masons were ones to fear in the vampire community.

"Layla, wait," he said in an even tone.

I angled my head as I gave myself a mental high five.

He smirked. "You better protect your other two children."

Rage commingled with fear as I inched closer to the glass door, desperately wanting to reach through it and pluck his yellow fangs from his gums. "Why do you need four of them?" I knew he wouldn't tell me, but I had to ask.

He burned his gaze into me, but his lips didn't move.

That familiar tingling in my belly reared up out of nowhere as fury clawed my insides. I bowed my head slightly, snarling as I dug deep for my inner banshee to take over. This motherfucker had no idea who he was dealing with. I wasn't just a lowly human with no powers. Goddamn it, I was Layla fucking Mason. But as quickly as my banshee came to the surface, I pushed her down. Norman Collier was immortal, which meant he was immune. Not that I could kill a human by unleashing what Sam called my Hollywood scream. But for fuck's sake, I wanted to try, if only to ease the inferno of anger that was making me see double.

"Woman, you can keep firing questions at me, but I'm not talking."

I wasn't giving up. I needed something, anything, to point us in the right direction.

Think, Layla.

"Are you working for Roman Brown?" Tripp, Sam, Conrad, and I believed either Intech was behind the kidnapping or my grandmother was, though she was included in Intech.

Cunning blood-cartel leader Roman Brown sold blood like crack to druggies, and now he was knee-deep in genetic engineering with Adam Emery. Not only would my children's blood be worth a lot of money but their DNA as well.

He grinned. "A lot of people work for Roman."

A silent scream blared in my head. The vampire was fucking with me. But I couldn't help thinking that Norman was on Roman's team. After all, Roman had broken out of the prison located in the council's administration building, which was where guardians like Norman worked. The SEALs said that Roman had to have inside help.

Ding, ding, ding. It had to be this asshole.

"Again, you're wasting your time. I don't care if you kill me. I played my role." He returned to his cot.

I pressed my hands on the glass barricade. "Mark my words. Your time on this earth is short. I will find my children, and when I do, anyone who had a hand in taking them will answer to me."

He let out a condescending laugh. "You'll never find them."

I itched to sever his carotid artery, but since I couldn't, I rolled back my shoulders and stomped toward Sam and the sheriff. I imagined both had heard everything with their vampire hearing.

Sam met me halfway, his rage evident as the vein in his forehead was about to pop. His face was red, his fangs out and hands fisted. "I will murder the fucker."

My brain was buzzing with ways to do just that. "You're powerful, but you can't break down that glass barrier."

"Pfft. Want to see me try?"

"Mason," the sheriff said, raising his voice. "Stick to the plan."

Sam blew past me, glaring into Norman's cell before he continued down the hall.

I prayed our plan with Rianne would work.

3

SAM

I was so fucking enraged I couldn't see straight as I waited for Stan to open Rianne's cell. Every word out of Collier's mouth had boiled my blood. I wanted to pound the fucker's head into the wall over and over again until he told us where our kids were.

My son would need my blood, and I knew exactly what happened when a vampire was blood deprived—fire coursing through the body, a burn in the throat like no other, the shakes, sweating, and a headache that felt like someone was smashing a hammer into my head. I didn't know if Orion would feel the same way, but he had to suffer in some way from bloodthirst.

I opened and closed my fists, still waiting for the first of the three barricades to open. Layla had joined Stan, and I could hear their conversation as clearly as if they were standing next to me.

"Do you think he'll kill her?" Stan asked, sounding worried.

As long as I'd known Stan, I had yet to see him in freak-out mode. He did his job and followed vampire law. The council had systems in place for sheriffs and police chiefs when it came to prisoners. But Rianne wasn't under council rule. There was no protocol for monsters like her who were made in a lab. Collier, on the other hand, could pose a problem for Stan if anything happened to him while in Stan's custody.

"Stan," I shouted in the brightly lit hall. "Open it, for fuck's sake." I was about to blow my top if we kept stalling or coming up against roadblocks.

"The most Sam will do," Layla said, her tone soft and sweet, "is punch my sister a few times. He promised he wouldn't kill her, and he won't. Stan, we need this. I believe she'll talk to Sam if he's in her cell. You'll have the whole exchange on camera to cover your ass, right?"

My huntress was barely keeping her emotions in check. Her heart was racing like a greyhound around a track.

The sheriff didn't respond with words but with action as the metal door glided open ever so fucking slowly.

I tied my hair back in a low ponytail with a leather strap I had around my wrist, preparing to spar with the bitch. A flurry of excited rage and hatred stirred in the pit of my stomach. I was beginning to realize that I might not be able to keep my promise to Stan. I was itching like a deprived drug addict to butcher anyone who didn't cooperate.

Man, take it down a notch. You want answers. Instead of using your fists, use your wits. Fuck with her head. Psychological warfare can be just as satisfying as seeing your enemy take her last breath.

I silently swore like the sailor I was. Rianne deserved to suffer. Besides, death was too easy for her.

Once the metal door was open, that voice spewing bullshit in my brain vanished when Rianne came into view.

The bitch was doing a headstand yoga pose with her body against the wall as if she didn't have a care in the world.

My ire simmered as the glass barrier opened.

"Look what the cat dragged in," Rianne said, sounding bored.

I expected her to be on her feet and in a fighting stance once she saw me, but she didn't move until the steel bars began to lift. Then she was upright, adjusting her sports bra and the waistband of her black leggings.

The air sizzled and crackled with heated tension and anticipation as I entered.

Glaring, her brown eyes flashed to red, her canines elongating. As a human, she'd been pretty. Long brown hair, big brown eyes, and a nice smile, although her rough and bitchy attitude got in the way of that beauty. Still, a genetically engineered Rianne Aberdeen with a buzz cut was hard to swallow.

Gradually, her cheekbones began to jut out, her forehead followed suit, and long, sharp nails curled from her fingertips. But she didn't have any hair growing on her face or arms like her cousin Noah had—or at least, not yet.

She grinned. "Are you here to fight me, dickwad? Because I'm so ready to show you that I can match you in skill."

Scratching my jaw, I choked out a laugh. "You'll never reach that level."

The suffocating stench of death hung in the air. I swore I could smell her organs dying.

The clicking sound of the steel bars closing seemed to ratchet up her heart rate as she licked her lips. "You're such a fucking asshole. You think you can beat anyone in a fight. Your ego is so inflated that I can't wait to squash it down."

My derisive laugh bounced off the walls as I crossed my arms over my chest. "You think your new costume scares me?"

She stuck out her chin, snarling and showing dingy yellow fangs. "Let's find out who can win this fight."

I could have her by the throat and be snapping her neck in three strides or less. But my wife would be disappointed if I didn't get answers first.

"Cat got your disgusting tongue?" she asked.

I continued to study every detail about her. Her transformation was odd and fucked-up—a monster head on what would remain a human body sans the claws. Yet she called *me* disgusting. How was it that she didn't see herself as an ugly beast? She looked like she had a Halloween mask on.

"You realize you will eventually become feral like your cousin Noah," I said. "Although I think your organs are dying as we speak." I wasn't bullshitting her on either count.

There was a pungent, almost-acetone odor in the room. Sadly, I knew what death smelled like. During our war with Edmund, we'd found hundreds of decomposing bodies with barely there heartbeats in the caverns in Alaska where Edmund had dumped them.

She lost her fighting stance, lowering her shoulders as if I had zapped her excitement. "Is Noah dead?" Genuine concern dripped from her tone.

To tell a lie or not? "What do you think? Most humans can't handle the serum."

Only two out of the hundreds my uncle had experimented on had lived: my friend Ben Jackson and Matthew Costner. Ben had no supernatural DNA—that we knew of, anyway. And Matthew came from a line of vampires, but he didn't carry the recessive gene. To Rianne's credit, she had supernatural blood in her lineage, so she could very well survive this. But there was one big difference. My uncle Patrick hadn't mixed vampire and shifter DNA.

"I can." She lifted her chest and chin, taking on a defiant pose. "I have vampire markers in my DNA."

Suddenly, I was looking at a frightened little girl who desperately wanted attention, wanted to be bigger than anyone around her. The word pathetic came to mind but so did a sliver of pity.

As an empath, I could feel her hatred for me but also sadness, jealousy, and dejection. While Layla had tried endlessly to save her, I believed Rianne, in her own twisted way, was trying to save Layla.

"I get that you hate me," I said, "but genetically altering yourself to stand up to me, or to think that your transformation will help kill more vampires, or to show Layla that life is better from your viewpoint is psychotic." I had no other word than that.

She snorted. "What are you, my psychiatrist? You don't fucking know me."

"I don't have to," I replied in an even tone, which surprised me as much as the fact that I wasn't using my elemental powers or punching the bitch.

Silence dangled like a pendulum until she returned to her human form, her brown eyes wide.

"What's going on? The asshole vampire I know would be bashing my head into the wall, not standing there analyzing me and acting like he's my doctor."

"I just want to have a conversation." My tone remained even.

A spark ignited in her brown eyes. "I see. Layla failed yesterday when trying to find out where our grandmother is. Unless you're here to convince me to join your military or some shit. That's it. Isn't it?"

A condescending laugh barreled out of me. "No way in hell would you ever join my military. Or any military."

I remembered that during their cellblock conversation yesterday, when I'd been listening and watching the drama unfold from a monitor upstairs. Layla mentioned that Rianne had once wanted to join the military.

She morphed into monster mode with a glint in her red eyes. "Afraid I might show you up?"

I sneered. "You wouldn't last a second in the military. You're pathetic."

"There's the asshole I wanted to see."

Before I could blink, she charged me and tackled me to the floor. Her fists connected with my jaw, then my nose as she whaled on me over and over again. "I hate you, motherfucker. I hate you so fucking much." Saliva dripped from one of her thick canines.

I could've stopped her but decided not to. One, if taking out her anger on me got her talking, then that was a win. And two, I was curious what type of powers, if any, she had other than strength.

I laughed, which only incited her rage.

She scratched her talons down my face before she dug them into my throat. "I should rip out your artery right now."

"Do it," I said in a casual tone, my fury biding its time.

She glowered. "Fight me, asshole."

I didn't move, though I wanted to slice and dice her to pieces.

She sank her claws farther into me. "I said fight me."

I still didn't react. But when she roared and lowered her head, her fangs on a collision course with my nose, I threw her off me.

She sailed across the room, taking skin from my neck with her as she landed on the cot.

I was upright in a flash, blood gushing out of me before slowing and eventually stopping when the wound closed. Best thing about being a vampire.

"For once in your life, Rianne, stop acting like a child and a bully. Layla chose her path, and you chose yours. It's time you move the fuck on. Do I want to kill you? You bet. But that isn't about to happen today."

She scurried to stand. "Then get the fuck out. I have nothing to say to you unless you fight me."

"Where's Harriet?" I asked.

She lost her monster mask. "I said fuck off. I am not telling you shit."

"Suit yourself. This was your only shot to take a swing at me."

I was about to threaten to compel her when footsteps pounded in the hall, growing louder as our guest approached.

Rianne whipped her head toward the doorway.

I didn't need to look. Layla's cherry scent mixed with her sweet-smelling sweat wafted through the steel bars. It was a welcome relief to the stench in the room.

My wife was fuming, her scowl lethal. "Rianne Aberdeen, tell us where Granny is right now or I'll have Sam kill you this instant." She planted her hands on her curvy hips.

Oh, how I loved my beautiful, sexy huntress.

Rianne spat. "He won't do anything. He said so himself."

"Then I will!" Layla shouted as the building shook. "Tell us right this instant." Her rabid tone was deadly, and I swore the floor beneath me rumbled.

Odd. I wasn't using my elemental powers to make the building move. But that phenomenon vanished when I heard Layla's pulse beating scarily high.

"Layla, leave us," I said in an even but commanding tone.

Layla seethed. "No. My sister will talk."

"I didn't tell you shit yesterday," Rianne said. "What makes you think I will today?"

Layla let out an evil laugh, wrapping her fingers around the bars as she swung her blue eyes my way.

Fear oozed from Rianne. "You two are up to something."

Thank fuck we were starting to see the bitch panic.

"Either tell us where Harriet is or I'll put you in a coma-like state. I know how you enjoyed that the last time." I belted out an excited laugh.

As if a lightbulb came on, her terror vanished. "Come to think of it, you can't. The sheriff tried to compel me, and he couldn't."

I gave her a cheeky grin. "You might be immune or smart enough to block normal compelling, but I don't compel like other vampires. Have you forgotten that?"

Like quicksilver, she shoved me.

I bounced off the wall but recovered quickly. Then I had her by the throat and was lifting her in the air, squeezing and squeezing as she tried to shed her human form but failed. "Either talk or I will compel you." I had her positioned so we were eye to eye. "Or I can erase your memories. Every single one of them from childhood until now."

I was digging the latter idea. She wouldn't remember vampires existed or anything else. Then we wouldn't have to deal with her anymore. Layla would feel much better that her sister was at least still breathing instead of buried six feet under. She might be all for taking Rianne out, but deep down, Layla didn't want to see her sister dead.

Terror drenched Rianne's clothes and radiated from her pores, the stench of her sweat permeating the air. She kicked and grabbed hold of my wrists in an attempt to pull my hands from her.

"Sam, let her speak," Layla said with a sigh, the exhalation lowering her pulse.

I tossed Rianne onto her bed the way I lobbed a basketball into the net.

She clutched her throat, choking as she adjusted herself into a sitting position.

I sneered. "So what will it be? Door number one, two, or three?"

Rianne glared at her sister. "Just kill me." She sounded defeated. "I'm not going through that compelling shit again."

Interesting turn. She would rather die than be compelled.

"So door number two is out," I mumbled.

"Fuck off, asshole." Rianne spat at me but missed.

"Sis, if you want today to be your last day on earth, we can make that happen," Layla said without any emotion. "Your egoistical, whacked-out decisions were always your downfall. Coming here to enact some idiotic scheme to change me in front of the nation was stupid. Also, your notion that we can be sisters again if I'm a monster like you is also insane. What happened to you? Don't answer that. All I know is you'll never be loved or have a family again."

Layla wasn't going for the jugular but the heart. Again, I loved my goddess to no end. We fit so well together, and my libido was enjoying her toughness too.

"I have Granny." Rianne frowned, looking like she'd lost her best friend. "She loves me."

"Then where is she?" Layla asked. "If she felt the same way about you, she would be here helping you."

Rianne's talons came out as she just sat there not responding to

Layla. But I could feel her hurt and sadness. Layla had definitely hit a nerve.

Still, I wanted out of this cell, and I was done dicking around.

I stepped toward Rianne. "If you won't cooperate, I'll compel you *and* erase your memories."

Rianne jerked her attention to me. "Fine. Our grandmother is at her cabin in Montana."

"Bullshit," Layla rushed out. "You want us to believe she doesn't have her nose up Adam Emery's ass, salivating for a cure for her blood cancer? In fact, you came here to kidnap my children for Granny and Intech. Didn't you?"

"I answered your question. I have nothing more to say." Rianne pressed her lips into a thin line.

"Answer me, goddamn it!" Layla screeched.

It wasn't her banshee scream, but my wife was on the edge of collapsing.

"We're done here." But I wasn't leaving this cell without doing the one thing Rianne hated.

Rianne darted around me, scared but screwed. "You're not compelling me."

My green eyes flashed to silver. "Oh, I am."

"Sam, wait," Layla said. "I have one last thing to say before you do anything."

Reluctantly, I held my ground.

4

LAYLA

My sister was maddening, driving me batshit crazy. The fact that she wouldn't confirm or deny that our grandmother and Intech sent her here told me I might be right. She came here for my children. Either that or she was here as a distraction so Intech could swoop in and take them.

I unhooked my fingers from the steel bars. "Granny sold that cabin two years ago before she left for Fiji. So you're lying."

Rianne pressed her back into the corner farthest away from Sam.

"She never sold it," Rianne said. "If you don't believe me, go there and find out."

"Did Granny take the serum like you?" I asked.

Rianne checked on Sam, who was watching her intently.

I knew Rianne hated Sam's compelling technique, but I was surprised she would rather die, which made me giddy inside. We finally had something to use to our advantage.

"Keep answering our questions, and I will consider sparing you," Sam said.

"I want you to promise you won't compel me," Rianne fired back.

"Sam," I pleaded. "We need answers."

He flashed his loving gaze my way. "Of course." Then he said to Rianne, "My promise will only go as far as I deem necessary."

Rianne slumped. "Granny didn't take the serum. She's holding out for a perfect batch."

Sam guffawed. "There's no such thing."

Rianne cocked an eyebrow. "No? Look at your friend Ben. Or Matthew, who, by the way, is helping greatly. Adam's new scientist is using Matthew's DNA, and it looks promising."

When will this crap ever end? I asked myself.

Never, my inner voice responded.

I massaged the kink in my neck. "Which one did you take? The one developed by Carly?"

She nodded. "I used one of the last three syringes. The other two I brought with me."

Sam slid closer to me as if he wanted to protect me in case Rianne could break through the steel bars. "Did you come here with the intent to kidnap our children?" he asked her.

"That would've been icing on the cake, but no," she said in an honest tone. "Although Roman and Adam think your spawns are the answers to their prayers. So does our grandmother. You know this, of course."

My stomach knotted, anger causing me to growl. "Are you saying they *took* our kids?"

Still hovering in the corner, her jaw dropped. "They're missing?" A slow grin emerged. She seemed to be enjoying this news.

"Careful," Sam bit out. "Deals can be broken."

I didn't trust Rianne, but her surprised reaction didn't seem fake.

"Are we done?" she asked. "I would like to be rid of both of you."

The feeling was mutual.

A muscle jumped in Sam's jaw. "There's something I don't quite understand. If Harriet is dying, why not take the chance on any batch of serum? She's dead either way."

"The people Carly experimented on who'd been dying from incurable diseases died instantly when they took the serum. Apparently, it sped up the disease's processes. My grandmother wants to live as long as she can, in hopes of a breakthrough," Rianne explained.

The Aberdeen clan was stubborn, so no big surprise that my grandmother wanted to hold out. Truth be told, I would, too, if I were in her shoes. Not that I would consider a gene-altering program.

"Unbelievable," Sam mumbled.

Rianne rolled her eyes. "Don't tell me, dickwad, that if Layla were dying, you wouldn't find a way to save her. All my grandmother wants is to live."

I gritted my teeth. "At the expense of my family. Look, we're not here to figure out how to fix Granny. How did you know where I was?"

Her nose wrinkled. "Really? You can't figure that out?"

"Cut the snarky comments." Sam's tone deepened. "Whether we know or not, I want to hear you say it. And think twice before you tell me to fuck off."

Her canines lowered.

Nausea climbed up my throat. Seeing my sister shed her human side wasn't natural.

"You have a mole." Her voice was strained. "If you want to know who it is, then ask Roman. But before I left Intech, I was walking past his office and overheard a conversation with a lady he had on speakerphone. I didn't recognize her voice, which was how I found out where you were. She also told him that you had four babies."

A lady? I thought the mole would've been Norman.

"Do you know Norman Collier?" I asked just to be sure.

Her forehead furrowed. "Never heard of him. But you were right about one thing. Granny is upset that I pissed off Adam. He severed ties with her. Also, I didn't come here to show Granny I'm worthy, like you accused me of yesterday. My intent was to make you see the light. Show the world that you need to fight fire with fire using lab-born creatures like myself to kill vampires." Her tone and expression indicated she was serious.

"How's that going for you?" Sam asked.

She threw him the finger. "Fuck off. I'm not talking to you."

That kink in my neck hurt. "Rianne, I do love you. You will always be my sister, and my heart breaks for you." I sighed. "But I'm tired of dealing with you. We will never agree on genetic engineering. I do hope you survive this change and that you truly are immortal. But this is the last time we'll see each other. If by chance, our paths do cross again, I hope you've come to your senses. If not, then I'll be ready to go up against you."

Rianne's future was dismal—a slow death in a vampire prison just like our cousin Noah. But I did hope that Dr. Vieira would study her. Maybe he could find a solution to either block the serum or reverse the process.

Red threaded through the brown in her eyes.

A chill skated down my spine. I couldn't get a read on her, and it wasn't like her not to respond. The last statement should've ignited her ego.

Sam twirled his finger at the camera overhead. "Stan, open up. Rianne, if I were you, I would make peace with your demons. You'll be lucky if you live another month."

Once Sam left the cell and the bars clicked back into place, I flinched. Not only at the sound but at the finality of my sister's life. Sam couldn't see the future, nor could he predict it, but he had that acute sense of smell. The body did give off a distinct odor when organs were in failure mode. However, I couldn't smell anything.

"I hope your spawns die." Her fear was gone now that Sam was on the other side of the bars. "And someone actually follows through with the contract that's on your head, bloodsucker."

Sam was breathing fire at her. "Who's behind the contract?"

My sister let out a bone-chilling laugh. "Sorry, I'm all out of answers."

"I should've compelled you, bitch," Sam spat.

I honestly had spaced on that million-dollar bounty on him. But Rianne and everything else faded when my phone rang. I plucked it from the pocket of my black jeans as I walked away.

Jordyn's name came across the screen. "Hey," I answered. "Anything wrong?" *Please say no.* "Are Ellie and Rorie okay?" *Please say yes.*

"You need to come home right now," Jordyn rushed out, sounding panicked. "Rorie hasn't stopped crying for an hour. I've fed her, held her, rocked her, and nothing is working. She's a bit warm to the touch. Plus, we need to leave. I have a bad feeling. I can't get that woman's voice out of my head and how she said they need all four babies." My poor sister was tired and frantic.

Sam marched alongside me as we headed into the computer area where Stan was tapping on the keyboard.

"Slow down, sis. I'm done here. I'll be home in a few. But has Rebekah checked Rorie?" I asked Jordyn, feeling helpless.

Sergeant Rebekah Whyte was a medic in the Army Special Forces, but she wasn't exactly an expert in newborn health. I wished Dr. Vieira was close by or Dr. Martin, the civilian doctor and friend of Doc's, who had delivered my babies. Other than the three of them, we couldn't risk or trust anyone else.

"She did, but she can't find anything medically wrong," Jordyn replied. "Rebekah says she feels Rorie's fear. She thinks Rorie is like this because you're not here."

"Maybe so. I'm hanging up now. See you in a few."

"Maybe Rorie needs your blood," Sam said. "She didn't stop crying when I gave her mine last night. Or Rebekah is right to think that Rorie senses something is terribly wrong, and her restlessness might be her way of telling us."

"But Doc said it's essential for a young vampire to feed on his father's blood." He hadn't gone into detail yet as to why.

Sam nodded. "That's true for humans who are born with the vampire gene and can't activate it until their teenage years, which doesn't apply to our children, since they're inhuman. My point is that they won't follow the norm."

It was worth a shot. "While I head home, can you talk to Tim Cox? Ask him if he'll interview me before he leaves. After I settle Rorie, I can come back."

Stan cleared his throat. "Tim's lawyer is here. I'll check with him first. He might have a legal reason why Tim might not be able to do anything until his news station approves." The sheriff left Sam and me standing at the bottom of the stairs.

If Tim couldn't interview me, then we would find another reporter in his place. I believed pleading with the public and offering a reward might help us. It was possible that someone between here and Boston had seen a woman with my babies.

Suddenly, my mind sharpened to a razor's edge. The mole.

"Rianne said Roman was talking to a lady. She has to be the one who was with Norman. Right?"

"Not necessarily," he said. "The mole and Collier's accomplice could be two different women. And I've been racking my brain. On our team, we have Petty Officer Olivia Brock. I trust her with my life. She would never put me or anyone in our SEAL family in jeopardy, including our children. There's Sawyer's sister, Harley. I can't see her working for Roman." His Adam's apple bobbed. "I would like to rule out Jordyn, but her track record is not good as of late, baby doll."

I snarled. "It's not her. She feels guilty as it is. What about Rebekah? I don't want to believe that, but her brother, Tucker, is missing and supposedly in the hands of Intech. She could've made a deal with Roman in exchange for help in kidnapping our babies." As I was talking, an icy chill blanketed me. "Not only that, she was on a run when Orion and Luna were taken. What if she had a hand in shooting the tranquilizer darts? Then, conveniently, she returned to the house barely minutes afterwards. She said she didn't see or hear anything. I find that hard to believe. She's a freaking wolf with sharp hearing." I turned to bolt up the stairs. I had to be sure it wasn't her. For fuck's sake. She was with Ellie and Rorie now. Jordyn had a bad feeling. Maybe Rebekah was the one making Jordyn nervous.

Sam caught my hand. "Wait, baby doll. Jordyn said she can't get that woman's voice out of her head. If it was Rebekah, then Jordyn would've said something by now."

I called my sister. I had to know.

Jordyn answered on the first ring. "What is it, Layla?"

"Where's Rebekah?" I asked as Sam watched me bite a nail.

"She's down on the beach with her cell phone to her ear. Why?"

"That lady who you heard in the nursery. Is it anyone familiar among us?"

"It's not Rebekah, if that's what you're asking. And I hadn't heard that woman's voice before last night."

"Thanks." After I hung up, I was ready to scream. My damn heart was having trouble slowing down.

Sam enveloped me into his protective arms, lifted me off the first step, and set me down. "Rebekah isn't Collier's accomplice."

"But she could be the mole, Sam, or have a hand in shooting the darts."

Sam tangled his fingers through my hair with one hand and tipped up my chin with the other. "I'm not discounting what you're saying. But Rebekah is a military soldier who lives by a set of rules that includes trust, honor, and integrity. I promise you, baby doll, she's not involved."

"Maybe as one military soldier to another, you see that, and your vampire senses probably get that vibe too. But I don't. Let's not forget that Jo, George, and Conrad felt Norman Collier was only doing his job as a guardian when he came to the house. But I didn't. I was right about him. We can't leave any stone unturned."

He pushed out a ragged breath. "Might as well confront her now." He curled errant strands of my oily hair behind my ear and touched my chest over my heart. "This is beating way too fast for my liking. Plus, you're pale again." A frown dented the space between his eyebrows. "Would you please do me a favor? When we get home, eat something." He pressed his forehead to mine. "I'm very worried about you. I can't lose you."

Quivering, I dipped my fingers just inside the waistband of his jeans. "You won't." Although I couldn't promise him that. "I will eat." I wasn't hungry, but I had to fuel up because I needed all the strength I could muster to search for our babies.

He kissed my eyes, cheeks, and then dragged his lips to my ear. "I love you, baby doll. So fucking much."

"I think we need some alone time, Sam. Maybe that will help both of us."

He nibbled on my earlobe. "Maybe when we get to the Catskills, we can play out that steamy dream we had together."

Even before Orion and Luna had been taken, Tripp and Sam had planned to pack up our kids and me and head to Dane Gray's compound. The alpha shifter agreed to take in our family along with Sam's niece, Abbey.

I let out a soft squeal. "It's a date."

He mashed his mouth to mine, pushing his tongue through my lips.

He tasted like heaven, sunshine, and happiness, and I wanted nothing more than to feel our naked bodies sliding together, to feel him on top of me, inside me, and to get lost in us. It seemed like it had been forever since we had that intimate connection.

But first, I had a she-wolf to interrogate.

5

SAM

After asking Stan to call me when he had a verdict on whether Tim Cox could interview Layla, she and I jumped into the SUV and sped to the house. She was anxious to talk to Rebekah, and I didn't want her to confront the shifter alone. I seriously believed that Rebekah was innocent and a solid addition to the team. Her Special Forces unit had been extremely helpful since joining the war with Intech. Regardless, I would kick myself in the ass if Layla was right about the she-wolf. That niggling doubt was a motherfucker, and Layla had brought up a good point about the possibility of Rebekah shooting the tranquilizer darts at George, Conrad, and the three deputies.

Seemingly lost in thought, Layla rested her arm on the open passenger window, her chin tilted up and her face angled toward the sun over the Atlantic.

"Why don't you let me speak with Rebekah while you take care of Rorie?"

She gave me one of her ball-squeezing smiles, although it was weak at best. "Absolutely not. We'll do it together." She propped her head against the back of the seat, closing her eyes.

35

I thought she would say that, but I had to try. I had to reduce her stress as much as possible.

I reached over the console and grabbed her clammy hand. "Stan says it could be a few hours before Tim has approval to interview you. So you have time to take a nap. I'll even lie down with you."

She giggled, a sound that had goose bumps popping up along my arms. "I would like that, with Ellie and Rorie between us."

"You need to laugh more, baby doll."

She squeezed my hand. "I will when our family is whole again."

I knew an excellent stress reliever. But sex was far from happening.

My muscles stiffened when we pulled into the driveway behind Tripp's vehicle. "Where is everyone?"

Before Layla and I left for the sheriff's station, the house had been surrounded with the townsfolk, Conrad, George, and Tripp. George's car was gone, as was Conrad's. I had Tripp's SUV, so he should be here. He'd better be. Someone had better be protecting my daughters.

"They must've taken off." She climbed out of the car. "But who's guarding Jordyn, Ellie, and Rorie?" Her auburn hair blew in the wind as she ran up onto the porch just as Tripp opened the front door.

"Oh, thank God you're here," Layla said. "Is Rebekah around? I don't see her car."

My lieutenant whisked a hand through his sandy-blond hair, looking haggard and spent. "Jordyn asked her to buy ice for the coolers you guys are taking with you to the Catskills. She'll return shortly."

Layla blew past him as Tripp stepped out and closed the door. "Before you say anything, I have George and Conrad taking care of a few things, and the deputies and the residents who joined the search are making another sweep of the town." He flicked a thumb at the house. "What's going on with Rebekah? Layla seems irritated with her."

Rubbing my burning throat, I lingered on the stone path at the bottom of the porch. My bloodthirst was beginning to make me see stars. "Rianne talked. Collier didn't. But our mole is a woman. Rianne overheard Roman's phone conversation. The woman told him where Layla was and how many children we had. From that, Layla surmised that Roman could've been talking to Rebekah, which leads my wife to think that the she-wolf might've made a deal with Roman in exchange for her brother, Tucker."

Tripp sat on the top step and adjusted the dagger on his leg. "No way. I don't buy that. Rebekah and her team have been loyal to us since she met Layla in the West Virginia mountains. The she-wolf doesn't strike me as someone to side with the enemy. She's Special Forces, man."

I raised a shoulder. "You're preaching to the choir. But we have to rule out every female in our circle."

"Agreed," he said. "Knowing it's a woman will help Sawyer narrow down the list faster. You don't think Jordyn could be the mole?"

I rested a foot on the bottom step. "I ran that by Layla. I doubt it. I put the fear of God into Jordyn after her fire-alarm-pulling incident."

The tree branches rustled as a hard wind blew, bringing with it a dose of salt air.

"Any word yet from Sawyer on the names of the guests from the Dewsbury Inn?" I asked.

"No. George is at the inn, shuffling through video," he said. "Conrad is with him but calling some of his contacts about those darts. Something will give." He sounded confident.

I briefly closed my eyes as another wave of bloodlust washed over me. I couldn't remember the last time I'd fed. Here I was, worried about Layla's well-being, and I might be passing out right along with her. But I shook it off for now. Besides, I'd gone days without feeding before.

"Your eyes are dull, Sam. When's the last time you had blood?" Tripp asked.

"Do you read minds now?" I knew that he didn't, but vampires could tell when another was starving. "I'll drink in a few. Any word from Webb? My dad? My sister?"

"I left Webb a voice message and followed up with an email, filling him in on the events up here. I don't have an update on how the vote is going either. As far as your sister, I didn't attempt to call her. Too much going on."

I certainly hadn't tried to reach Jo. But she would find out soon enough about Orion and Luna.

"We should just lay our cards on the table in front of the nation." I ground my back teeth together. "The longer we wait for our government to make a decision, the worse things will get between us and humans."

Tripp leaned his elbows on his knees. "I'm with you. But some of us don't think the way we do. It's not an easy decision for those vampires who've enjoyed a quiet life. How do they tell their human neighbors they're bloodsuckers? We're in a catch-22. Damned if we do and damned if we don't." He scraped a hand down his face. "Most humans will always see us as a threat. Not to mention, scientists and assholes like Adam will want to study us." He paused for a second. "Although now that our existence has been compromised, there's no going back. So we need to move ahead and deal with whatever comes our way. In doing so, we can only hope to reduce the fear, which will cut down on the chaos."

"If humans understand that we can't turn them, I think that would alleviate some fear. Not all, because they will always see us as hungry predators out for human blood."

He pressed his fingers into his temple. "Speaking of predators, what else did Rianne tell you?"

I proceeded to give him the important highlights regarding

Harriet's whereabouts, that Adam ditched her, and Rianne's barb about the contract on my head.

"Do you think Roman has initiated the hit on you? Or Harriet?"

"Could be anybody, man," I said. "But my guess is either one."

Right now, the bounty was the last thing I was worried about.

A strong wind whipped up errant leaves and dead flower petals.

Tripp toyed with the sheath on his leg. "Harriet is in Montana, huh?"

I shrugged. "Who the fuck knows? Rianne isn't exactly the bearer of truths. I mean, Harriet doesn't strike me as the type to crawl into the woods and die." I bit the inside of my cheek. "The only way to know is to confirm Rianne's story. Are you cool if *I* head to Montana? It's time we confront Harriet, bring her in, and rule her out once and for all."

"Doc informed me last night that Jack Aberdeen is out of the infirmary, and he left for Montana a couple of days ago. He's worried about his family. We can have him check on his mother."

"If my children weren't involved, I would say yes. But I can't rely on Jack. I also can't sit around. I have to keep moving. I don't plan on leaving until Ellie and Rorie are safe at Dane's compound. Maybe by then, we'll have stronger leads."

"I would go with you if I didn't have other fires to put out," he said. "We also don't have any field personnel to spare, except maybe Conrad."

I inhaled the salt air, which had a way of quieting my nerves. "Conrad is perfect." Layla was going with me, but I would feel better if I had a SEAL brother or scout with us.

He scrubbed a hand over his jaw and released a heavy sigh.

"When this is all over," I said. "We need a big blowout."

"I'm all for it, but it depends on what you mean by *this*. With all the shit piling up higher than Mount Everest, it will be years before we can breathe."

"I meant when we find Orion and Luna." I knew the war with Intech, humans, and other crap wasn't going away anytime soon.

His phone dinged, and he removed it from the side pocket of his cargo pants. "I'm ready to throw this cell in the ocean."

I was about to go inside to give him some privacy to read his text message, but he held up his hand. "Listen to this. The fucking Feds didn't find Adam or Roman at Intech. All they found during the search and seizure were dead bodies."

Motherfucker. "Did someone tip them off?"

He shrugged. "Seems that way. The master chief for Viking II confirmed that the missing DOD officials were among the dead." He lifted his bronze gaze. "What a fucking shitshow."

"So Adam moves his operation from Chicago to West Virginia, then back to Chicago, and now he's cleared out?" I asked. "That doesn't make sense to me. People were lined up outside of Intech, hoping to get that hundred-thousand-dollar signing bonus to be experimented on. This sounds like Edmund. Remember, he kept moving from one location to another."

"It says here that the human government is up in arms. Apparently, there's a divide going on in their chain of command. The master chief overheard that some high-level human officials are demanding their military eradicate all vampires." He growled so loud that I swore the birds flew from the trees. "This was our shot to stop Adam and Roman."

"What about Matthew? Has he sent any more coded messages to Wyman like he did the other day?"

Matthew Costner, Alia's son, was an enigma. He'd been kidnapped by Roman, and he'd made his debut TV appearance at Adam's news conference, spilling his guts to the world about vampires and even going as far as showing the world his fangs. However, several days ago, Tripp learned that Matthew had sent two messages three days apart to a secure server on his grandfather's estate. How he had done that was a mystery, since he was supposedly a prisoner. Still, he'd indicated that he was fine, but the experiments were failing.

"I'll have to check," Tripp said.

"Rianne told us that Adam has a new scientist who is using Matthew's DNA, which looks promising. But Matthew's message said otherwise. I don't know if I trust Matthew. Anyway, my thought is that this new scientist could have his own lab somewhere."

"Mmm," Tripp said.

"I want to help." I truly did. "But with Orion and Luna missing—"

He waved me off. "Stop. Your family comes first. You worry about them and nothing else. This crap will be here when you're ready to return."

"I don't know what I would do without you. I owe you."

He always had my back. Others on my SEAL team did as well, but Tripp and I had been joined at the hip since he'd become my bodyguard when I first turned.

His bronze eyes met my green ones. "We're family, Sam. You know I would die for you."

I choked up. "Same, brother. I feel responsible for what's happening with the elders. I hate that I've put our entire community in jeopardy."

Lines dented his forehead. "What the fuck? Do not blame yourself. In the heat of certain moments, our emotions drive us, which makes it harder to control our vampire side. Do you think Webb would've done anything different if he were in your shoes and your sister was taken? I can tell you he's done the same thing."

"Yeah, but no one was taking pics or videos of him and blasting them on the Internet," I fired back.

He gave me a stern look. "Fuck the council. Your father will handle them. Things might get rocky for a while, but your dad always comes out on top."

The front door opened.

"Sam, get in here. You have to see this," Jordyn said excitedly.

Layla squealed.

Tripp and I exchanged a wide-eyed look before I rushed inside.

6

LAYLA

I was sitting in an oversized chair by the accordion glass doors with my jaw practically in my lap, watching the throw pillows on the couch float in the air.

Sam and Tripp ran in and stopped abruptly behind the couch, their eyebrows disappearing into their hairlines.

Sam pointed at the floating pillows. "Who's doing that? Rorie?"

Ellie was asleep by the fireplace in her baby rocker. She could very well be the little witch. But my guess was Rorie, since she was awake and sucking on my finger.

"It seems we have a vampire witch," I said. "My blood did the trick. You were right, Sam."

Knowing I had inhuman children was one thing, but to witness Rorie's talent was mind-blowing and awe-inspiring. I was accustomed to vampires, had recently met shifters, and learned that my Vel-negative blood indicated I came from a line of witches, which was how I'd gotten pregnant by a vampire, but I had yet to see magic in action other than Sam's elemental powers.

The men were still amazed as the pillows continued to float.

Jordyn sat down on a barstool. "Rebekah said she can feel their magic, and when the babies are together, their power is stronger."

"She's right," Tripp agreed, finally coming out of his trance. "I can attest to the magic I'm feeling right now."

Sam skirted the couch, strutting over to Ellie. "It's always been strong. The second I walked into the birthing suite right after they were born, I felt it. But I didn't think they would show their powers so early. Unless it's you doing this, baby doll." He flashed his swoony green eyes at me.

I lifted a shoulder. "I'm hoping I have some magical ability other than my banshee scream. But I don't think so."

He bent over and smoothed a gentle hand over Ellie's reddish-brown hair. As if that act was an off switch, the pillows dropped to the couch. Then he straightened. "How soon you forget the power we had in the birthing suite when you were holding Rorie."

I ogled my beautiful mahogany-eyed daughter as I pulled out my finger from her mouth and took a quick jaunt down memory lane. I'd been sitting in a rocker, holding Rorie.

Sam came over to me, crouched down, and grasped my hand. Instantly, a bolt of electricity zipped up my arm, and I wasn't talking goose bumps and flutters and gooeyness from holding my husband's hand. Rather, it was a feeling of magic and mayhem and a connection that could probably fry everything in this room to a crisp.

His eyebrows slashed down. "Did you feel that?"

Mine shot upward. "I know you're upset, vampire." His anger always brought out his elemental powers. Or was it Rorie giving off magic?

"I am, but our connection is more than that. Are you still feeling the energy?"

I nodded. "But it's you, not me. Or is it our daughter?" It felt like a million electrical pulses throbbed along my arm.

He studied our conjoined hands, then glanced at Rorie. "It's not me. My powers only go one way. You're the one zapping me. Or maybe it is Rorie feeding you power."

"I could understand if she was. After all, they had given me my banshee scream and mind-control abilities."

The memory was zapped from me when a sudden surge of electricity coursed through my body. I sucked in air, rounding my gaze on my husband standing over Rorie and me.

He had his hand in mine. "There's your answer. Rorie is feeding you power. It's strong too. Same thing happened in the birthing suite."

My eyebrows came together. "Will I be able to make pillows float on my own?"

Jordyn giggled. "If Mom and Dad were here, they would shit their pants."

"For sure," I mumbled as Sam released me, and the electrical charge fizzled. "I don't understand why I only feel it when you touch me," I said to Sam. "It's got to be your elemental powers. You're the one doing it."

Jordyn hopped off the stool. "Why don't we try? I don't have any magic." She passed Sam, who was heading into the kitchen.

As soon as Jordyn grabbed my hand, she screeched and jumped backward. "It's you and Rorie." She shook her wrists. "That hurt. It felt like I stuck my finger into an electrical socket."

Sam and Tripp were standing behind the island, drinking blood, not fazed at all.

Rorie squirmed in my arms. "If she's feeding me her magic, will that be the only way I'll have any powers?"

Tripp lowered his bottle of blood. "Strong emotions tend to reveal one's true magic. But Rorie might be unlocking your latent powers—if you have any, of course."

Hopefully, I did. After all, vampires and witches were steeped in my mom's family history.

"Layla did light up when Rorie sucked the blood off her finger," Jordyn said, resuming her seat. "It was like my sister had a halo around her, bright and sunny. Then the pillows began to float.

Seems to me that qualifies as a strong emotion. Look at your banshee scream. That surfaces when you're boiling mad."

She was making good points.

Sam got another bottle of blood out of the fridge. "Jordyn, maybe it's time you have your DNA tested."

"I was thinking about that very thing, Sam," she said.

My mouth parted. "You're ready now? You weren't interested in having any testing done when I recommended it to you months ago."

She shrugged like it was no big deal to her. "I've thought a lot about it, and it's best if I know. That way, I'm not blindsided like you were, especially if I sleep with a vampire."

Tripp froze while Sam almost spit out his drink.

I placed Rorie in her rocker next to Ellie's then yawned. I felt like I could use a hot shower and comfy bed. That nap that Sam had talked about seemed appropriate now.

I slid onto a stool next to Jordyn. "Do you plan on having sex with a vampire?"

"Okay," Tripp said. "That's my cue to leave." He scraped a hand over his day-old scruff, dumped his empty bottle in the trash, and went outside and onto the deck.

Jordyn and I laughed. I was dying to know which of Sam's friends or teammates she had in mind. We'd hardly had any sister time to catch up. The attention had been on me for so long that I was feeling like a terrible sister.

Sam finished off his second round of blood before dumping the empty bottle as a smile flirted with his lips. "I'll be with Tripp," he said, though he seemed as interested as I was about Jordyn's unabashed announcement.

That light and airy feeling in the room dissolved into tension when the front door opened and closed.

Sam darted in that direction.

"It's just me," Rebekah said, carrying bags of ice.

Anxiety wormed its way into my stomach as the pretty she-wolf of average height, toned body, multicolored hair, and sparkling, golden-yellow eyes shoved the bags into the freezer.

That tension was clogging the air.

"I feel an icy chill in here," Rebekah said. "What did I miss?"

No one said a word.

I was eager to confront Rebekah, but I was waffling back and forth. One part of me trusted her, and the other didn't. She'd gone out of her way for me when we first met at her family cabin in West Virginia. Sam made a good point about her military oath. Yet, she and I had shared the heartache of having a missing loved one. I needed to do everything I could for Orion and Luna, so I understood she had to do the same to find her brother.

"Seriously. What's going on? What happened at the station? Did you find a lead?" Rebekah asked.

"We need to talk," I said to her as Sam lingered near me.

The Special Forces soldier lifted her shoulders, ready to fight. "You don't have to say it, Layla. I was wondering when you would put me on the suspect list."

She was quite perceptive, but I wasn't surprised by that. Whether it was her military background or her supernatural abilities as a shifter or both, she could read situations and people quite well.

"Do you blame me?" I asked.

Rebekah regarded Sam. "Do you think I had a hand in your kids' abduction?"

"No, I don't, and Layla knows that. But my wife brings up some good points. Such as, you could've shot the tranquilizer darts."

I dug my elbows into the top of the island. "You believe Intech has Tucker. Did you make a deal with Roman?"

"Would you believe me if I said no?" Her golden-yellow eyes glowed amber, her wolf rising to the surface.

I shrugged. "Frankly, I don't know who or what to believe anymore."

She placed her hands behind her back and stuck out her chin as if she was addressing her superior office. "Then there's no need for me to say anything. I can tell you I was on a run all day long, but from the suspicious look in your eyes, you won't believe a word I say. I understand where you're coming from. So to save you the time, I'll take my leave. When you find Orion and Luna and uncover the culprits, then you can apologize to me."

I wasn't about to stop her or trust her until I had hard facts, so she was right—it was best that she left.

Sam, Jordyn, and I didn't speak.

"I need to talk to Tripp before I take off." She walked out with her head held high.

When she was out on the deck with Tripp, I released the air I'd been holding.

"I want to hear what she's saying," Sam said, then joined Tripp and Rebekah.

My stomach growled. "Well, that went better than I expected."

Jordyn climbed off the stool. "I'll make you something to eat."

Jordyn gathered all the ingredients to make a turkey sandwich. "Do you still believe she's guilty?"

"I still don't know. But I won't be comfortable with her here. Can we talk about anything other than moles and enemies? Tell me more about sleeping with a vampire. Who is he? Or who do you have in mind?"

She giggled, piling turkey on a slice of bread. "Would you laugh if I said I have a thing for Sawyer?"

One eyebrow went up, the other down. "For a second, I thought you were going to say Tripp."

She wagged a butter knife at me. "Who wouldn't want to sleep with him?" She briefly glanced at the closed accordion doors. "He hates me. But a one-night stand, sure. Long-term with him? No way. He's rough, tough, and possessive. That's your kind of man. Not mine."

The boys she'd dated in high school were more the studious type, so I could see her with Sawyer. Tripp, not so much.

"You just described Sam. Anyway, Sawyer is handsome, geeky,

likes computers and programming. He's right up your alley. I can see that. Does he know?"

She hadn't had time to strike up a relationship with the hot techie, although she'd worked on his team briefly, and I'd been so absorbed with my own problems I wouldn't have noticed.

She slid a plate with a sandwich and chips over to me. "He doesn't know. Harley says he doesn't date much."

"How can he? The vampire works 24-7."

Jordyn proceeded to make herself a sandwich. "Please don't share any of this with Sam or Tripp. I don't want them to think that the reason I'm so dedicated to working with them is because I want to sleep with a vampire."

I bit into a chip. "Sam might ask me. But of course I won't say anything."

"He and Tripp probably suspect I might be guilty like Rebekah, huh?"

I wouldn't lie to Jordyn. "They do. But I don't. You're not Rianne or Granny. You're not vindictive. You would never put anyone you love in harm's way."

"Well, I did with cousin Junior," she said sadly.

"That was an accident, Jordyn. I know you'll live with regret for a long time, but you understand what I'm saying. To be clear, if Tripp or Sam really felt you were guilty, you wouldn't be standing behind this island, no matter what I did to convince them otherwise."

"You have a point." She took a bite of her sandwich. "On another note. Something has been bothering me." She swallowed. "Everything last night happened so fast. But George, Conrad, and the three deputies mentioned smelling a strong fragrance of euca-lyptus that made them dizzy just before they passed out. Well, George mentioned he thought the odor was bitter. Anyway, remember Mom used to make scented oils, and eucalyptus was one? She used it in a diffuser to promote relaxation and sleep. Granny loved that oil."

I ate as she talked, remembering our mother and her creative projects. "Are you thinking Granny was here? She came into the house last night?"

"Possible," Jordyn said. "Granny, of course, wasn't the speaker I heard. That woman's voice had a mousy squeak. If I heard it again, I would know. My point about Granny is that Rianne is in town, and I believe her presence was a distraction. Granny has been pretty clear about wanting your kids' DNA or Sam's to cure her."

Nothing Jordyn had said was surprising, except I'd forgotten about our mom's eucalyptus oil.

"Rianne talked, but she's adamant that Granny went to her cabin in Montana," I said. "Though that doesn't mean she's not involved."

Sam, Tripp, and Rebekah were still talking. I was tempted to go out there but decided a nap was in order. We had a long day ahead of us. "I think I'm ready to lie down." I pushed my plate away. "Can you let Sam know I'll be in the bedroom?"

"Sure. Go, and I'll watch the girls."

"Jordyn, if I haven't told you lately, I love you, and thank you for all your help. Sam and I can't do this alone."

"Layla, I will do anything for you, and I will never break your trust." Tears pooled in her eyes.

"You know I will do the same for you."

I would protect her as fiercely as I would Sam and my children.

7

SAM

Thirty minutes later, I was lying on the bed with Layla, Ellie, and Rorie. Ellie was holding my finger, her bright blue eyes wide open, and Rorie was tucked close to her momma.

Layla yawned. "I didn't think we would have time to take a break." A tear leaked from the corner of her eye. "I feel empty inside, Sam. It's like there's a piece of me missing without Orion and Luna here. This might sound strange, but I think I can feel them. It's like they're alive and calling out to me."

I plucked my finger from Ellie, reached over the girls, and wiped away Layla's lone tear. "It's not odd. You carried them inside you. Plus, I'm certain that in some magical way, you're connected to them. We'll never know for sure, but when Orion was born and his vitals were dropping, then they improved, you followed suit as though you two were linked. It's possible you still are." I wondered if she was pale because she was feeling Orion's hunger or something along those lines.

She traced circles on Rorie's belly. "Care to tell me about your talk with Tripp and Rebekah?"

The confrontation Layla had with Rebekah went better than I

expected. As empaths, Tripp and I were in tune to other's emotions, especially when people lied, no matter if they were human or supernatural. He and I were certain that Rebekah didn't have any involvement with the Orion and Luna kidnapping. Still, it was the right move to confront her, just to be sure.

"It was all military stuff. She's joining her team on the naval base."

"I hope that in the end, I will be apologizing to her, because I really like her."

In my book, the she-wolf was a top-notch soldier, but I was with Layla. We had to be extremely cautious who we trusted.

Layla's eyes were droopy.

"Sleep," I said as Ellie's pacifier fell out of her mouth. "You have to rest, baby doll."

"I was until you came in with the girls," she said with another yawn. "You should as well."

I couldn't shut my eyes if she paid me. "Vampires don't need as much rest as humans."

She stuck out her tongue at me as she played with Rorie's tiny foot. "I think our girls are growing faster than normal, which would make sense since they grew faster in my womb. They're about due for their one-month checkup. I guess we'll have to wait, though."

"Safety first, baby doll."

"We should inform Doc that Rorie likes my blood and not yours. I also want to know if their DNA results are back and whether Doc can tell if they're all vampire witches. Speaking of that, are there any known vampire witches? You're kind of both, with your elemental powers."

"Not really. I can't make shit float. The only spell I know is chanting a series of numbers to compel someone. My niece Abbey, on the other hand, could be classified as both once she becomes a vampire when she hits puberty."

"What's her prophecy again?" Layla asked.

I stuck Ellie's pacifier in her mouth. "Supposedly, as Abbey ages, she will slowly shed her humanity, which means she won't require her father's blood to turn vampire. Also, if the prophecy surrounding her is correct, she'll be the first female vampire to have children."

"I hope our girls have that option, and I also pray my mother was wrong about the prophecy targeting one of our children. Which reminds me, I need to call Kendra." She yawned again.

"Baby doll, close your eyes. Sleep. For me, please."

As if I had her under my spell, her eyelids shut and she sighed, snuggling into the pillow. "Just for an hour. I love you, vampire."

I sized up her curvy body, my mind going to places that weren't appropriate with Ellie and Rorie between us. "Right back at you, baby doll."

I wasn't tired at the moment, and someone had to watch Ellie and Rorie. Tripp was in the living room. He'd gotten a call from Sawyer when I'd been walking Rebekah to her car. I was dying to know if Sawyer had found anything on the names of the guests at the Dewsbury Inn.

I waited a few minutes to be sure Layla was sleeping before I moved. I took in the beauty of my precious daughters.

Rorie's bright mahogany eyes flashed at me as if to say, *I love you, Daddy. I'm your vampire witch.* In contrast, Ellie's blue eyes were sharp and clear like the ocean off the coast of the Caribbean. Both had a head of reddish-brown hair. Rorie, despite her eye color, reminded me more of Layla, with the same shaped nose.

Love poured into my heart as I continued to gaze at my daughters. It angered me that my children would never live a normal life. I didn't want to lock them up and take away their opportunity to be children—playing sports with other kids their age or having friends over. Jo and I didn't have the best upbringing, but we had friends, went to the park, the movies, and played sports.

Hell, my ten-year-old niece Abbey didn't even have that luxury. She had no friends, was tutored at home rather than attending school with other kids her age, and hanging around adults wasn't ideal for her social growth. But we had to protect her and would continue to. She was just as much a target as her cousins, and that pissed me the fuck off.

What made me even angrier was my promise to Layla. My family deserved a happily ever after, the beach house, and anything they desired. But was that a pipe dream—at least for the foreseeable future.

The sound of Layla's deep breathing wormed its way through my thoughts.

I eased off the bed and grabbed Ellie first. "We'll let Momma sleep," I whispered.

After the girls were in their baby carriers, I tiptoed out with them in tow. As I wound my way down the hall, the aroma of coffee lingered in the air.

Inhaling a large dose of it, I strutted into the living room to the *tap, tap, tap* of Tripp's fingers flying over his laptop and that muted the sound of waves breaking along the shore. It seemed the Atlantic was angry, whipping up whitecaps in the distance.

After I set my girls by the fireplace sans the fire, I closed the accordion doors. The weather was warm to me but probably not warm enough for them.

Tripp glanced up from the couch. "Can't sleep?"

I went into the kitchen and poured a cup of coffee. "I'm not tired. Too much on my mind. Where's Jordyn?"

"No clue. Don't care. Give me a second, and I'll be finished with this email."

I dropped into the oversized chair opposite Tripp. "You don't like her either." I kept my voice as low as possible, not sure where the Aberdeen sister was.

"Not a fan." He tapped on a key, then closed his laptop. "And I certainly don't want to know about her sex life."

Tripp had loads of patience, but not when it came to women and certainly not with Jordyn or Rianne. He dated but didn't talk much about the lucky ladies who graced his bed. Not that he and

Jordyn would make a good match. As long as I'd known Tripp, he liked his women blond, curvy, and with tits he could get lost in. His words, not mine.

I took a drink of coffee. "Bro, you need an outlet."

"I don't have time," he said. Quick as a whip, he changed the subject. "Is Layla asleep?" he asked, meaning *Shut the fuck up, Sam*.

"Finally." Part of my soul was at peace over the fact that Layla was resting. "Does she look extremely pale to you?"

He picked up a mug that was on the table next to his laptop and eyed Ellie and Rorie. "She does. But sleep should help."

I hoped he was right. But something told me that her lack of color might be related to her connection to Orion and Luna, and if that were true, we might be in for a rougher road than we assumed we were already on.

"Your phone was ringing earlier." He drank from his mug. "Stan has been trying to reach you, so he called me. Care to fill me in on Layla's interview?" His lieutenant mask morphed into place, and his tone hardened. "*You're* not going on television. The last thing we need is to incite the council and heads of state any further. And by the way, Petty Officer Kraft told me about Layla's idea to talk to the press. We are not doing a show-and-tell."

"Did you not just say outside on that porch"—I pointed behind him—"to focus on your children and family? Fuck the council. Your father will handle them."

"Sure, but what I meant by that was what is done is done. Your father will handle the aftermath of your *prior* TV appearances. Any new public displays might have the council reissuing your warrant."

I swallowed down the anger as best I could. "Chill, man. Layla's goal is nothing more than pleading with the public to help find Orion and Luna. We have to do everything we can, right? And I would like to know what the council is going to do about Collier. They'd better not sweep his actions under the rug." If they did, I would be flushing the elders' ashes, excluding my father's, down a sewer drain. "The nation wants to know if Layla is fine. So why not play on their sympathy for her? Mothers everywhere would help." I was sure of it.

Although throwing Rianne in front of the camera wouldn't be a bad idea. The public would see a before-and-after shot of her, and maybe then they would think twice before signing up for Adam's experiment despite the $100,000 signing bonus.

He relaxed against the couch. "It's not that I don't agree with you. You and I are usually on the same wavelength. I just want to cover *your* ass. Not only does your family need you, but the SEAL team can't lose you either. Fuck, man. You're someone I call a brother, and I would hate to see you rot in a prison cell. We need to be strategic about our moves and actions."

"I'm not going on TV. My reasoning has nothing to do with the council but more about how humans see me as a bloodsucker and not a grieving father. That wouldn't help our cause."

The tension visibly left his hard features. "You know, if I weren't a vampire, you would've given me a full head of gray hair by now. Anyway, Stan says Tim Cox has the approval to interview Layla. Can we agree that she doesn't answer questions like, 'Are vampires real?' The narrative needs to be about Orion and Luna. If I see the interview spiraling in the wrong direction, I'll pull the plug. Clear?" He used his lieutenant tone on the last few sentences.

"Yes. She knows what's at stake."

"Good," he said.

I smirked. "I'm glad we got that figured out. I thought I would have to kill you."

He threw me the finger. "I would like to see you try, asshole."

Layla walked in, stealthy and sleepy, twisting her hair up into a messy bun. "What are you two arguing about?"

"You didn't sleep at all," I asked. "What's wrong?"

She rubbed the corner of her eye. "I thought I could. But my mind is too busy with stuff." She grabbed my mug from me. "Plus, we should pack. We're leaving today, right? Jordyn has done some preparation, but with all the baby things we need to bring, we're nowhere near ready."

"How come I didn't hear you?" Tripp asked, his forehead creasing.

I didn't either. Odd. He and I should've heard her heartbeat, breathing, walking—something.

"You two were in a heated discussion." She took a swig of coffee and wrinkled her nose. "That coffee is weak."

"You would kill us with your version," I retorted.

She used an entire bag of grounds for one pot. Nasty tasting and probably strong enough to knock out a vampire.

After placing the mug on the coffee table, Layla sat on my lap, hooking an arm around the back of my neck. "Did I hear 'TV interview'?"

"You did. Tim's news station gave us the thumbs-up." I regarded Tripp. "Did he say what time?"

Tripp crossed a leg over the other. "Three p.m."

According to my watch, we had two hours.

"Layla, I—"

She held up her hand at Tripp. "I heard you when I was coming down the hall. I know the drill about the interview."

I could see Tripp's wheels turning over the idea of others listening. He despised when people did just that. I made a mental note to share that with Layla.

Placing his cup on the coffee table, my lieutenant opened his laptop. "We got a hit on a name of a guest who was staying at the inn in town. George sent a video of the woman. Patty Smith. It seems she checked in under an alias. The address she jotted on her paperwork when she checked in belongs to the Garcia family from Ohio. Sawyer tracked down a phone number for the Garcias, but they don't know a Patty Smith, nor have they been to Maine. The Garcias are a couple in their early sixties. They settled in Dayton, Ohio, many moons ago. Three children—two married, one is single. But none of their names are Patty Smith or have Smith as a surname." Tripp pressed a key, then turned his laptop screen toward us.

Layla grabbed the computer and brought it over to me and resumed sitting on my lap. "It looks like she's wearing transition glasses that change in the light. I can't make out her facial features. It also looks like she's wearing a brown wig. I don't recognize her."

"The front-desk clerk, who is a vampire," Tripp said, "told George the woman was human. She doesn't resemble anyone we know. So we can assume she's not the mole."

"But she could be the woman who was in the nursery with Norman," Layla said.

"Maybe," Tripp replied. "But we think we narrowed down who the mole is."

Layla tensed, biting her nail. "Who is it?"

"We're still investigating," Tripp said. "But her phone records indicate that she called two different burner phones. Numbers associated with them are usually hard to trace but not impossible with the right tools. Sawyer has Murphy, his top computer expert, working on this as we speak."

"I don't care about all that. Just tell us," Layla squeaked out.

I was waiting with bated breath myself.

Tripp was studying Layla and me with a watchful eye. He knew what I would do.

"That nurse, Beverly," he said. "Do not tear out of here. You won't find her. The nurses who were on your medical team are no longer on base."

Layla's jaw came unhinged. "The redhead?"

"Wait." I lowered my gaze to the floor, then to Tripp. "She works at our Boston medical facility. I met her when my dad was brought in after the explosion. She also befriended Abbey. I bet Abbey would've been taken if she were here. That is, if Roman is part of this road show."

Layla continued to gnaw on her thumbnail. "They were vetted before Doc brought them in for the births."

"You're right." Tripp pressed keys on his laptop. "According to Beverly's background, she's clean. Her phone records from before she joined Doc are as well. Amy and Wendy, the other two nurses, are squeaky clean. I have Kraft tracking down Beverly."

I shoved both hands through my hair and growled. "She's the woman that Roman was talking to when Rianne walked by his office. Fuck! Are we assuming the human Patty Smith is Collier's accomplice? If so, can we connect all of them to Intech?"

"If not, then Collier isn't working for Roman," Layla said. "Which means someone else or some other organization is involved. But who? Though I keep thinking about my grandmother. Jordyn brought up a point about the eucalyptus odor the guys smelled. I forgot my mom used to make eucalyptus oil, and my grandmother liked it. She might've been here last night."

Not that I was surprised, but the knowledge that Harriet could've had her grubby hands on my children sent waves of fury through me. I mean, I would have the same reaction with any of my enemies, but Harriet took my rage to a whole new level.

"Harriet is on the list. As soon as we can talk to Steven, he can release all the records on the guardians, including Collier's," Tripp said. "I am fucking livid that Orion and Luna were taken under our noses. I can assure both of you that with my fucking life, I will find out who's responsible. We have a dedicated team putting all their efforts into this. And with Adam and Roman having disappeared, we're hoping we can kill two birds with one stone." Tripp glanced past me.

"There's a *but* coming," I said.

Tripp nodded. "Here's what you two will do. Layla will do the interview with Tim Cox. Directly afterward, I want you guys on the road to the Catskills. I've spoken to Dane and brought him up to speed. He and his pack have decided to join our Intech fight. But he will also dedicate any resources we need to Orion and Luna's search. Once you have Ellie and Rorie settled at the compound, then we'll discuss next steps. If Rianne is right and your grandmother went to Montana, then I'll send Sam and Conrad to bring her in. But first, we'll check flights from Chicago to confirm if Harriet was on any passenger list."

"Well, I'm going with Sam to Montana. There's no way I'm sitting around. My family. My fight." Layla stood, body stiff, daring Tripp to stop her.

I cocked an eyebrow at Tripp. "My queen has spoken."

"No argument here," he said.

Layla went over to Tripp and hugged him. "Thank you so much. I know you don't like my sisters or my family in general. I promise Jordyn won't act out anymore. Speaking of my sisters, what is the plan for Rianne?"

Tripp squeezed his temples. "I will be escorting her myself to the naval base. She'll be in a cell alongside Fred Emery. I have a special vehicle coming up tomorrow just for her." It was the first time since we arrived that Tripp cracked a smile. One that was dripping with excitement.

I took comfort in knowing if Rianne fucked with Tripp, he wouldn't hesitate to chop off her head.

Maybe things were looking up. We had a decent plan. We had suspects, including the mole. Tripp was leading the charge, for which I owed him my life. My daughters were sleeping and content, and color had returned to Layla's face. Now we just needed Orion and Luna back home and in their warm beds.

8

LAYLA

S am, Tripp, and I climbed out of the car at the sheriff's station later that afternoon. Storm clouds were rolling in, the temperature had dropped, and the trees in the park across the street were blowing in the wind.

"I need a minute," I said as I glanced out at the Atlantic.

The car ride from the house to the station had been disquieting —at least for me.

Tripp and Sam talked about Intech while I continued stewing about everything. What would I say on TV? Would I vomit like I wanted to at the moment? Was I making the right decision in telling the world about my children?

Plus, I felt a little weird around Tripp after what Sam had told me about him when we were packing. Apparently, Tripp wasn't a fan of eavesdroppers. That wasn't in my nature, and I'd never intended to spy on anyone. Yet I couldn't help myself when I'd heard Jordyn's name. I knew Tripp despised Rianne, and he wasn't a fan of Jordyn's. After all, Jordyn had screwed up by pulling the fire alarm on base. She'd admitted her mistake, and since then, she was back to her old self. I also felt like I was the problem. My family had basically turned the Vampire Navy SEAL world upside down. Of course, the Aberdeens weren't the only ones. But in some ways, I felt Tripp only tolerated me because of Sam, although Sam would disagree with me on that.

Sam snapped his fingers. "Layla, is anything wrong?"

"Just nerves. I've never been on TV before." All true. "Also trying to connect the dots with the facts we have."

I still believed Norman was working for Roman. I didn't believe we had two independent groups after our children. It made sense that Roman had sent Norman to confirm that I was in Maine with the babies, and that we, in fact, had four children. Roman wasn't about to make a move until he knew for sure. Case in point: Roman had held Jordyn hostage until I found out the SEALs had a little girl named Abbey. That was the day my life had changed in a way I'd never expected.

Then there was Beverly. I couldn't recall any suspicious activity on her part or from the other nurses.

"Focus on the interview for now," Sam said. "You'll do great."

I gave him a weak smile. "I hate not knowing if Orion and Luna are hurt. Or if Orion is suffering from lack of blood." I held my nauseous stomach, feeling as if he was giving me a sign. Maybe, in part, he was.

"Then show the nation exactly how you feel." He shook as he hugged me. "Can you do that?"

I squeezed him, inhaling his woodsy scent. "For sure."

He let go of me, blinking away the moisture in his eyes.

My heart burst open at seeing the formidable vampire shed a tear.

I rose up on my toes and brushed my lips over his. "After we settle Ellie and Rorie at Dane's compound, you and I are going hunting, vampire. I can't wait to sink my nails into my grandmother or anyone who has a hand in all this." It was time to end my family's involvement in my life, period.

He chuckled. "I fucking love you."

Stan called me over. "Layla, Tim is ready."

Those pesky nerves took flight. "Showtime," I mumbled.

"We'll be right there," Sam told Stan, then he rubbed his nose against mine. "Breathe, baby doll."

"Before we go in, tell me something snarky or anything to make me laugh." I needed a mood boost. The last twenty-four hours had been harrowing and nail-biting.

A glint sparkled in his green eyes as a wolfish grin deepened his dimples. "You know I'm good at predictions, unless you forgot."

I rolled my eyes as the word prediction provoked a memory of when we'd first met. "The elevator scene." I giggled. He'd bet me I would be in his bed in two days, tops. If I remembered correctly, he'd won. "I asked for something snarky, not a wager."

His goofy grin belied the predator that he was. "You're thinking of me naked, aren't you? I can smell your lust." The low rumble of his raspy voice had a direct line to my core.

"Of course I'm not," I lied as I pictured him naked. "What's your prediction?"

"Tonight, I'll be chasing your gorgeous ass through the woods surrounding Dane's compound."

I choked through a snort. "Are you delusional?" Then again, Sam loved a good game of cat and mouse.

"For you, yes."

I laughed all the way into the sheriff's station. I was adventurous, and sex with my husband was definitely a need. In fact, my stomach fluttered at the idea of Sam's huge cock inside me. But the Catskills had to be cold at night despite the summer season.

Live a little, girl. Sam chasing you through the woods just might be what you need to clear your head. Or chase his ass instead. Now, there's an idea.

When Sam and I entered an interrogation room several minutes later, my nerves went back to doing a number on my stomach.

Tim Cox rose from a wooden chair, his brown eyes glistening as if he were about to interview his favorite celebrity.

In a roundabout way, Sam and I *were* celebrities. His face had been plastered on news stations from coast to coast. Some humans thought my hunky husband was a monster, while others were fascinated with him. As for me, people thought I was being held by a bloodsucking vampire against my will or had been compelled by Sam to fall in love with his snarky and handsome ass.

I giggled silently, remembering our first encounter at the nightclub in Massachusetts way back at the beginning of February, which seemed like years had gone by when only six months had passed.

Regardless of the timeline, the only one Sam had compelled that snowy night was my sister Rianne, and that hadn't been a pretty sight. Yet, the sexy vampire had thrown me for a loop that had made my head spin and my sex hormones to go haywire. I'd wrestled with the need to kill him or fuck his brains out.

Sam's hot breath breezed over my ear, making me shiver back to reality. "I love that smile on your beautiful face. It must be one hell of a thought," he whispered.

I flushed as Tim extended his hand to Sam. "I'm Tim Cox, a news reporter with Chicago's TNN cable news network." He stabbed a finger at his cameraman. "This is Bob. He'll be taping the segment."

"Sam Mason." The two shook hands, but Tim winced during the process as if Sam had clamped his hand with a vise. I would guess Sam was giving Tim a warning of sorts.

"I'm Layla Mason. We met yesterday, of course, but not officially."

Toying with his camera near the two-way mirror, Bob smiled at me. The husky, big-gutted, and curly-brown-haired man was now angling a spotlight at the two lone chairs in the room. "Nice to meet you, Layla. You did well yesterday." He sounded sincere and appreciative.

He and Tim had been in the diner, and Bob had been impatient to film every detail of Rianne's interaction with Jordyn and me. Rianne had coaxed the reporting duo to accompany her to Maine for the story of Tim's news career. That was, until Rianne's beastly side materialized. Then Bob and Tim had flown out of the diner faster than the Flash.

Tim's warm-brown eyes were kind as he regarded Sam and me. "Before we start, do you have pictures of your babies? Also, Stan has told me you want to offer a monetary reward. How much will that be?"

Sam and I had discussed the amount earlier. "Twenty-five-thousand dollars," I said.

"We don't have pictures, but their hair and eye colors are distinctive," Sam added.

Tim adjusted the collar of his white dress shirt. "Also, I've gotten the green light to air this segment tomorrow night. Once Bob and I return to our station in Chicago, we'll pretty things up, run the edited segment by our boss, and it should air tomorrow night on our network at six p.m. central time. Any questions before we start?"

I couldn't think of any at the moment as I began to sweat. There was something about a camera that set me on edge. Maybe it was the coldness of talking to a piece of equipment and not knowing whether or not people watching were agreeing with me, throwing something at their TV, or having any kind of an emotional reaction.

Sam rested his hand on my lower back. "You'll do fine," he said, tapping into my emotions. "I'll be in the next room, watching through the two-way mirror. If you need me, just tug on your ear." Then he kissed me lovingly on the lips.

Tim seemed like a man who wouldn't tear me apart for answers, unlike some reporters I'd seen on the news. Even if he did, I wasn't fragile. I could handle myself. But I was comforted to know Sam would be in the next room and would come to my rescue if need be.

"Sam, please reconsider joining us," Tim pleaded. "Your message will have more of an impact as a husband-and-wife team. Plus, it's clear you love each other. That alone will resonate with my viewers and show them you're not the deadly vampire they think you are."

Oh, my husband was deadly but also had a big heart. Yet, the news about vampires that was spreading like wildfire around the country and probably the world, coupled with the number-one vampire celebrity, Sam Mason, who was someone the public feared, would definitely overshadow our desperate plea for help.

Tripp cleared his throat from the doorway. "Petty Officer Mason, stick to the plan." His tone was commanding and businesslike.

Ignoring his lieutenant, Sam flashed his pearly white fangs at Tim. "This interview isn't about me. It's about our missing babies. You know as well as I do that humans wouldn't hear our message if they saw me on TV." Sam loomed over the reporter, tall and intimidating. "I'll make you a deal, though. You help us find our babies, and when the time comes, I'll give you an exclusive. And by help, I don't mean just this interview. Any lead you might find or hear about my children, my family, me, Intech, prototypes—you get my drift—you come to me. No one else."

Tripp was tense and wearing an inscrutable expression, reminding me of Webb London, Sam's brother-in-law and the commander of the Vampire Navy SEALs. Deadpan looks must be a requirement for promotion in the military.

"I would greatly appreciate an exclusive." Tim's voice hitched.

Sam retracted his fangs. "Good. Then it's a deal. But if you grill Layla to the point where I see she's uncomfortable or I have to stop the interview for some reason, you can kiss your exclusive goodbye."

A sheen of sweat glistened on Tim's face. "My job, as a reporter, is to ask the tough questions. If Layla doesn't want to answer, she doesn't have to."

I gently nudged Sam to leave. "Go. I'm a big girl. I can handle this." I knew what was at stake aside from my children. I also didn't need to look at Tripp to know he was boring a hole into the back of my head.

Once Sam left, closing the door behind him, Tim and I took our seats, which were at a slight angle to each other. Bob was across from us with his camera ready. Behind him was the two-way mirror.

"One more thing before we start." Tim crossed one leg over the other, causing my gaze to drop to his shiny black loafers. "I want to apologize to you. When I approached your sister, Rianne, outside Intech, I had no idea that her meeting with you would escalate to the magnitude it had. I'm happy to see that you're okay. How is your other sister—Jordyn, right?"

Now that he had kick-started my synapsis, I did have questions for him. A few I'd planned to ask him yesterday, but I'd never had a chance.

I laced my fingers together in my lap. "Jordyn is fine. But what were you expecting when you came here with Rianne? Did you think that I would give in and take the serum like she had? She held hostages. She put people's lives in jeopardy. For all I know, she used meeting you as a distraction to have her team kidnap my babies. Is that what reporters do these days? Help criminals?"

He leaned away, lifting his hands. "I had no idea Rianne would take hostages or had planned to inject you and your other sister. She sold me on a meeting with you and that she wanted to show you and the nation what Adam Emery's prototypes looked like. In part, she was extremely upset about what she had done and wanted to warn everyone."

I had a hard time controlling my laughter. Then again, Rianne was a good liar. "And you believed her, obviously."

"Given the state of unrest in this nation and her plea on national television about your well-being, I had no reason not to. I quickly realized I'd made a mistake when she shot the darts at the cook and the two ladies. Then she threatened Bob and me when we tried to leave. We have it on tape." He sounded sincere and regretful.

"It's true," Bob added.

I didn't see any light on the camera to indicate it was on. But if it was, they were implicating themselves.

Tim frowned and continued. "Layla, I'm not your enemy. I want to help. And you have to agree that the knowledge of vampires is galvanizing. We have several schools of thought out there. Some humans are running scared, some are ecstatic that immortality could be real, and still others are indifferent. The landscape of this world has drastically changed. Add in what Adam Emery is doing with his prototype program, and I would rather hang out with vampires than someone like what Rianne has become. I can now show and prove that Adam's prototypes are worse than we ever could imagine. My news station manager and I are in agreement. The idea that Adam Emery could've kidnapped your babies to support his efforts is one of the most horrific things in all this. We want to help."

My eyebrows rose. "Do you know for sure if he has?"

"Sadly, I don't. But Rianne mentioned how Adam thought your children might have the right DNA for a successful experiment."

Rianne had shared that very piece of information with Sam and me earlier. But hearing Tim say it caused my entire body to cramp. If the world got wind of how special my children and their DNA were, it would spread like wildfire, and others like Adam would come out of the woodwork.

I was impatiently desperate to find Orion and Luna. I wasn't sure pleading with the nation was the right idea. We had a decent plan. We knew who the mole was. We could possibly connect Norman to Roman. If Rianne was telling the truth, we knew where my grandmother was. We had to use our in-house resources. Tripp and the Vampire Navy SEALs were working overtime. I believed in them. Plus, Dane and his pack had joined us, which meant there was an army of shifters available if Sam and I needed them.

"I think I might have been too hasty to engage a reporter."

Tim flinched. "What? Why? I want to help."

I sat up straighter. "My family is everything to me. I will die to find Orion and Luna. But I can't have you reporting that their DNA is unique. Those who know my husband might be aware, but I can't have the nation knowing that information. They will fear my kids and hunt them down. Again, I wasn't thinking clearly." I got up to leave.

Sam blew into the room. "Are you sure, baby doll?"

"Absolutely." My intuition was screaming not to do this. "I'm sorry to have wasted your time."

Tim stood. "Layla, please. I will not report on anything specific about your children other than the fact that they're missing."

I shook my head. "Considering what happened yesterday, you have enough for a story. I appreciate you want to help, but the best way to help on your part is by saving human lives. Show them just how bad the results are from Adam's experiments. On the flip side, I will extend the same offer my husband has. I will give you an exclusive about the Aberdeen family myself, and I'll help to convince the nation that Sam and the supernatural military are not the enemy. My children have no business in this war."

"But they *are* in it," Tim argued.

Sam, who'd been at my side, piped up. "You're right, Tim. But we don't need to publicize it."

Tim bobbed his head, clearly disheartened. "My reporter side wants the story. The father in me agrees with you, and family is everything. You have my assurance I will keep your children out of my segment. I'll stick to the facts I have. Regardless of an exclusive, I will alert you to anything I come across."

Tim gave me the impression that he was a man of his word.

"You'll help us no matter what?" Sam scrubbed a hand along his chin.

"I'm not going to lie. I want both of your stories," Tim said. "But Layla said something a few minutes ago about saving human lives. We have to work together." He twirled his gold wedding ring. "But I would like to leave you with one thought. It seems you're the good vampires, and I can tell the public that all day long. However, if you want to stop Intech and ease the disorder in this country, then someone in your organization needs to explain the science behind vampires and how that differs both from what Adam Emery is doing and from folklore as well. That knowledge could save many lives."

He wasn't kidding. Now that humans knew vampires lived among them, it was imperative to educate them on all things vampires. Otherwise, mayhem would be the norm, and soon enough, no one would be safe.

9

SAM

After Tim and his cameraman left the building, Layla dropped down on the chair in the interrogation room, threw her head into her hands, and pushed out the sigh of the century.

"What was I thinking?" Dragging a hand along the side of her head, she sat back. "While he was talking about Rianne and our children's DNA, I felt sick. In that moment, I knew it was wrong to go on TV. We don't need the nation knowing anything about our children. We would put them in more jeopardy than they are already in. Humans would want to kill them like they do you."

I crouched down in front of her and grasped her cold, damp hands. "Hey, you didn't go through with it."

She pressed her forehead against mine. "I almost did, Sam. If humans didn't know vampires existed, or Intech and my sister hadn't thrown us to the wolves, a public plea might've worked. I couldn't risk Ellie and Rorie either. I fucking hate this. I want our children back."

"We *will* bring them home, baby doll." My heart splintered in two. I hoped I could follow through on that statement. "We have a good plan."

She eased away, her eyes locking with mine. "Why didn't you stop me, Sam?"

"Would you have let me?"

"Not on your life." She laughed. "I probably would've cut off your balls."

I chuckled but winced as if I could feel her doing just that. "I rest my case. Layla, you did the right thing. There's no easy decision in all this." I traced her full lips. "But you need to know something. It doesn't matter whether the world finds out about our children today or next year. They were in danger the minute they were born. It fucking torments me to say that." I gritted my teeth.

Frowning, she flattened a hand on my face. "I know." She shuddered. "I need to use the ladies' room."

After she glided out, I mumbled several swear words. I was ready to punch walls or feel someone else's bones crack as I rammed my fist into them. Anything to feel physical pain rather than emotional. The latter feeling was a thousand times worse than breaking my bones or even a dagger in the heart. Being an empath sucked the fucking big one. If something didn't give soon, I was afraid Layla wouldn't make it. As it was, she was holding on by a thread.

I snagged my phone out of my jeans pocket to see my father's name flash on the screen. I couldn't answer fast enough. He must've heard about Orion and Luna.

"Pops, are the votes in?" My voice was shaky. "Are we telling the world we exist?" I didn't know why I was even asking that, because right now, I didn't give a fuck.

"Son, Webb just told me about my grandkids. I'm gutted."

I didn't know if it was everything up until now that had happened or hearing the heartache and rage in his voice, but I felt like someone had flipped my emotional switch as tears burned my eyes.

I began pacing, cloudy gaze on the floor, heart sputtering, chest tight. What the fuck was happening to me? Maybe I would be the one to pass out. *You don't have time for a breakdown.*

"Samuel, breathe, son." His voice had softened.

"I'm trying, Pops. This is fucking killing me. I should've heard those fuckers coming into the house last night. I wasn't there to protect my family."

Man, give yourself a small break. You were on the beach, and sounds were drowned out by the waves crashing on the shore.

There wasn't room for a break. Not when my family would always be in danger. I was failing as a husband and father.

"Don't you dare blame yourself," he said. "I read Tripp's email to Webb. He explained everything so far. I'm assigning a guardian to track down that nurse Beverly. Collier will return to Boston, and I will deal with him. He's about to regret that he ever met me. I also understand Harriet Aberdeen is no longer with Adam Emery. Find her and bring her in. In the meantime, we have Viking II leading the charge to find where Adam and Roman disappeared to. Webb will handle the Feds. I've asked the Special Forces unit to join Viking II. And I've given Sawyer access to all guardian records. I want you to focus on your family."

"What about the council and their screwed-up idea to use me as a scapegoat? You've held them off, but is that permanent?" I scraped a hand along my beard that had grown overnight. "Because I am not sitting in a jail cell while Orion and Luna are missing. No fucking way. Orion will need my blood soon, if he doesn't already. Pops, you know what happens when a vampire is blood deprived."

A loud boom sounded in the background as if he'd thrown something. "Fuuuck!"

"My sentiments exactly, which is one of many reasons I can't have guardians hunting me."

He sighed through a growl. "I'm happy to say I've finally convinced the elders you're an asset, not a problem. They'd initially panicked."

My fangs lowered and embedded in my bottom lip. "At my

expense and my family's." My voice boomed in the small space. "I didn't have to run. I could've been with Layla and my newborns, protecting them."

Motherfucker.

"I'm sorry, son. I feel responsible." Regret threaded through his words. "I led you to believe that I had a backup plan in the event the elders didn't see things my way. While I did, one of my colleagues decided to screw me."

I sat down and stared at a speck of dirt on the floor. "No apology necessary, Pops. When are you going to lead our government? It seems you're the only one who isn't living in the 1800s."

"That might happen, son. But right now, I'm trying to be as diplomatic as possible and keep anarchy at bay among our ranks."

"All this chaos started because of me," I muttered.

I'd never intentionally sought to show humans that vampires lived among them, but as vampires, our emotions were difficult to control in heightened situations, which had been especially true when Layla was taken by Roman and his goons.

"Samuel, don't you dare blame yourself for what's happening with our government or the public. You're not the first vampire to stand before a group of humans with your fangs out. Also, we're at this juncture because of Roman, Adam, and genetic engineering."

I snorted. "That parking lot wasn't a group but a damn concert crowd."

He clicked his tongue. "I haven't shared this with you yet. We have protocols in place to prevent videos like the ones taken of you from going viral. Someone on our team failed in executing that protocol. Either they were lazy or they're working against us. The security and tech teams here at the administration building are looking into who's responsible. The bottom line is, we can't change what happened. We now have to press forward."

I wanted to murder the asshole who hadn't done his job. "It seems we have more than one mole on our team."

"Maybe so," he said. "I have to run soon, but tell me—how's

Layla holding up? In Tripp's email, he said Layla was interviewing with a reporter." His tone was indifferent, so I couldn't gauge how he felt about that.

I clutched the back of my neck. "Layla is a mess. She's starting to have visions too. But she decided against the interview. She felt it would only increase the threat against your grandchildren."

"She's probably right, but it's only a matter of time before the world knows about them."

"Pops, I'm beginning to realize why you didn't take Jo and me out of foster care when you returned from deployment. I hated you for that, but I understand now."

"You don't know how much I despised myself for that, Samuel." His voice cracked.

Emotion clogged my throat. "I love you, Pops. By the way, it seems your granddaughter Aurora—or Rorie, as we call her—is a vampire witch. We don't know about Ellie or Luna yet, but so far, Orion appears to be a vampire." All my children could be vampire witches.

"I can't wait to see them," he said, clearing his throat. "I'll pool every resource I have from this end to help, and I will personally deal with Collier."

I would love to be a fly on the wall when he did.

I leaned my forearms on my knees. "Wait, Pops. Is the vote still tied?"

A door squeaked in the background on my father's end. "On the topic of announcing us to humans, yes. We are also voting on whether to dissolve the council or not. There's a lot going on here behind the scenes that I don't want you to worry about. I love you. Hug your wife and my other grandkids for me. Oh, and Samuel—if for any reason something happens to me, stay the course. Those babies are your most important priority. I'll be in touch soon." Then he was gone.

I flinched. What the fuck? What would happen to him?

Nothing will, a voice in the back of my head whispered. *Your father is important in this war.*

Suddenly, I was taking a trip down memory lane to a conversation I had with Tripp, Webb, and my dad not long after my father had recovered from the explosion at the vampire administration in Boston several months ago.

"What's going on, Pops? You're thinking really hard."

He swiped a hand over his black hair. "There's something all of you should know." He groaned out a heavy sigh. "I'm still trying to understand it." He glanced anywhere but at us for a few seconds. "When I was under, I saw my father."

Tripp, Webb, and I exchanged a frightened look. Anytime my grandfather had graced Jo's dreams, it was never good. The air in the office thickened with a fear that we had buried five years ago.

Dad pressed his hands together in a prayerlike position against his mouth. "A war is coming. One that could wipe out our existence."

"You mean erase vampires, humanity, and all supernaturals?" Webb asked.

Dad straightened. "I don't know. The last thing he told me before I woke up was that I couldn't die. I had to help my son."

I sucked in a breath. "Me? Are you saying I have something to do with a war breaking out?"

Dad lifted a shoulder. "I don't know, Sam. But it sounds to me like you'll be in the thick of it."

"Aren't we always?" I asked. "We're Navy SEALs. We fight. We protect. I don't see the big deal here." Unless I was the one to start a war. Maybe I would.

"Holy shit!" I said, shaking off the memory as Layla's cherry scent filled my nostrils.

The second I laid eyes on her, I forgot everything else. Her silky auburn hair was tied up in a bun, her black yoga pants molded to her toned thighs, and her ribbed tank top accentuated her voluptuous tits. *Stunning* came to mind, especially when she batted her long lashes that framed obscenely blue eyes and gave me a smile reserved only for me.

She sashayed closer. "Vampire, are you okay? You were mumbling before you shouted, 'Holy shit.'"

"I am now. You're fucking stunning, baby doll."

She blushed, licking her lips.

Oh, how I wanted those full, sensuous lips around my cock right now. I needed a distraction, a fucking release of pent-up energy. Short of ramming my fists into a wall or a punching bag, sex would be a terrific way to release my frustrations.

She straddled my lap. "Want to talk about it?"

"Maybe later. I just talked to my dad."

She tensed, her hands digging into my shoulders. "I'm listening."

"Good news. Regardless of the vote, I'm free. He managed to call off the hounds."

She squealed. "That's awesome. Another worry off our plate."

My growing cock was pushing at the zipper of my jeans. Oh, the desire to be inside her was driving me mad. "Tonight, baby doll. Somehow or somewhere, you and I need some alone time."

She combed her fingers through my hair as she squirmed against my erection. "It's a date. I called Conrad. He's bringing Jordyn and the girls down to the station, so we can leave from here."

I cupped her face with my hands and kissed her tenderly. "Before we go, I have to talk to Tripp." I thought he might know something about my father. But I also needed a gut check.

I lifted her up and off me. "Come on. Let's find Tripp, and I'll fill you in."

I couldn't shake the notion that I *was* the spark that had ignited a war of mass proportions.

10

LAYLA

As Sam and I went in search of Tripp, I was elated that my husband wouldn't be pursued by guardians. I also felt good about my decision not to interview with Tim Cox, even though I had a niggling of doubt, which completely vanished when I thought of my children. Was Orion in need of blood? Were the kidnappers hurting Luna and him? And if Roman did have them, was he experimenting on them?

Nausea, thick and acidic, churned in my stomach as we entered the lobby.

Jo was running from her car toward the sheriff's station with her adoptive daughter, Abbey, on her heels. My beautiful sister-in-law with glossy black hair and diamond-colored eyes looked like she'd been crying. There wasn't any doubt she'd heard about her niece and nephew.

A warm breeze from outside whooshed in with Jo and Abbey. My niece by marriage had sadness written on her adorable face until she saw her uncle Sam. Then her blue eyes brightened as she jumped into his arms.

Jo swallowed me up as she hugged me. "Webb told me about

Orion and Luna. I am so, so sorry, Layla. I've been crying and berating myself on the drive up. I should've stayed."

Mother and daughter had gone to Boston at the crack of dawn yesterday morning, mainly to pick up Alia Costner, who was coming to stay with us because she needed protection. Her son, Matthew, had been taken by Roman, and her father, Victor, was supposedly MIA.

"Don't blame yourself," I said to Jo. "Everything happened so fast."

Whether she had stayed or not, the outcome wouldn't have been any different. No one who'd been at the house had heard or sensed a fucking thing, which still bothered me. We were missing something.

Sam set Abbey down as she shed tears. "Hey, it's okay. We'll find Orion and Luna." His confidence always melted my nerves.

Abbey played with the end of her braid. "I know."

My antenna went up. "Did you have a vision?" I checked with Jo when Abbey didn't immediately answer. "Did she?" Hope sprouted like a flower after a hard rain.

Jo shrugged. "It sounded to me like she had a nightmare last night. But she didn't want to talk about it. My daughter doesn't share many of her visions with me."

Sam gave Jo a stern look. "That's because she doesn't want to frighten you."

"I talked to a woman in a vision I had yesterday," Abbey announced like we were talking about the weather.

My curiosity sharpened as I wondered if she'd seen the same woman I had in my vision that morning. "What does she look like?" My heart punched my ribs like a boxer in a ring.

The station phone rang, blaring in the echoless silence of the room. It was then I noticed Grace, Stan's administrative assistant, behind the glass-encased counter.

Abbey closed the short distance between us, still fidgeting with the end of her braid. "The lady has white hair and orange eyes."

I didn't believe in coincidences. This revelation was huge. The white-haired lady was definitely trying to send us a message. I was sure of it. But concerning what? My children?

I sat on the lobby bench. "That's the same woman I saw too. What did she say?" I'd only gotten a glimpse of her before my vision was cut short.

Abbey touched my knee. "She vanished when Mom called my name, but before that, she asked if your name was Layla and if you had four babies. I told her yes."

Sam sat on the edge of the bench next to me. "Abbey, is she friend or foe? Did she seem evil?"

I bit a nail like a hungry chipmunk, fleetingly glancing at Grace, who hung up the receiver and curled her brown hair around her ear.

Abbey lifted her small shoulders. "She was nice. She told me that your babies are special but also feared because together, they're the perfect storm."

"Sounds to me like the woman is a dream walker trying to send a message," Grace said as if she were an expert on magic and witchcraft.

My mind was stuck on the message *Your babies are special but also feared because together, they're the perfect storm.* What in the fucknation did that mean?

"Layla and I shared a dream," Sam announced with a hitch in his tone.

Heat flooded my cheeks at the memory of our steamy encounter, especially when he batted those long lashes that framed his sexy green eyes while wearing that lopsided grin I adored.

From behind her desk, Grace said, "There's a difference between shared dreaming and dream walking."

Everyone turned their attention to Grace as though we were her students in a history class.

She eyed each of us, her soft-brown eyes framed with a heavy coat of mascara. "Dream walkers make deliberate efforts to walk into a person's consciousness and gain control over their space, and the powerful ones can control your actions, whereas a shared dream is done without control. So when you and Layla shared a dream, it wasn't intentional—or was it?"

Sam shook his head. "No. I wouldn't even know how to do that."

I giggled. "But you're welcome in mine anytime."

He gave me a cheeky grin, and my lady parts sparked to life.

Jo propped her elbow on the counter. "How do you know all this?"

"My mom was good friends with a witch." Grace frowned. "I used to love talking to her. I was sad when she died."

"Are you saying dream walkers can put you in a trance and make you do things?" I asked.

She bobbed her head. "Again, the powerful ones, who are mainly witches, can. They can go as far as making you sleepwalk."

"So can I learn how to dream walk?" Abbey asked, intrigued.

"Yes," Grace said. "With the right teacher and practice."

Abbey regarded her mom. "Can Alia teach me that?"

Jo moved Abbey's braid off her shoulder. "Alia isn't a powerful witch, and let's not get ahead of ourselves just yet."

Sam regarded Jo. "Sis, I'm just throwing this out there—but you should think about sending Abbey to a private school. I'm sure there are academies for children with abilities like hers. I mean, we went to a vampire high school. Briefly, of course."

I didn't know that about Sam and Jo. But none of that mattered.

I went over to Grace. "How do we find this woman? Seems to me she's either trying to help or she might know where Orion and Luna are."

Grace clicked her tongue. "Unfortunately, you can't. She's the dream walker, not you. But it sounds to me like she found you through Abbey, because you had a vision of the same woman after Abbey did. Which tells me she'll probably reach out to you again."

Jo whipped her head toward Grace. "How does she know my daughter? Or was able to find her?"

Abbey was on the most-wanted list of evil assholes like Roman Brown. I didn't want her harmed in any way either.

"Witches have their ways that I'm not up to speed on," Grace explained.

Jo and Sam exchanged a worried look.

Abbey glanced up at Jo. "It's okay, Mom. The white-haired lady won't hurt me."

Silence zipped around the lobby until Tripp strutted in from outside. His sandy-blond hair was tied at his nape. He was sporting a close-shaven beard, and the badass vampire was dressed to fight with weapons strapped around his legs and waist. "What's wrong?"

Everything. "Do you know anything about witches?"

He raised his hands. "Not my area of expertise."

Vampires were my specialty, and I could add shifters to that list. But witches, not so much. My brain felt like someone had smashed it with a hammer, and I needed a reprieve for the moment.

11

SAM

I inhaled the crisp mountain air from the cabin porch, and the sweet rich scents of balsam firs and birch trees invaded my nostrils as I glanced up at the star-laden sky.

After a long drive from Maine to the Catskills, we'd arrived at the shifter compound around midnight. The property was bathed in darkness with the exception of yellow bulbs glowing from cabin porches and the occasional automatic spotlight that turned on in driveways as someone pulled up or walked by.

The journey with Jordyn, Layla, Ellie, Rorie, and Abbey hadn't been as bad as I thought it would be. Traffic through Boston had been a breeze. Aside from the occasional bathroom stop, the girls slept on and off the entire time, especially Ellie and Rorie.

I was relieved Layla had finally slept. Her nap earlier that day at the house couldn't really be classified as one. She'd probably gotten ten minutes of sleep at most.

My niece had tagged along while Jo stayed behind. She wanted Abbey in a safe location while she returned to Boston to be with Webb. He'd loaned his car to Alia so she could make the journey to the shifter compound, which meant Webb would need transportation when he was ready to leave.

Regardless, I'd used the quiet time behind the wheel to clear my head and think through our next steps. From here, my dad wanted us to bring Harriet in if she was in fact in Montana. His goal no doubt was to extract information from her with his mind-reading ability. She certainly could be a wealth of information regarding Adam, Roman, Intech, their strategy, where they were, who had my children, and even a location on Orion and Luna. Frankly, I didn't give a shit about Intech unless Adam and Roman were the masterminds behind the kidnapping. They very well could be. But Harriet stood out as a top suspect in my book.

Her desire to cure her blood cancer would drive that woman to use and abuse my children. Plus, the one defining element that was sticking in my brain was that eucalyptus scent. Right before the men outside the house were shot with the tranquilizer darts, they'd detected that distinct fragrance. According to Jordyn and Layla, their mom had made eucalyptus oil that Harriet loved.

I stretched my neck one way, then another as the cool air breezed over my heated skin. Greta's cabin was as hot as a sauna with its crackling fire and space heaters in the bedrooms. I'd found it odd that a shifter would keep her place that hot until she explained why. She'd wanted her home warm for the babies' arrival. But damn, it had to be ninety degrees inside. That tent I'd stayed in on the property last week was looking like a better option—for me, at least.

Regardless, once the shifter enforcers at the main gate had waved us in, my muscles had loosened. I'd been on edge, constantly looking in the rearview on the drive up to make sure no one had been tailing us, and no one had. Thank fuck.

With Ellie's and Rorie's lives in danger, the last thing we needed was our location compromised. Above that, I would feel like a shithead if I was the one responsible for putting the lives of the shifters in peril as well.

The good news was that the compound was up in the Catskill Mountains and hard to find. There wasn't a soul around Dane and his pack. They took living off the grid to a whole new level, which was something I needed to take notes on in order to protect my family at some point in the near future. Between the location and the security, I felt comfortable leaving Ellie and Rorie with Jordyn and the Gray pack while Layla and I trekked to Montana.

I was so looking forward to confronting Harriet Aberdeen. I couldn't wait to see what lies spilled from the old woman's mouth. There was no way on this planet she had given up her quest for immortality to cure her blood cancer. I would stake my life on that.

Yet before we jetted off, Tripp and I agreed we would videoconference as soon as he returned to the naval base with Rianne. I growled at her name. I would like to think that bitch was doomed to die by the serum—but my gut was telling me otherwise.

I shoved her out of my mind. It would be a brighter future without her or Harriet in it. Grandmother and granddaughter were their own worst enemies.

Nevertheless, once Tripp was settled, he'd have confirmation if Harriet was on any passenger lists for flights to Montana. He would also give me an update if he heard anything about my father.

I hadn't been able to shake my dad's last words to me. *"Oh, and Samuel, if for any reason something happens to me, stay the course."* We couldn't afford to lose him. I couldn't afford to either. As far as the vampire nation went, he was the only one who could prevent a world war between humans and vampires. Above all that, I would burn down the vampire administration if the elders fucked with him. I was not losing my dad. I needed him as much as my children needed me.

The door opened, and Greta's mutt odor hit me between the eyes.

"There you are, Sam." She sidled up to me. "Sorry about the heat inside."

The she-wolf was a sweet middle-aged lady and one of the few shifters to address me by my first name. The majority of pack members called me bloodsucker, which didn't bother me. Regardless, Greta was the resident chef and in charge of running a well-oiled staff in the chow hall and had been gracious enough to offer up her home to my family.

I'd complained about the heat the second I'd crossed the threshold. "No worries. I might sleep in my tent."

"Beautiful night for sleeping under the stars—and romantic, if you ask me." She smiled knowingly.

I smirked. "Are you giving me a hint on how to cozy up to my wife?"

The sweet sound of her laughter cut through the quiet of darkness. "Maybe. I have plenty of blankets and sleeping bags. You two could probably use some alone time." Her cheeks reddened.

"Is Layla feeding the girls?" I asked, changing the subject.

We'd been here about an hour, but the minute we arrived, our daughters seemed to be in sync, both crying and hungry.

"Abbey is asleep. Jordyn is feeding one girl and Layla the other," she said. "Your daughters are precious and powerful. I can feel their magic."

I stared out at the cluster of trees that made up the front yard. "Funny, your alpha said the same, as have others." That had been the first thing that had come out of Dane's mouth in the infirmary outside the nursery. "It seems Rorie can make pillows float."

Her eyebrows lifted. "See? You'll have your hands full."

I didn't know much about witchcraft, but I guessed Layla and I were about to learn.

She rested her small hands on the railing. "Ever since you and Layla told me about the dream walker and her message, I've been thinking. Now, this is just a theory. Together, the four of your children are what the dream walker calls a perfect storm, which to me means they're weaker on their own. Therefore, whoever has Orion and Luna won't harm them. They just want your kids for their powers and nothing more."

I knew she was trying to make me feel better. Yet no matter what theory she had, the kidnappers were fucking with my children. Orion and Luna were suffering—especially Orion, if he needed blood.

"You're saying a witch has them?" Vampires couldn't steal others' abilities, and trying to extract powers from DNA didn't work.

She nodded. "Dream walkers are witches, Sam. I've met a few over the years. None who could enter a dream, though. But they're always trying to hone their craft. In their world, magical power is everything. They strive for it." She slipped her hands into the pockets of her robe.

When Grace mentioned something similar, I didn't put much thought to it. But if witches were involved, then that threw a monkey wrench into the mix. Maybe we were assuming too much with Harriet. Nah. I couldn't take Harriet off the list.

"Do you know a witch I can talk to?" I asked.

"It's been a long time, and the witch community is tight. I'll see what I can do," she said.

Alia Costner had the ability to craft spells, and she'd been around a long time. She might know one as well.

"Do you know if Alia Costner showed up today?" I asked.

Greta stared out into the night. "She's here. She's staying with Dane's grandmother."

In my three weeks as Dane's guest, I'd learned that the alpha of the Gray pack adored his grandmother. She'd stepped up to care for Dane and his brothers when his parents died several years ago at the hands of a rival pack. Greta had warned me not to broach the subject with Dane or Cooper. Neither was over the loss of their parents, and they might never come to terms with how brutal and bloody their deaths had been.

My feisty huntress called my name before she breezed out of the house through the open door. I guessed Greta was trying to cool off the inside for me.

"What did I miss?" Layla asked with a lilt in her tone.

Greta pivoted on her heel. "I'm going to make some valerian tea. Would either of you like some?"

I opened my arms, welcoming my gorgeous huntress, who looked ready to party with electric-blue eyes, color in her cheeks, and a smile that warmed my damn soul.

"A hard pass for me," I replied. I'd never drunk a drop of tea in my life. Not even iced tea.

She snuggled into me. "Ooh, that would be wonderful. It helps with stress too, right?"

"You know your tea leaves," Greta said as she went inside.

Layla slipped a cold hand underneath my T-shirt. "You're burning up, vampire."

I pressed my ass into the railing. "Just hot for you." I waggled my eyebrows.

She rolled her eyes, mashing her hips into me. "Someone has a surprise for me. A gigantic one." She giggled, her tongue darting out to lick those full lips.

My brain short-circuited at what that mouth of hers could do to me.

She tossed a quick look over her shoulder at the open door before she grabbed my dick, squeezed, and let out a soft moan.

Lust coursed through me at warp speed. "How does sleeping in a tent tonight sound?"

She wiggled her hips into my groin again. "Romantic." Rising up on her toes, she pressed her tits into my chest. "I want you inside me so fucking bad," she whispered, brushing her lips over mine.

I dipped into my back pocket and whipped out a condom. A wild, fucked-up laugh shouted in my head. I'd never used a condom. Never had to, since the women before Layla had been vampires, and even if any of them had been human, I wouldn't have worried about their blood type. Females with Vel-negative blood were rare, and I'd never been with one until Layla. Still, she and I agreed that we couldn't risk her getting pregnant again. Not after she'd died three times during childbirth.

She busted out laughing. "Where did you get that? Dane?"

I had yet to see the imposing alpha shifter since we rolled in.

I cupped her face. "I want to hear that laugh over and over again. But I bought a box at one of the gas stations on the way here. I wanted to be prepared."

Her cheeks were rosy red. "I'm impressed, vampire. I started birth control a few days ago, but it's best to double up for now, since I have to wait a week before the pill is effective. I've been assuming we could reenact that dream we shared. Remember the one in the birthing suite where we were in a sixty-nine position?"

My cock was impossibly hard, and I might lose my load before we even left this porch.

12

LAYLA

After Sam and I informed Greta we would be staying in the tent, Sam guided me through the compound, away from the cabins. The night was quiet, the air fresh and crisp, and a myriad of scents floated in the breeze. It smelled as if we were traipsing deep into a forest filled with Christmas trees. I couldn't see too much but didn't have to with Sam leading the way.

When we cleared a fat tree trunk, the tent came into view. I was expecting a small one that fit two people and having to duck my head to enter, but the structure I was walking into was big enough for Sam to stand at his full height.

He switched on an LED lantern that was on the ground next to a folding, fabric camp chair.

"This is where you stayed?" I asked in awe. "I was expecting a little tent fit for two."

His dimples emerged as he tossed the blankets and sleeping bags on the ground. "Dane has this for his shifter guests. I liked the tent. It's quiet, and the mutt smell isn't as strong out here as it is in a cabin."

"Plenty of room for monkey sex."

He full-on laughed, a deep throaty sound that sent sparks of heat and tingles to my belly. "I'm in for wild monkey sex." He kicked off his boots, not wasting time in undressing.

I spread out the blankets, then crawled on top of them while toeing off my flats. The temps were much cooler than in Maine, but at the moment, I was burning up from the oven-like cabin. Greta had a blazing fire going when we arrived, in preparation for the babies. My daughters didn't need that much heat.

Sam already had his shirt off and was unbuckling his belt when I moved my shoes out of the way.

"Horny, vampire?" I giggled, raking my gaze over him, wild and free.

It felt like ages since I'd seen my husband naked. All that wood chopping he'd done for the shifters recently had only served to define the cut grooves of his biceps and enhance the peaks and valleys of his ripped abs.

But what had me squirming where I sat was that thin line of hair that led to the bulge straining through his jeans. For a second, I lost all thought, feeling light-headed and giddy in anticipation of what was to come.

"Starving is more like it." He gave me a boyish grin. Yet there was nothing boyish about Sam Mason.

My heart sputtered, my pussy throbbed, and my throat became as dry as a damn bone.

"Take off your yoga pants." His tone was husky and commanding.

I obeyed, stripping from the waist down. Then I splayed my legs open as wide as they would go.

Silver banished the green in his eyes, and in a blur of motion, he shucked the rest of his clothes, his lustful gaze glued to my lady parts. "It's been too fucking long, baby doll." He stroked his long, thick cock.

Licking my lips, I played with my clit, my eyes rolling back in my head. He was right. It felt like eons since we'd had sex, and I wasn't counting that dream he and I had shared. Sure, it had been mind-blowingly awesome, and I'd felt everything as though it had been real. But reality topped a dream. I shivered at the thought of him inside me, on top of me, all over me.

We played with ourselves, our eyes locked, lust and love stringing us together.

Then I dragged my hand down to my inner thigh—the one spot other than my pussy and tits that he craved.

As if I'd flipped the switch, his canines slid out, and I shuddered.

He pumped his cock faster. "Top off."

My breath hitched as I obeyed. As soon as my bra came off, my tits bounced free, heavy and needy.

He growled, hiking his gaze up and down my naked body, opening his stance wider as he continued to please himself.

I pouted. "I want your cock in my mouth, vampire."

Before I could track his movements, he was on his knees between my legs, studying me through heavy-lidded eyes.

A sharp longing spiraled through me, and suddenly, I felt what he felt—love, lust, and happiness but also sadness. I swallowed the knot clogging my throat, feeling as though we were doing something wrong while our babies were missing. I couldn't stop the emotional change as a tear shot out and slid down my cheek. *What? No. No. No.*

Sam inclined his head, his midnight-black hair falling to the side. "Fuck. What's wrong?" He began feeling my body as if he were a doctor. "Are you hurt? Nauseous?"

Sitting up on my elbows, I blinked away another tear. "I'm fine. I'm sorry. I can feel your emotions. You're sad, and I feel guilty. We should be out finding our babies, Sam."

Pensive silence filled the tent until an owl hooted somewhere nearby.

He shoved a hand through his hair, releasing an epic sigh. "I know, baby doll. But we need sleep and each other." He went to grab his jeans. "Let's go back to the cabin. Maybe this isn't the right time."

When will it be the right time? We would always be hiding and running or putting out fires. We couldn't live on edge the entire time. We had to give ourselves a moment, minutes, or even a couple of hours to decompress and recharge our batteries.

I sat on my haunches. "Wait, I *need* you. Again, I'm sorry."

He tipped up my chin with the knuckle of his finger. "No need to apologize. I get it. There's nothing more important than bringing Orion and Luna home. That sadness you're feeling from me is partly what I'm feeling from you." He touched my heart then his. "You and I need this moment. Not just because I want to fuck your brains out—even though I do, desperately. It's more than that. I need to feel your love pouring into me. It's a balm to my crumbled nerves and weakens the agonizing pain stabbing my heart."

I tackled him. "I love you so fucking much, vampire." I cried as I kissed him, and as our tongues twisted together, little pieces of my soul mended.

I felt his heart beating in time with mine as an electrical charge raced through my body. From the moment I'd met him, we'd always had a metaphysical connection. At first, I hadn't understood it, but the longer we were together, the stronger our otherworldly link grew along with the love we had for each other.

We became two wild, starving animals, rolling around, mouths fused, hands everywhere, him on top, me on top, and sweat slicking our skin.

The world outside vanished, and before long, we were in a sixty-nine position. I laughed. He didn't. Instead, he licked an area on my inner thigh, and my pulse blasted out of the tent in anticipation of that initial bite. He kept up his assault as if stuck on repeat.

So I gripped his shaft, flicking my tongue over the tip of his cock.

He bucked once, and as though that was the nudge he needed, he sank his fangs into me. Swallowing a scream, I took him deep, sucking and licking, then playing with his balls as my orgasm was on the precipice of exploding. There was something about his fangs in me that was sensual and erotic—painful pleasure.

After he had his fill, he flattened his tongue on my clit then suckled. It took one hot second, then an ocean of ecstasy crashed into me. My body was on fire, my toes tingled, and my belly was a flutter of bat wings.

As my body relaxed for the first time in months, Sam jumped up. Startled, I stiffened until I saw him ripping open the condom package. Then I pouted. I would prefer to feel the velvety skin of his cock, but we needed that double protection—at least for now.

In vampire speed, the condom was on and he was hovering over me. "I can't tell you how desperate I've been to feel your pussy walls clenched around me."

"Stop talking, vampire, and fuck me like you mean it."

"There's my sex goddess. Legs over my shoulders," he commanded.

As soon as I was splayed open, he fucked me like a madman.

"Harder, vampire."

He chuckled, flipping us over until I was on top. "I need to see those tits bounce." He reached up and pinched my nipples hard.

I rolled my hips, tilted my head back, and began a slow and steady movement, squeezing my pussy walls around him. It had been way too long since we'd fucked, and I felt that fullness and friction I needed more than I'd even realized.

He grasped my hips, helping me move. "That's it. Faster."

I righted my head to find a fang embedded in his lower lip as he watched his dick slide in and out of my soaked pussy.

Blood dribbled down his jaw, the sight of it igniting a fire in my throat. I shot forward and licked the blood from his chin and groaned when my taste buds exploded with an array of sweet, salty, and spicy tastes. As his life essence slid down my throat, cooling that burn, his emotions commingled with mine—happiness, elation, love, lust, and satisfaction.

He flipped us once again and drove into me, his fangs gleaming, his silver eyes high beams in the muted light. "So fucking wet and tight."

I squeezed around him, then bucked forward, urging him to move.

His silver eyes became molten liquid as he thrust into me, hard and fast, rough then soft.

Skin slapped on skin. Moans, groans, and grunts peppered the air.

I latched on to his hair and kissed his chin, his lips, his jaw.

He shoved his tongue in my mouth as another orgasm dangled just out of reach.

"Fuck me harder, Sam. I'm almost there."

He obeyed and pounded into me.

I tuned out our heavy breathing, feeling every thrust as blinding white sparks flashed behind my eyelids, then I was falling over that orgasmic cliff, flying, soaring, and feeling free. No problems. No wars. No drama. Just pure freedom.

I slowly oriented my vision when Sam released a low growl as his cock pulsed inside me.

For a long minute, an outpouring of love tethered our gazes together. I could stay like this forever, watching him watch me. No words between us were needed. Yet I had the desire to shout out to the heavens how much this formidable, imposing, and gentle vampire meant to me—a passionate lover, a fierce fighter, a protective husband and father who had a heart of gold.

I rubbed my hands up his slicked chest, thanking the heavens above that he was all mine. "I love you, vampire. I would endure hell for you if it ever came to that."

His heartwarming grin awakened the butterflies in my stomach. "You and I could rule hell. Though our enemies wouldn't like us being there."

I giggled while he peppered kisses along my jaw to my ear.

"Love isn't a strong enough word to describe how I feel about you or us. You're the best thing to ever happen to me, Layla. I would marry you a million times over."

After a long, sensual kiss, I was ready for round two, until he got up.

"You're shivering." He tore off his condom and cleaned himself off with his T-shirt. "Let's head back to the cabin."

I didn't expect us to sleep out here, although on a warmer night, it would be the perfect spot to curl up in Sam's arms.

Once we were dressed, we started for the cabin.

"I've been thinking," he said. "In the near future, when our life is settled, we're going to buy land and build a place like Dane has here." He drew in a deep breath. "I'm done serving in the vampire military. You and our family come before anything else."

I stopped abruptly near a balsam fir. "You love the Vampire SEALs. You can't leave them." As much as I wanted a quiet life to raise our kids, Sam was a soldier and fighter. He lived for the action and the kill. He and his teammates were dedicated to protecting not only humanity but his kind as well.

The moon hung high in the sky, its rays beaming down and dancing across the hard planes of his face. "I love you more. Besides, we have to protect our children." Guilt coated his words.

"Sam, what happened with our babies is not your fault." I was pretty darn sure he was blaming himself, and I couldn't say I wasn't sharing the guilt because I was.

His forehead kissed mine. "For fuck's sake. It *is*. I'm immortal with sharp hearing."

"Is that why you want to leave the military? Because you feel guilty?"

"Remember when I told you at the sheriff's station that our kids were in danger the second they were born? Well, it's going to take two of us to protect them. I can't do that if I'm off on missions."

We resumed walking.

"Webb and Jo do just fine keeping Abbey safe," I replied.

"That's one child, Layla. We have four. You're strong and resilient, but you can't do it alone. Please don't say you have Jordyn because the two of you can't fight off a group of vampires or even humans."

He had a point, and I wasn't arguing. Our emotions were high and affecting our decisions, so he might see things differently later.

"I will support whatever decision you make about the military," I said. "But just know that humanity needs you." I wanted to be selfish, but that wasn't me.

Our children stood a better chance at a normal life with Sam leading the charge to save humankind. If he decided to leave the military, then I would endure anything for Sam and our family, even if it meant running and hiding until the day I took my last breath.

13

LAYLA

I *ran under a canopy of trees as the familiar scent of wintergreen hung in the night air. A crescent moon peeked through the branches from high above.*

Sticks, rocks, and dead leaves embedded in my feet, the adrenaline keeping me from feeling any pain.

"Go back. Momma," a boy said, fear coating his small voice.

I stopped cold and searched all around me, looking for that boy with green eyes and black hair. But I came up empty. "Orion, is that you?"

"Momma, you can't be here," he said.

The hackles on my neck flash froze, as did the limbs of my body. "Where are you?"

"This way, Layla. Keep walking forward," a woman said in a sugary tone.

I lost the ability to breathe. "Granny?" The woman sounded like Harriet Aberdeen but at the same time didn't.

Wolves howled in the distance, jarring me out of my stupor. I swallowed down my nerves and darted in and around fat tree trunks and low branches that scored my arms every now and then.

"I'm coming for you, baby boy," I shouted, breathing heavily as fear clogged my veins, but the adrenaline cleared them.

97

"That's it, Layla. You're getting closer," the woman said in a croaky voice. "Just another twenty feet."

I sprinted, pumping my legs faster and faster, my lungs burning like an out-of-control inferno, searing and scorching. "I'll kill you if you harm my children," I struggled to say as I crested over an incline.

Then everything became a blur. I couldn't stop my fall as every muscle in me went rigid, and my arms flew out in front of me. My stomach hit the ground first, and the air whooshed out of me.

I slid down a hill, arms out in front of me as gravity took the wheel. Faster and faster I went. I was on a collision course—to where, I didn't know. I fought for purchase, frantically feeling for something to stop me, but found nothing.

My heart was in my throat. Breathing became a monumental task as I scrambled to save my life.

You can't panic.

I laughed at the fucking voice in my head until I oriented my vision. The moon's rays sprayed down over a ravine, the edge of doom coming up fast. Terror careened through me, and death loomed. In about two seconds, my body would be splattered on the ground miles below.

The woman laughed, sounding ominous and unfamiliar. "You'll never see your children again."

"Fuck you, whoever you are," I shouted, or at least it sounded like that in my head.

If there ever was a time I needed an angel or fate to help me instead of screw me, it was in this instance. As if my prayers were answered, my foot caught on something thin but strong. I jerked to a stop, my hands and head mere feet from the edge.

My pulse hammered in my ears. I swallowed down the horror, afraid to move, afraid to look behind me, even afraid to scream for help. The tiniest of movements could send me to my death.

I was staring out over the chasm that cut through two mountain ranges when a white-haired woman materialized as if floating in the air.

I narrowed my eyes. "I swear, if you hurt my children, I will kill you." My voice was barely audible.

Her eyes flashed to orange. "I'm not your enemy."

"The fuck you aren't. You have my babies." However, she didn't sound remotely similar to the woman I'd just heard. The white-haired woman had a younger and softer lilt to her tone.

She shook her head. "I don't, Layla. But you need to listen to me carefully. If you don't wake up, you'll die." She glanced over her shoulder as if she'd heard someone. "I have to go. They're coming."

"Wait! Who has my children?"

"I can't talk. Just know that they're alive. I'll contact you soon." Then she began to fade into thin air. "Wake up, Layla," she said as her voice grew fainter, then a wolf howled somewhere nearby.

Then another wolf followed suit.

I shivered and jerked awake.

I was about to sit up when my eyes bugged out of my head.

What? Where was I? A quick glance sent terror through me. I was lying on my belly, my arms out in front of me and the cliff's edge deathly close just like in my dream. How did I get out here?

A piercing pain and pressure registered in my right foot that felt as if someone had tied it to a tree.

I pressed my hands into the damp earth and squealed when my body slid down an inch closer to death. I definitely wasn't dreaming. This situation was as real as the wetness seeping into my clothes.

I looked behind me ever so slowly and found my foot was caught on a vine. I didn't know whether to be relieved or not, since it was the only reason I wasn't sailing over the edge and into the ravine.

Think, girl.

That was my problem. My head was foggy as panic dug its claws into me. I could scream, but who the fuck would hear me?

The wolves, my inner voice supplied.

Ding. Ding. Ding. Shifters.

In order to scream, though, I had to suck in a ton of air, and that tiny movement could cause my foot to come loose, then my death would be imminent.

I laid my cheek on the wet leaves, squeezing my eyes shut for the briefest of moments and trying not to freak out.

It was becoming harder and harder to separate the dreamworld from the real world—the conscious from the unconscious.

I pushed out a scream, or attempted to, but I grunted instead.

Maybe I could use the vine to pull myself up. So I turned my head inch by slow inch, twisting my upper torso, feeling along the ground for something to grab on to when the vine gave way.

A scream barreled out of me, echoing through the dense forest in the dead of night.

14

SAM

A scream followed by wolves howling had me running out of the dining hall with Greta on my ass.

"That sounded like Layla." I stopped in the middle of the road and listened.

After Layla had crawled into bed, she'd fallen asleep in what seemed like seconds. I couldn't sleep, so I decided to sit out on the porch. That was around the time Greta had been getting ready for work. She was always at work preparing for the breakfast crowd before the crack of dawn since she managed the kitchen in the chow hall.

The she-wolf had asked if I could help prep the food because one of her employees would be late. I agreed. I knew what to do in the kitchen since I'd worked for her when I stayed at the compound while Layla had been in Maine. I thought my family would be okay for a couple of hours. I'd even left a note in the event Layla woke up.

"I'm going back to check on my family," I said to Greta just as another scream echoed somewhere nearby.

I ran for my life toward the cabin, which was the direction of the sound.

"I'll call Cooper," Greta shouted behind me.

The second I reached the porch of Greta's cabin, Jordyn flew out and practically jumped the steps to the ground next to me. "Layla's not in bed or anywhere inside. I saw your note. I was just coming to find you." Terror washed over her sleepy face. "The front door was wide open, Sam. Was that her banshee scream we heard?"

I couldn't imagine why Layla would be outside.

The rumble of an engine split the morning air. Cooper Gray, Dane's younger brother, skidded to a stop in the ATV, fear swimming in his blue eyes.

"It's Layla, isn't it?" Jordyn hugged herself.

"I'm afraid so. Sam, come with me," Cooper said.

Jordyn swallowed audibly. "This can't be happening." She was on the verge of tears.

I gripped her shoulder. "I'm sure she's fine." I didn't sound convincing. "Go inside. Can you start a fire?"

If the front door had been open, then all the warm air was gone. I was sure Layla would be the one needing the cabin at ninety degrees, depending on how long she'd been outside.

Jordyn snapped her spine straight. "I'll take care of things here."

She was a good egg, even though I'd wanted to strangle her. She'd pulled the fire alarm the night I'd rushed Layla to the infirmary where my beautiful huntress died three times during childbirth.

Whoa! Layla is not dead. Stop thinking the worst. Fucking hard to do just that when our lives were riddled with bad shit after more bad shit. Fate wasn't our friend, and the way the road ahead of us twisted and turned, I doubted we would ever catch a break.

Again, dude—shut the fuck up. Think positive thoughts. Layla is okay. Layla is okay. Repeat it ten times.

I did as my subconscious ordered even though horror slithered through my veins like a snake on the hunt for its prey.

I jumped into the passenger seat of the ATV.

Cooper peeled out like a NASCAR driver coming out of the pit.

Darkness waned as twilight set in.

I grabbed on to the roll bars overhead. "Tell me what happened."

He sped down the dirt road alongside Greta's cabin. "As far as I know, two of our pups decided to run this morning before the sun came up. On their way back, they smelled her, then followed her scent. One of them returned to get an ATV and gear to rescue her."

I was squeezing the roll bar to the point that I was crushing it. "Rescue her?"

My breathing was on a death-defying roller-coaster ride to hell, especially knowing the terrain outside the compound. I'd run in the mornings when I'd been a guest here for the last three weeks. The forest was dense alongside the ravine that dropped down several miles.

My stomach pitched and rolled. "Please tell me she's not dead."

"She wasn't when Jake got the ATV." Cooper drove through an open gate several yards from Greta's cabin.

My damn soul was crying like a newborn baby as Cooper headed toward the chasm that separated two mountain ranges.

"Does Layla sleepwalk?" Cooper asked.

"Not that I know of," I said as I mentally replayed the timeline from our monkey sex in the tent until Layla crawled into bed at the house.

After we'd returned to the cabin around three, we'd checked on Ellie, Rorie, and Abbey, who were soundly sleeping in the same room as Jordyn, then we showered. Afterward, we chatted for maybe fifteen minutes, touching on topics about my dad, the council, her grandmother, and Kendra. Layla had left her a voice mail on our way to the Catskills.

I'd been talking about looking for property when Layla had fallen asleep, which had to have been around four a.m. and about the same time Greta had gotten up for work. I'd gone out to sit on the porch when Greta asked me for help.

"She couldn't have been out here long," I mumbled. "I left the cabin with Greta around four thirty."

Cooper skidded to a stop at the top of a hill next to the other ATV that was shining lights directly toward the ravine.

I jumped out and literally lost my breath.

A shaggy-haired shifter was kneeling on the edge of the cliff, looking down.

My heart stopped, literally, when I didn't see hide nor tail of Layla.

Cooper sidled up to me. "Dear God. Did she fall over?"

My pulse was pounding for freedom, and my legs were locked into place.

"Please, Jake, just get Sam. He can save me." Layla's frightened voice echoed. "I don't want you to die because of me."

My heart restarted, and my body kicked into high gear. I ran to the edge beside the young teenager and peered over. My wife was barely hanging on, and I was flabbergasted as to how the fuck she ended up out here and over a fucking cliff.

Grace's explanation of dream walkers crystallized in my brain. They could put their victims in a trance and make them do things like sleepwalk.

"Sam." Layla's siren voice cracked. "Help me."

Her fingers were gripping a rock that jutted out from the mountain face as she teetered on a ledge.

I couldn't decipher whose pulse was beating off the charts. Hers? Or mine?

Stay focused, man.

I crouched down. "Here's how this will go. Layla, Jake and I will pull you up."

I regarded the teenager. He was broad and built, so he had the muscle to help.

Jake's friend and Cooper were lingering close behind us in case they had to step in to help.

I would like to think that with my vampire speed and strength, I could save my wife on my own. But man, my nerves were doing a number on me.

Her pulse was unstable, and she was breathing heavily. "I trust you."

I nodded at Jake. "Ready. We have to lift her together."

"Ten-four," he said.

We positioned ourselves with our knees on the ground.

"I'm right here," Cooper said. "Once you two lift her, I'll grab her."

As Jake and I pulled Layla up, Cooper slid his hands under her arms and tugged her to safety.

The second she was out of danger, I released the huge breath I'd been holding, then whisked Layla into my arms. As soon as we were on flatter terrain at the top of the hill, she passed out.

Cooper got on the ATV as Jake and his buddy ran up.

"Thanks, guys," I said to the teenagers. "I owe you."

If he and his buddy hadn't been on a run, I would be attending my wife's funeral. I stared at Layla's blotchy cheeks and scratched arms as my eyes clouded over. I wasn't one to cry, but I was ready to wail.

I was so fucking ready for a quiet life—away from the madness, the missions, the wars, deaths, and the list went on. I wasn't one to give up. But when would any of this end? When would our enemies give up and go home? When would we find our happily ever after? Could we?

15

LAYLA

Sweating like a pig, I kicked off the blanket and opened my eyes. As sleep began to fade and my mind awakened, I slowly registered stiffness and soreness in my muscles. I felt as though someone had beaten me with a meat tenderizer. I stretched my body and was working out the kinks when the deep timbre of Sam's voice caressed my skin, firing goose bumps to life along with my heart.

"Hey, baby doll, you're awake."

I sat up on the couch and turned from the blazing fire in the stone hearth to the kitchen on the other side of the room. The cabin was homey, rustic, and in a way reminded me of Uncle Jack's ranch. But the sweet aroma wafting around was taking me on a trip down memory lane. To Christmas morning, in fact. My mom had always baked cinnamon rolls for the holidays.

Sam strutted over, his long legs and thick thighs encased in jeans. His shoulder-length inky-black hair was tied in a low ponytail at his nape. My husband was clean-shaven, green eyes alight with pleasure, and wearing that lopsided grin that I loved seeing every fucking time.

As if he knew what I was thinking, he said, "Greta makes the best cinnamon buns."

But I didn't see the she-wolf, only my sister, who was cutting a roll.

"It does smell like home," I said, adjusting my T-shirt that was covered in mud.

Mud? Icy horror drenched my veins, my eyebrows knitting so hard it hurt as the events of my dream rounded to sharp pinpoints before me. As if that one word set off a bomb, pain registered in my sock-covered right foot. Actually, both feet had thick blue fuzzy socks on them.

The cushion dipped beside me as Sam sat down. "Dr. Hammond, the shifter's resident doc, stopped by to examine you. She cleaned your wounds, then bandaged your feet. Your soles were bloody. Do you remember what happened?"

Cliff. Ravine. Death. My breath halted in my lungs. I remembered it vividly.

Jordyn brought over coffee and a plate with a gooey cinnamon roll on it and set them on the wood table between the two couches.

Suddenly, I wasn't hungry. Instead, I was ready to heave.

She sat on the couch opposite me. "You scared the bejesus out of us, sis."

I brought my knees to my chest. "I frightened myself."

Truth. The sweat on my back was making me shiver. Weird that I felt hot yet chilled to the bone. I could use a shot of bourbon or whiskey, especially to settle my nerves. I'd almost died in a fucking dream. My head ached more so than the rest of my body.

Jordyn's brown eyes glowed with concern. "What happened? You've never been known to sleepwalk."

I inhaled. "I wish I knew."

"It was a dream walker, wasn't it?" Fear and worry etched Sam's tone.

I hugged my knees, resting my chin on top. "She was trying to kill me. Why? It's beyond me or my realm of thinking."

Jordyn's mouth parted. "Can someone really do that in a dream? This is your world, Sam. Do you know?"

He raised his hands. "I'm not accustomed to witches and their craft. Grace and Greta, who both know witches, have explained that dream walkers are powerful witches. My dad always says to believe in your dreams and the messages in them and never take them for granted. But this is out of my expertise. I'm afraid things are starting to take a different path."

"No shit," I mumbled. "First, our kids are abducted. Now some witch wants me dead. I wonder if the two situations are related— meaning, are witches the reason they were taken?"

"Tell us more about your dream, baby doll." Sam settled in as if I was about to tell a ghost story around a campfire.

In a way, I was. We even had the fire going. A psychotic laugh blared in my head. Maybe I was still asleep. I dug my chin deeper into my knees just for the sake of feeling a sensation to confirm I was among the living.

"There were two dream walkers," I started. "One good. One evil. The good witch is the white-haired woman I'd seen in my vision yesterday morning. She told me our babies are alive."

Sam flinched, and his mouth dropped open.

"Great news, right?" Wings of hope fluttered in my stomach at the notion that Orion and Luna were not dead. "Sadly, she didn't say where they were. She had to go. She seemed frightened and mentioned *they* were coming. Again, I don't know who she was referring to. That was as far as she got, other than saving my life by telling me to wake up." If she hadn't, then I wouldn't have screamed, and those shifters probably wouldn't have found me. Just telling them the story was making me shake. "Oh, and she is supposed to contact me soon. Please tell me I am not about to sleepwalk again." Another round of cold chills burrowed into my bones.

"For fuck's sake. Over my dead body." His tone was tight, his words clipped. "I'll be guarding the front door myself."

Jordyn was fascinated, but concerned creases lined the area around her brown eyes. "And what did the bad witch say?"

"The other woman sounded like Granny, but I don't think she was." I stared past my sister and directly at the trees swaying in the yard.

A vortex of dread, fear, and grief stabbed my chest. "Do you think the prophecy plays a part here?" Those damn words my dead mother had spoken felt like shards of glass etched in my brain.

One of your children is prophesied to change the course of humankind that will have a ripple effect, upsetting the balance of the world.

Sam's hypnotizing green eyes filled with questions and turmoil as he gave a quick shake of his head. "I don't think so. Greta mentioned that witches are always trying to hone their craft. Magical power is what they strive for. My guess is, if witches are involved, then they're after our kids' powers. Didn't the white-haired lady tell Abbey—"

"That our babies are special but also feared because together, they're the perfect storm," I finished for him. "That has a double meaning, though." I was ready to scream. "I just want to talk to that white-haired lady. Why is this so fucking confusing?" Frustration blazed like a fire burning my veins. "I can't make sense of any of it or figure out if it's true. I don't know what to believe anymore. We need an expert on witches."

Jordyn snorted. "For real?"

Sam handed me the mug of coffee Jordyn had brought over.

I shook my head. "I'm too wired. Caffeine will only make me more jittery right now. I'm second-guessing if my grandmother even has a hand in any of this."

A sardonic snort dropped from Jordyn's lips. "Oh, don't discount Granny. You know how resourceful and desperate she is. For all we know, she might've met a witch to do her dirty work since Adam kicked her to the curb. After all, our grandmother has been living among supernaturals a lot longer than we have."

I pulled on my hair as I kicked out my legs to rest my feet on the scuffed hardwood floor. "Okay, but the same boy in all my recurring dreams was also there. I didn't see him, but he called me Momma. He's definitely an older version of Orion. He warned me to go back, saying I couldn't be there. The older woman kept egging me on with 'This way, Layla. Keep walking forward. You're getting closer now. Just another twenty feet.' That was when I slid down the hill, and my foot caught on a vine." A round of chills blanketed my body. "Then I moved when I was trying to find a way to save myself." I shivered. "Next thing, I was sliding over the cliff."

Sam turned as white as a ghost.

"I latched on to the rock, and at the same time, my feet landed on the ledge. I swear that white-haired lady had to be helping me somehow." That was the only reasonable-yet-unreasonable idea I could think of for why I hadn't plummeted to my death. "This supernatural world—dream walkers, witches, shifters, vampires, who's our enemy, who's not—is causing me to lose my fucking mind. I just want our babies back, Sam."

He scooted closer until his arms were around me. "Greta might know a witch we can talk to. If not, I'll find one."

"Honestly, I think Kendra is still the one we need." I felt it in my gut, and I swore if that vampire didn't return my call today, I would hunt her down myself. Granted, I'd had other shit on my mind since I'd given birth, but it was time to chat with her. Not only did I believe she could shed some light on the prophecy, but she'd known my mom. She'd also known my aunt Vanessa, who was supposedly Abbey's grandmother. "We need to see Cooper." The enforcers confiscated our phones for security purposes at the gate last night. "I need to check my messages. Kendra should be back stateside by now. If we have witches on our mother's side, then Kendra might know them."

"I still think you can't discount Granny," Jordyn added.

"We're not," Sam chimed in. "Cooper stopped by earlier to check on you and informed me that we have a video conference with Tripp later this afternoon. He might have an update on passenger lists and whether Harriet took a flight to Montana."

I was beginning to wonder if we were on the wrong track or if maybe the witches were connected to my grandmother like Jordyn had speculated. Hell, maybe Norman Collier, Roman Brown, Rianne, Harriet, and the entire Intech band of merry fuckups were all working together.

I glanced up at Sam. "If Kendra is in the States, can Sawyer track her phone's location?"

"Sawyer can do anything." Jordyn swooned.

Sam cocked an eyebrow. "Is he the vampire you're hot for?"

I smiled at my sister. "You spilled those beans."

Jordyn huffed as she got up off the couch. "You two check your messages. I'll babysit Ellie and Rorie."

I needed a shower first, followed by some hugs and kisses with Ellie and Rorie. Then I might be in a better frame of mind to deal with whatever cannonballs people might fire at us.

16

SAM

Layla and I wound through a tunnel of trees on a narrow dirt path as we walked to the administration building. The August temperature was in the seventies. The air was fresh. I had my wife at my side. Thank fuck. I still couldn't shake the memory of her barely clinging to the ledge over a ravine. I didn't think I would ever be able to unsee that ever again. It hadn't helped when she articulated how she ended up out there. My life had flashed before me when she did.

"Are your feet hurting?" I asked. "We could've taken an ATV."

"I'm fine, Sam. The cuts aren't that bad. I want to walk. I love it here. It feels so quiet and peaceful." She threaded her fingers through mine. "I can't shake the feeling that the white-haired lady is trying to tell me something about Orion and Luna. I want to see her again."

"Fuck, Layla. My heart can't handle another round of sleep-walking."

"Maybe she'll come to me in a waking vision like she did yesterday morning."

As it stood, I wasn't sleeping ever again.

The sweet, fragrant mountain air swirled around us, filling my nostrils and giving me a sense of calmness for the moment. Just for five minutes or even ten, I didn't want to talk about witches, enemies, her grandmother, or sleepwalking.

What she and I needed was a good dose of laughter. Something to take the edge off.

"Can we talk about us?" I asked.

She hooked her arm around mine. "Sure, vampire. What do you want to talk about? I could use another distraction. I need something to forget my almost death, for sure. I have an idea." She flicked her head to the left. "Follow me."

Who was I to disobey?

She led me off the road and between two trees. The second we were shrouded amid balsam firs, she threw herself at me.

I lifted her up as she wrapped those mouthwatering thighs around me. "You want to make out?" I asked even though I knew what she was up to.

"We have lost time to make up for." She nipped my chin. "You have a problem with that?"

"Fuck no."

She pulled on my hair, making my head fall back as she kissed me. I felt her passion, her love, the energy emanating from her skin, and the beating of her heart as I ran my tongue along the seam of her lips.

We teased each other with soft flickering touches, coaxing, persuading, and finally giving in like two animals in the wild.

She dragged her lips down my jaw, neck, then back up to my ear. "I want to fuck you, vampire. Right here. Right now." She slid down my body until her feet were planted on the ground and her hands encircled my erection, then she squeezed it.

Stars danced in my vision. Birds chirped. Branches rustled, and leaves kicked up around us until all sounds began to fade except the beats of our hearts. I felt as though I were standing on the edge of a mountain high above, with a sense of freedom at my fingertips. No more strife. No more grief. No more feeling as though I couldn't breathe.

I buried my nose in her hair, basking in her essence that had a way of driving me mad.

She dipped her hand into the waistband of my jeans and froze.

"What's wrong?" I whispered in her ear. "Afraid of the big bad wolf?"

She dropped into a fit of giggles, a sound that was sultry, sending waves of warmth to my soul and me hurtling into her web of beauty, a thriving force that tugged, twisted, and snaked into my entire being before filling me with an unconditional love that set me on fire.

My fangs shot out as I yanked on her hair, studying her gorgeous face, mesmerizing blue eyes, and sensuous mouth that I wanted wrapped around my painfully hard cock.

Her tongue snaked out. "You're commando beneath those jeans."

It was my turn to chuckle. "That's why you're shocked?"

"No, but I'm trying hard not to suck you off."

"Fuuuck, baby doll. I don't think you'll have to. I'm about to lose my load right now."

She fixated on my mouth as she ran her finger over the tip of a fang. "You're a beauty to behold, vampire. I love seeing those fangs. That lust and love in your silver eyes. God, I would give anything to feel you bite me."

I sank my fangs into my lower lip, holding back the urge not to strip her naked. "Careful, baby doll," I said in a voice that didn't sound like my own. "I have no problem ripping off your clothes."

"Do it," she urged. "Let's throw caution to the wind. I need this. I need us. This might be our only chance for a while." She pushed me, or I let her. Then she walked deeper into the tree-infested area. "Come get me, husband."

I shoved a hand through my hair, glanced at the dirt road, and scanned the immediate area to be sure we were alone. The hub of activity was half a mile down the road, and not many shifters trekked through the woods—at least they hadn't when I'd been staying on the compound. Plus, we were nowhere near a cliff or ravine.

I sniffed the air, the fragrances of nature and Layla the only scents around. No dog smell. No additional heartbeats. It was just Layla and I cloaked beneath the enormous trees.

I darted in her direction. My pulse was high, my fucking cock ready to explode, and the idea of tasting her had my throat scorching hot.

I slowed to a walk. "I can hear your heart beating."

"Only for you, husband," she tittered, peeking around a tree trunk, her blue eyes shining in the shaded area. She sized me up, her gaze lingering on my groin. "I want him. Now."

Chuckling, I unbuckled my belt as I approached, staring at her mouth-watering tits poking through her white cotton shirt.

The second we were hidden in a cluster of fir trees, she unzipped my jeans, pulled them down, and pounced, sucking me into her mouth.

My legs went weak, and I almost stumbled as the area around me spun. "Fuck" dropped from my lips as I grabbed on to her head and dug my feet into the ground.

She licked, pumped, and nipped, but the second the tip of my cock touched the back of her throat, I bit down on my bottom lip, holding back a roar as my release hit me like white lightning.

She suctioned her lips around my shaft as she swallowed, moaning and giggling.

I thanked the vampire gods in heaven for bestowing this gorgeous woman upon me—a woman who was no doubt meant for me in every way possible—mind, body, soul.

I pulled lightly on her head, urging her to stand. Her cheeks were flushed, her eyes half closed, and she wore a smile that sent a bolt of love to my soul. I bent over slightly and captured her lips with mine. "Thank you."

She peered up at me. "Nonsense. I love tasting you."

In a flash, I had her leggings around her ankles and was on my knees, teasing her swollen clit with my tongue.

She pushed my head down to her inner thigh. "Bite me, vampire. I know you want to."

I wanted both her pussy and her blood dancing on my tongue. I grazed my fangs along her soft skin, peering up at her.

She watched me watch her before her hands coasted through my hair as she blinked once as if to say, *I'm ready.*

I peppered kisses along her leg, giving her a chance to breathe and allowing me a moment to enjoy her excitement. But when she began flicking her swollen nub, I struck, quick and hard, and groaned when her blood hit my tongue—sweet, salty, and savory.

She gulped in air, tensing, then released a sigh. "Fuck, Sam. I love when you do this."

My cock sprang to life, my chest exploded with warmth, and my fucking stomach was fluttering to no end. Drinking from her was a high like no other—seemingly forbidden, pure, and refined. I felt what she felt—lust, happiness, unconditional love that overpowered her guilt, despair, sadness, anger, hurt, and anxiousness.

She played with herself, frantically rubbing her clit.

I sucked with great pulls one last time, retracted my fangs, and moved her hand out of the way. I dove in hard and fast, running my tongue between her soaking-wet folds, sucking, licking, and eating like a madman. The taste of her juices coupled with her blood on my tongue was drug like no other.

"Sam. I need you to suck on my clit. Right now." Her tone was scratchy, sultry, and so fucking sexy. "That's it, Sam. Suck hard."

I did as she commanded, and the second I did, her legs started shaking, her nails dug into my scalp, and she whimpered as she rode out her orgasm.

I peered up at her to find her gaze locked on me. A beauty to behold—red cheeks, heavy-lidded eyes, and her signature smile reserved only for me.

"Sam," she said in a throaty voice. "Would you do me a favor?"

"Anything, baby doll."

"Can you slit your wrist?"

"Why does that sound so fucking sexy?" I think I fell in love with her all over again. There was something erotic and possessive about my blood inside her. Sometimes, it was better than anything in this world to see her drinking from me. Maybe even better than her blow jobs.

She lifted a delicate shoulder, her shyness making her more beautiful than I'd ever seen her.

Standing up, I bit down on my wrist as she stared at me with breathless eagerness, licking her lips as if she were the vampire and I were the human. The second the blood oozed out, her pulse quickened, her eyes flashed with hunger, and she drank like she'd been bloodthirsty for days.

I was quickly reminded of when she was rabid for my blood when we first met. She'd been so desperate for it that she used a dagger to slit my wrist open. Then, she'd been sweaty and had complained of a headache—symptoms vampires had when blood deprived, though we knew she couldn't turn. However, we had learned not long afterward that she was pregnant.

I went ramrod straight for a mere second until I realized she couldn't be. We'd used a condom, and she was on the pill.

Lifting her head, she sighed. "That was delicious."

I snorted. "Call me crazy, but why the raving hunger?"

She shrugged. "I don't know. I got this craving and burning sensation in my throat, which is reminiscent of when I first drank your blood. Weird, right?"

A siren blared with a high shriek and propelled us into action.

We hurriedly pulled ourselves together, fixing our clothes before darting out and onto the road.

"Rorie and Ellie," she said, breathing heavily as she started in the direction of the cabin.

I ran alongside, not sure what the fuck was happening. This

place was locked down tighter than a high-security prison. Then again, Layla had gotten out earlier this morning because one of the pups had left the gate open. Maybe someone had done the same now and our enemies had found us.

A blinding light flashed before me as I mentally kicked myself in the ass for letting my guard down.

"I wished we had our fucking phones," Layla pushed out through a breath.

"Cooper will give us radios today," I said as we banked right toward Greta's home.

I wasn't about to explain Dane's rules about security and phones. I understood why he was cautious. Well, I didn't know the details behind the entire story, but he had enemy shifters sniffing up his ass, and I would bet his anxiety had something to do with the death of his parents. I couldn't blame him.

She mumbled swear words when I spotted Dane driving a golf cart in our direction. The massive alpha looked odd with his head practically touching the hood of the cart.

I slowed to a walk, but Layla didn't. She kept running for her damn life.

"There's no threat," Dane said, holding out his arm in front of Layla.

Stopping abruptly, she fastened her hands on her hips. "Then what the fuck is it? My heart is my throat."

Dane slid out, his white hair ruffled, his features tight, and he was holding a two-way radio. "I'm sorry. I truly am."

His radio crackled. "Dane," the caller's voice blared.

"Go, Waters," Dane said into his radio.

"We're all clear. She's back with her mom."

"Copy that," Dane responded, then slipped the radio into the back pocket of his jeans. He eyed me then Layla, his human gaze shifting to a deep red—a sign his wolf was having a tough time staying hidden. "One of my enforcers opened the east gate on routine patrol, and he was met with a bear cub. I was heading out to help him when the cub slipped by him. We engage the siren as a precaution. Children here like to approach the cubs, and it's too dangerous. We've been trying to locate the momma bear, with no luck. Again, my apologies."

Layla was trying to regulate her breathing. "All I could think about was that someone had broken through and kidnapped Ellie and Rorie. We need those radios, Dane, for times like these so I can talk to Jordyn."

I wasn't about to disagree with Layla, but it had been crazy since we arrived. Cooper was giving us radios, which was another reason we were on our way to the administration building.

Sorrow washed over the alpha, softening his hard features as he enveloped Layla in a hug. "Again, I'm sorry to have frightened you. Also, I'm glad you're okay. When Cooper told me you were dangling off the cliff, I wasn't sure I heard him right." He released her. "That gate should've never been open."

I was beginning to think that maybe his compound wasn't the safe hideaway I'd thought it to be. "Dude, I know you run a tight ship. Do we have anything to worry about? I mean, Layla and I are leaving for Montana soon. I need to know if I can trust that some fucker like Roman doesn't invade this place."

Dane scrubbed a large paw across his chin. "Believe me, if someone like Roman finds us, we'll know about it from our spies in the town five miles from here."

Layla angled her head, her hair billowing in the breeze. "Doesn't Roman know where you are? He dated Vera's sister." She regarded me with wide eyes, her skin pasty. "We should rethink our plan."

Vera? I hadn't heard that name in a while. She was one of Dane's pack members and had been instrumental in stopping Dane and me from ripping off each other's heads that snowy night we'd met on the naval base in Massachusetts.

"Hold up," Dane's baritone voice echoed through the trees.

"Vera's sister never brought that asshole here. She'd been living in Boston. And any meeting I had with Roman was also in Boston."

I hadn't forgotten the brief conversation on that day after we'd carted Roman off to prison. I'd been shocked to learn that Roman had saved a shifter in Dane's pack. The alpha felt he owed Roman a favor, which prompted Dane and Vera to storm the naval base with him. On the flip side, Dane despised the cunning vampire. Roman had not only kidnapped Dane, but we were convinced his brother Ross was in the hands of Intech.

"Dane, do you swear and promise that my children are safe here?" Layla asked in a pleading tone. "I will still worry about them as a mother, but I need to know Ellie and Rorie and my sister will be okay while Sam and I are gone."

My mind was scrambling to figure out an alternate location, just in case. If Layla suggested we leave this instant, I wouldn't hesitate. The only backup we had was the naval base. That might not be the best place with the mob outside the gates, but it was guarded.

Dane crossed his bulky arms over his chest. "My pack are the most important people to me, Layla. I would die for them. The same goes for your children while they are under my protection. Can I tell you without a doubt we won't have any threats? No. In our world, and with what's happening in the human community, threats will always be there, which is what keeps me up at night. But that's the best answer I can offer you."

She flicked hair from her face. "For now, I need to check on Jordyn and our daughters. My sister is probably freaking out."

Dane nodded. "Then take the cart. I'll meet you in the conference room in the administration building. You know the way, bloodsucker, right?" The alpha seemed more agitated than usual.

Layla regarded me. "I'll go. I'll only be a few minutes. Wait here?"

This would be a good time to corner Dane without Layla to make fucking certain he knew I would gut the shifter if anything happened to Ellie and Rorie.

Once Layla had driven away, silence dangled like a branch hanging on by a thread as Dane and I stood staring at each other. The thrum of power was strong, twisting and stretching between us. But I wasn't about to cause trouble, although I would love to have that sparring session we hadn't yet had, if only to release some bad mojo.

"You owe me a sparring session, mutt," I said as I laughed.

He threw me the finger. "Good to see you, bloodsucker."

I feigned a pout. "Aren't you going to hug me?"

His canines lowered, seemingly for effect. "Not on your life."

"Glad to know you still love me."

He retracted his incisors and laughed. "You're such a snarky asshole."

I had plenty of barbs queued up, but it was time to ask the serious question. "Were you pulling our legs about the cub? Or were you trying not to freak Layla out?"

He held up his paws. "On my parents' graves, I wasn't lying. Also, I wasn't blowing smoke or placating anyone's feelings. I will die to protect your family while they are here. You have my word, bloodsucker."

I bobbed my head. "That's all I needed to know. Trust is a tall order right now."

"This fucking state of affairs with humans, Intech, Ross missing, your government, the shifter community, and supernaturals everywhere is out of control. I don't sleep a fucking wink anymore. When, not if, I get my hands on Adam Emery and Roman Brown, I'm carving out their intestines. We might not be best buds, but rest assured I have your back."

"Thanks for all that, man. I owe you big time."

"You do whatever is necessary to find Orion and Luna. And just to drive home my point one more time, Sam. I will decimate anyone who dares to touch, take, or harm your other two children on my watch."

The fact that he called me Sam and not bloodsucker was confirmation enough that he was true to his word. It also helped to hear the conviction in his voice and see the determination in his expression.

"I'm sensing you've been through something similar?" I asked.

"It's a long story for another day, but Cooper was taken at a young age by a rival pack. The wolf that took him is no longer alive, and I'll leave it at that."

I didn't know how our relationship had turned from wanting to break each other's skulls to a growing trust and friendship that was building like wildfire, but I wasn't complaining. I liked the pack dynamic—trust, family, friendship, dedication, bravery, and a fighting spirit. All those attributes resonated in me. That was what I stood for, and the Vampire Navy SEALs lived by those codes.

Now I felt like I could leave and not worry about anything other than finding my son and daughter.

17

LAYLA

I wasn't sure how much longer I could go on before my brain shut down completely or my heart gave out. I was beginning to question my sanity. When that siren went off, I'd lost the ability to breathe. To say I was on edge was an understatement. I understood that shit happened. But given what Sam and I were dealing with, anything, no matter how small or accidental the situation might be, would instantly rattle my nerves. Jordyn was in the same boat.

Earlier, when I'd sped home in the golf cart to check on her, she was pacing and panicked. I promised her there wasn't anything to worry about. Once I had her calm, I made a promise that after my family was whole again, we would discuss her, what she wanted out of life, and what her future looked like.

If she wanted to leave and start a quiet life somewhere, I would support her. If she wanted to fuck Sawyer's brains out, I would make that happen. How? I wasn't sure. If she never wanted to be part of the vampire world and felt the need to leave the country, I would help her do just that. It would break me if she ever left, but if anyone needed a chance at happiness, it was Jordyn.

"Earth to Layla." Cooper's kind tone penetrated my thoughts.

I blinked as I straightened in a chair in his office.

He slid my phone across his desk, his blue eyes appraising. "Are you sure you're okay?"

"I will be when I have Orion and Luna in my arms. This shit has to stop." I was on the verge of tears.

He traded his desk chair for the one next to mine, studying me. "I feel your anguish, believe it or not. I don't talk about this much, but it might help you. I was six years old when a rival pack kidnapped me."

I reared back, holding my chest, but I didn't say anything.

He flicked his wavy brown hair from his forehead. "My mom lost her mind. She couldn't sleep or eat. She had nightmares. She was so distraught that the only saving grace for her was shifting. She took comfort in her wolf and could feel that I was alive through her wolf senses." He paused for a breath. "I know you can't shift, but you have magic, Layla. I can feel it. It's not strong, but it's there. See if you can tap into it. Maybe then you'll feel your babies and sense that they're alive. That might relieve some of your anxiety."

The white-haired woman had said they were, but I didn't know if she was telling me lies or not. I wanted to believe her. Still, in a way, I did feel Orion and Luna. I wasn't sure how, though.

Cooper was sweet for trying to make me feel better. Also, it was good to know I wasn't the only one who'd experienced the loss of a child—or in my case, children.

"Thank you for sharing that. I'm so happy you survived," I said.

He patted my leg. "Whatever I can do to help."

Dane and Cooper—and even Greta—were good people. I was feeling much better about leaving Jordyn, Ellie, and Rorie here. Plus, Abbey was on-site as well, which also helped. Jo and Webb wouldn't leave her with just anyone.

"On another note, you're giving us radios today, right? My sister needs a way to communicate, particularly when Sam and I are gone."

I liked that the Gray pack had strict rules about the use of cell phones—the traceable kind, anyway. In all fairness to Cooper, my family and I had only been on the property less than twenty-four hours.

"I have them ready for you. Sorry I didn't give them to you sooner. We usually don't have so much excitement around here. Also, we have a communication room in this building set up with landlines for our pack. While you and Sam are in Montana, Jordyn can call you at any time." He pointed at something on his desk. "If you need to make a call now, you can use my phone. Also, all lines are secure and will show no caller ID to the person you're calling." He crossed the room to the door. "I'll be in the conference room down the hall with Sam and Dane."

"Can you tell Sam I'll join him in a few?" I asked.

"Sure thing. Also, I'm sorry about the gate last night. Jake mistakenly left it open. I'm assigning an enforcer to stand watch outside Greta's cabin tonight." Then he strutted out.

I didn't think the gate issue would've mattered. If that evil dream walker was trying to kill me, she probably could've somehow forced me to do anything.

I turned my cell on and walked around Cooper's office as I waited for it to power up. His space was neat and tidy with pictures of his family displayed on a bookshelf and on his desk. I zeroed in on a framed photo of Dane, Ross, and Cooper with a dead deer and another picture beside it of the Gray family—Mom, Dad, the three boys, who looked to be teenagers, and a young girl with brown curls who resembled Mom.

I didn't know the Gray brothers well. But Sam had shared that their parents weren't alive. He hadn't mentioned anything about a sister, and the third brother was Ross, who had supposedly been kidnapped by Roman.

Once my cell was on, I noticed I had a text message but didn't recognize the number until I saw Kendra's name in the body of the message.

Kendra: *Hi Layla. This is Kendra. I'm texting you from a burner phone for security purposes, which I can't go into right now. I apologize for not reaching out sooner. I was out of the country, but now that I've returned, I've had some issues I've had to deal with. I know the situation with your father is probably on your mind, and I would love to explain everything. But first, we have a different matter to discuss. So please call me at this number as soon as you read this message.*

My interest was piqued, and I couldn't pick up the desk phone fast enough.

"Hello?" the woman answered.

"May I speak to Kendra?" I asked.

"This is Kendra. Layla?"

I picked up a stress ball from Cooper's desk. "Yes. Finally."

"Sorry to be blunt, but I believe you're in danger," she said, quick as lightning.

What else is new?

"I know I am," I fired back in an insolent tone that came out more harshly than I'd intended.

Since I'd taken the job to capture Sam many months ago, every action taken on my part was a life-threatening risk. Danger was an everyday occurrence, not only as a vampire hunter but also as the wife of a bloodsucker. That last part was a gas. I was married to a powerful vampire who had a bounty on his head, his DNA was in high demand, most humans would probably try to kill him, and I could be used as a pawn to lure Sam out of the shadows. Fun times.

Yet that was only the half of it. I had my screwed-up Aberdeen family trying to change me into a monster, lock me up and throw away the key, or even kill me like that dream-walker witch had been attempting to do.

"But why do *you* think I am?" I asked.

"The prophecy," she said casually, as if we were chatting about old times.

The blood drained to my achy feet. "The prophecy is about a child of mine, not me."

She made a noise in the back of her throat. "So you know about it?"

I squeezed the stress ball, hoping to relieve some frustration. "Not really. When I died, I saw my mother, and she told me about a prophecy that is tied to a child of mine. She also told me to find you. That is, if you're Kendra?" When I'd met her, she'd only spoken two lines. Since then, she and I had only exchanged text messages—though she did sound like the woman in her voice mail greeting.

She harrumphed. "If it helps, I first met you at an abandoned airport outside of Chicago. Your asshole uncle Ray dragged me there. I will explain about your father at some point but not today. The important message here relates to your maternal great-grandfather. He wants to meet you and speak to you about the prophecy. Sadly, he can't travel."

My jaw hit the desk as my tongue stuck to the roof of my mouth. A chill like no other hit me like a Mack truck, and I was having trouble finding words. I should be excited that someone from my mom's family was interested in meeting me. I was more than interested in learning more about my mom's past, yet the timing was suspect given Orion and Luna's kidnapping.

"Why hasn't this man tried to contact me before now? Did he even know I existed? I need more to go on. I'm on a secure landline. You're on a burner phone. Therefore, we're okay to talk freely."

Her sigh sounded agitated. "You're right. My apologies. Everett Drake, your great-grandfather, didn't know anything about you until I found him. This is not my story to tell, and honestly, you need to hear it from Everett. What he has to say relates to a prophecy about you and your children."

Anxiety was a bitch, constricting my chest, my nerves, and short-circuiting my brain. How did I fit into a prophecy? I was supposed to save humanity, according to my mother.

"Are you saying he knows where my babies are?"

"Wait. Are they missing?" Her fear rang through loud and clear. "Please tell me they're not."

I was crushing the stress ball in my hand. "Two of them were taken two nights ago."

"Fuck," she said. "Who took them?"

"We caught a vampire guardian by the name of Norman Collier." I was imagining the stress ball was his head. "He had an accomplice who we think goes by the name of Patty Smith," I said. "Have you heard those names, or do you know them?"

"I don't. I'm sorry," she said on a sigh. "For the last few weeks, I've been looking for anyone in the Drake family."

"My mom's family? Why?" Given that my mom kept her past a secret, I was surprised to hear she hadn't lied about her maiden name.

"I grew up with your mom and her sister. They told me about a prophecy that affected the Monroe coven—your maternal grand-mother's coven, to be exact—and a set of quadruplets."

The picture of Cooper and his two brothers that sat on his desk went blurry. "Are you about to tell me that a coven of witches has my children?" I was ninety-nine percent sure this was where her conversation was headed. If so, then Harriet might be off my suspect list.

"That I can't say for certain," she said. "However, when I over-heard you were having four, I couldn't believe my ears. That's why I took off. I couldn't remember every detail of the prophecy, but knew I had to find anyone in the Drake family, in particular your grand-mother Agnes, who is a Monroe witch. I struck out in finding her. I did locate her father-in-law, Everett. He's in an assisted-living facility in Great Falls, Montana. I can't stress enough how important it is for you to hear what he has to say, particularly now that I know that two of your children are missing." The fear in her voice was becoming stronger.

"What are you afraid of? Tell me, Kendra." I felt as though she were sucking the air out of my lungs.

"Partly because witches scare the crap out of me," she said. "I had a run-in with one many years ago. Look, I know what I'm telling you might be hard to comprehend—" Her tone softened. "—but I promise you that I'm seriously trying to help you. I liked your mom, Layla. I didn't murder your father either."

"I know you didn't. Fred Emery admitted to killing my dad."

"I hate that fucker," she said through gritted teeth. "Roman Brown too. I can explain everything about your dad but not today. Talk to Sam about coming to Great Falls."

I didn't see an issue about going. After all, we were planning on confronting and bringing in Harriet. But if what Everett had to say was urgent and related to my children, then there was another way to chat.

"I'm at a place where we can set up a secure video call with Everett," I said.

"That won't work. Everett is insistent on meeting you in person. He has something of your mother's he would like to give you and only you. Whether this helps or not, Layla, he's dying of some type of liver disease. I'm not sure how much time he has. Sure, I can tell you about the prophecy or what I remember of it, but I wouldn't do it justice. The only thing I will say is that the prophecy shouldn't be ignored. Everett has firsthand knowledge of the Monroe coven. I really wish we could find Agnes. Everett told me he hasn't seen your grandmother in several years. He doesn't know if she's dead or not."

I was beginning to think that maybe the dream walkers were the witches in the Monroe coven. "Do you know what Agnes looks like? Also, are you thinking that the Monroes might have my babies?"

She blew out a breath. "It's been such a long time since I've seen Agnes. Then, she had long brown hair and eyes to match. As to your second question, I don't know. I also don't know where the Monroe coven is. I told you that I'd gone out of the country. I went to Regina, Saskatchewan, in Canada, which is where Agnes is from. I struck out. The Monroes aren't there anymore."

Maybe Sawyer or Cooper could do some digging on the Monroes.

"Give me a few hours, then I'll have an answer on when we can be there," I said.

I had to run this by Sam, but I didn't see any reason why he would shoot down the idea to talk to Everett.

"Don't take too long, Layla," she said before the line disconnected.

I sat there for a moment, mentally laying out the puzzle pieces we had so far—the vision of the white-haired lady who saved my life, Abbey having a vision of the same white-haired woman, a dream walker trying to kill me, and everything Kendra just shared. All of it was pointing to the kidnappers who had Orion and Luna being witches. The questions now were: Did the Monroe coven have them? Or did another coven?

On top of that, we had an opportunity to understand the meaning behind the prophecy that was tied to one of my children. I was beginning to believe that was the reason they'd been taken. Still, how had the witches found my children? I would like to say it had been with the help of our mole and Norman Collier. But we were dealing with witchcraft now, so anything was possible.

I hurried out of the office in search of Sam.

Tim Cox's voice filtered out from the conference room as I approached it. I'd been wondering when his story would air. Rianne's beastly picture was on the movie screen in front of the conference table when I entered.

Sam, Cooper, and Dane were riveted as they watched and listened to Tim. I was suddenly engrossed, seeing before-and-after images of my sister. Tears stung my eyes at the picture of her before she'd turned. She'd been beautiful with her long brown hair, big brown eyes, and a smile that warmed my heart. She'd resembled our mom in so many ways.

Sam's hot breath in my ear jarred me out of my pity for Rianne. "Have a seat. You look like you've seen a ghost."

Every damn time I saw my sister with canines and talons, I cringed.

"We don't have time to sit. I spoke to Kendra. She found my great-grandfather, Everett Drake, who can tell us about the prophecy."

Dane picked up the remote, and a second later, the sound was muted. I now had their undivided attention, so I dove in and explained everything Kendra and I had talked about.

After I finished, Cooper was flipping open his laptop on the conference table. "You said the Monroes are originally from Regina, Saskatchewan. I don't know that I can dig that deep into a foreign database, but I can try. First, it might be best to work backward. We have Agnes Monroe. Layla, where did your mom grow up?"

"If Kendra knows your mom," Sam said, "then try Shelby, Montana. Sawyer dug into Kendra, but that was all he found on her."

Dane leaned back in the leather chair. "Are you sure it's not a trap?"

I regarded the white-haired alpha. "One hundred percent sure? No. But the fear in her voice tells me she's not lying about anything she told me." I craned my neck up at my husband, who seemed to have his thinking cap on. "What do you think, Sam?"

"Tripp confirmed Harriet is in Montana." He held his chin with two fingers. "I find the timing suspect."

"I do as well. But I would bet my life Kendra isn't working with Harriet. She hates my uncles." Granted, that didn't mean she despised Harriet by proxy. "However, my intuition says we need to talk to Everett."

Dane pushed to his feet, dragging his knuckles over his jaw. "I have to agree with Sam. I hate to say this, but the entire world is against you two. I wouldn't be surprised if Roman made a deal with witches or the other way around. Think about it. That fucker has his hands in everything. You could be walking into a trap."

I didn't want to piss off the alpha. Dane was a scary dude. But he wasn't helping me.

"Guys," Cooper said. "Check this out."

My pulse soared into the heavens as I rushed over to Cooper. "What?"

He pointed at the screen. "Agnes Monroe Drake was reported missing six years ago by her husband, Derrick Drake, who perished in a house fire two years later."

"Does it say anything about their daughters—my mother, Meredith, and my aunt Vanessa Drake?" I asked, standing over Cooper's shoulder.

He typed like the wind, and another article popped up. "There's an obituary for Vanessa Drake. She died ten years ago of ovarian cancer."

Sam leaned over Cooper slightly. "Vanessa was Abbey's grandmother. Does it say anything about her having a granddaughter?"

Cooper scrolled down. "It doesn't."

Sam pushed out a huge breath. He was worried about his niece. I got that. But even if the article confirmed Vanessa had a granddaughter, it wouldn't matter. Roman already knew Abbey existed.

I pressed my lips into a thin line. "This is all good. But we need to decide when we're leaving." The more I thought about what Kendra had said, the more urgent I felt it was to meet Everett. I was going with or without Sam. I suspected he would try to stop me, but I was ready to fight him if he did. "We're going to confront Harriet, so why not Kendra and Everett too?"

As if a lightbulb came on, Sam bobbed his head. "You're right. But someone is trying to kill you. I want to be as cautious as we can. In my book, Harriet is easy. She's human. Witches, on the other hand, could be quite the challenge. There's a reason your mom never told you about her family, and that also makes me nervous."

I hadn't asked if Everett was a witch, but I was certain Kendra wouldn't have left out that part.

I touched Sam's chest. "I know you're worried about me. But we have to think about Orion and Luna. Their lives are just as important as ours."

His jaw flexed. "Fuck, Layla. I know that. I don't want to lose anyone. But please understand something. I can't live my life without you, and I will do everything I can to make sure I never do."

I gave him a loving smile. "May I remind you that I've faced danger hunting bloodsuckers most of my life, and I'm still here." Even though I was out of practice, no one and nothing would stop me. "You know you can't keep me sidelined. So if it helps, I will follow your lead, orders, and commands like I'm your soldier. Suit me up with armor or whatever. I need you calm and the badass vampire you are and not freaking out about me. If you do, you could get hurt or killed as well. Deal?"

He chuckled. "How can I say no to that?"

"You can't and won't. You know I'm stubborn," I teased, trying to infuse some lightness into the discussion.

My husband was worried about me. He was trying to protect me. One of many attributes I loved about him. But we were in a catch-22. No matter how much we were concerned about each other, we had to put our children first.

18

LAYLA

Orange, yellows, and reds streaked the sky outside the Meadow Oaks nursing home in Great Falls, Montana. Sam and I were scoping out the backside of the property that sat along the Missouri River on the east side and was tucked off a main thoroughfare in a populated area of the city.

Despite Sam's skepticism about this meeting, we'd arrived thirty minutes early to ensure we weren't walking into an ambush, which was normal protocol for my military husband.

"All clear on the street. No signs of suspicious activity," Conrad said through the comm.

He was the only one with us. We'd been hoping for more field personnel to accompany us to Montana, but we had several fires going on, including tracking Adam and Roman's whereabouts. The Vampire Navy SEALs speculated that Adam and Roman had been tipped off that the Feds were converging on Intech's headquarters in Chicago, so it was possible there was another mole somewhere, either on our side or on the Feds'.

Unless Intech was calling the shots with kidnapping, I didn't give a shit about them right now—or about my grandmother, for that

134

matter. All signs were pointing to witches. Sure, Jordyn could be right about our grandmother teaming up with a witch, but I was banking on Everett giving us something of substance or hoping I had another vision involving the white-haired woman. I'd even forced myself to sleep the last three nights. I'd struck out. Not even a glimpse at the other dream walker, who wanted me dead. Sam had said I'd tossed and turned the majority of the time I was trying to sleep, which was probably why I hadn't been able to dream. I'd never dropped into the REM state.

Yep, my overprotective husband had watched me like a hawk while I slept, even going as far as barricading the bedroom door with a dresser. He wasn't taking any chances. He'd been kicking himself in the ass for leaving to help Greta in the dining hall that morning I'd been hanging off the side of the cliff.

"We're heading your way," Sam said to Conrad.

I lingered for a moment on a concrete path that led from the small lake behind the building to the parking lot, watching a nurse push a gray-haired woman in a wheelchair toward the lake.

Sam backtracked. His radar fired to attention, his voice rising an octave as he asked, "What is it?"

"Nothing to worry about," I said. "Instead of going inside, we can have Kendra bring Everett out." If he wasn't bedridden. "We can sit by the lake." The sound of the water sliding over a rock bed would drown out voices for sure.

Besides, the August temperature was a balmy eighty degrees with a soft breeze. The sweet smell of fresh-cut grass and nice scenery definitely trumped the inside of a nursing home or any indoor facility. More importantly, we wouldn't risk anyone hearing us or recognizing Sam.

As it stood, he was trying to look inconspicuous with a ball cap shadowing his face. The operative word was *trying*. The imposing vampire's height alone turned heads. Not to mention the aura of danger he exuded, especially when he was tense and wearing his soldier mask—jaw flexed, eyes hard, and nostrils flaring.

"Good idea," Sam said as we continued to the SUV where Conrad was waiting.

Unlike Sam, Conrad exuded an aura of calmness despite his tall height and had a softer look to him.

Then again, Conrad was a scout—a detective, in human terms—for the vampire government. He had to blend in for his job. Instead of military boots like Sam was wearing, Conrad had black loafers on and was wearing ripped jeans and a white dress shirt that brought out his black hair and hazel eyes.

My husband was dressed in civilian clothes as well, but whereas Conrad reminded me of a businessman, Sam exuded a badass gang-member vibe.

Conrad slid his cell into his jeans pocket. "Still no response back from my contact in Boston about those darts." He sounded more frustrated than I'd ever heard him.

"Something else is bothering you, man. I can feel it," Sam said. "What did you leave out of what you told us when we landed earlier?"

Conrad had flown commercial and met us at the private airport outside Great Falls with a rental car. He'd given us an update on the state of affairs at the council's headquarters—chaos, tension, and shouting matches. There was no resolution on the vote, and from what Conrad had seen, it didn't appear a vote would be decided upon anytime soon. Steven was so enraged that a guardian was responsible for kidnapping his grandchildren that he'd put the council's political affairs on hold until further notice.

But the elders weren't listening to Steven. They were proceeding with or without him. Well, that didn't go over well with my father-in-law. So he gathered his close-knit team of guardians who he trusted and had them lock up the ancient elders until further notice.

I had my jaw on the ground when I'd heard that. Steven was the most revered and powerful vampire among his kind, yet he'd always been diplomatic—at least, toward me. I'd never witnessed him going off the rails. But everyone had a breaking point.

Sam hadn't been shocked. His response had been, "It's about fucking time."

Silence strung us together as Sam and I waited for Conrad to speak. He seemed to be struggling for words, glancing out in the distance where oak trees shrouded the view of the nursing home from the road.

"Dude, just come out and say it," Sam told him.

Conrad and Stan had escorted Norman Collier from Maine to Boston. Conrad had informed us that it went off without a hitch. Unless he'd lied.

I stiffened. "Did Norman get away?" Rianne flitted through my thoughts, but she was locked up in the prison building on the naval base. Tripp also hadn't experienced any issues transporting her from Maine to Massachusetts.

A muscle jumped in Sam's jaw. "Fucking talk, Conrad. We don't have all day." My husband was operating on his last nerve.

His ire had multiplied over the past seventy-two hours since I'd spoken to Kendra on the phone. It had taken that long to round up a plane and pilot for Sam and me. A commercial airline had been out of the question given Sam's so-called celebrity status with humans.

In the meantime, the tension had been mounting. Cooper had failed to find anything on the Monroe witches, Sam was deathly afraid that I would sleepwalk again, and the more days that passed, the more both of us were dropping into a wild state of madness. If we didn't find a hot lead on Orion and Luna soon, he and I would explode. But his patience was thinning faster than mine, and before long Sam would be leaving dead bodies in his wake.

Conrad scratched his close-shaven beard. "I don't want you guys distracted. I wanted to wait until after we were through here. As I told you earlier, your father sent Jonah to tail Harriet Aberdeen in Bozeman. Well, Jonah just sent me a text. Harriet's at a casino, meeting with Claude Irving."

I had to think about that for a second. "She despises that man."

Claude Irving was a thorn in the Aberdeen family's side because of my uncle Ray's love for the game of blackjack. He'd wagered the Aberdeen bank account and drained every penny of it at Claude's casino.

Sam shrugged. "So what? She's probably gambling her money away since she's dying."

Conrad's grin was congratulatory as he gave Sam a slight nod. "Oh, she's gambling, but not on cards or roulette. She's got her money on you, Sam."

Sam threw his head back and laughed, a sound that was eerie but contagious. He had me joining him as I realized what Conrad was inferring.

"You're telling me she's the one who put the bounty on my head?" Sam asked through a deep chuckle.

"Not one hundred percent sure, but Jonah overheard Harriet say something to that effect to Claude Irving. He'll find out more."

I was grateful that Conrad had chosen to tell us now because it zapped the tension from Sam until a blue Honda Accord wheeled into the parking lot.

The blonde driver smiled at us before she pulled her car alongside our SUV. It was hard not to remember Kendra or that snowy day my uncle Ray had brought her to a fight she didn't belong in.

She got out, shoving her keys into the pocket of her black jeans as she smiled at us. She had a look about her that reminded me of runway models—sleek and beautiful. Her long wavy hair spilled down her shoulders, and her eyelashes were covered with a thick coat of black mascara that framed her shimmering green eyes. Her makeup was painted on to perfection, and she had a beauty mark near the corner of her right eye.

After a round of introductions, she summarized what she had relayed to me on the phone and told us what to expect from Everett, which was that he was as sharp as a tack but tired easily.

"Before we go in," she said, "I take it you guys made sure you weren't followed?"

"Of course we did," Sam bit out. "Were you?"

She raised her hands. "Full disclosure—someone has been tailing me, but I lost him two weeks ago. I'm pretty sure it's one of Roman's goons. Since Roman knocked me out at the hotel in Massachusetts, I think he's been trying to see what I'm up to." Her green eyes flitted to black as her anger caused her vampire side to show.

Steam practically came out of Sam's nose. "You're just telling us this now?"

She narrowed her gaze at Sam. "Chill. I've eluded assholes tracking me for years. This isn't my first rodeo, Mason. Besides, if you'd known before coming here, would that have changed your mind?"

I doubted it would've made a difference for me. Anywhere we went, we had to be cautious, and today wasn't any different.

Sam growled. "If you put my wife in danger, I will yank out your fangs."

She half smiled. "You have no reason to trust me. I get it. But know this. I owe your father my life, which is one reason I'm helping. But the other reason, you'll hear from Everett. When you leave this place, you'll be glad you came."

I would be the judge of that.

19

LAYLA

Conrad guarded the front of the property while Sam and I waited by the lake for Kendra to bring out Everett Drake.

She hadn't anticipated any hiccups since Everett wasn't bedridden. He actually liked the outdoors, and meeting out here was his suggestion when Kendra had visited him a few days prior. Apparently, he liked sitting out by the lake with a rock-bed waterfall, flowering trees, shrubs, and benches completing the Zen-like area.

If I were dying, I wouldn't want to spend my remaining time in a hospital-style room if I didn't have to. In fact, I certainly was enjoying the calming vibe. Sam wasn't. My gorgeous vampire, who was quite sexy wearing his ball cap with his hair in a low ponytail, was pacing up and down the concrete walkway that circled the lake while I sat on a wood-slatted bench with wrought-iron arms and legs.

Every minute, he glanced at the building, flexing his hands as if preparing for a fight. I didn't anticipate any threats even though Sam wasn't thrilled about Kendra's announcement that Roman's men had been tailing her. He'd mumbled swear words the entire way from the parking lot.

"Sam," I said as he sped by me. "You're making me nervous."

He flashed a lopsided grin, his dimples on display. "Sorry, baby doll. I know it's best to talk out here, but I feel like we're being watched."

I jumped in front of him. "Do you hear or smell anything?" He had the senses to know for sure, and his gut feelings were hardly ever wrong.

He threaded his rough fingers through my soft ones. "No." He pressed on his comm. "Conrad, is it all good your way?"

"Clear," Conrad said.

"See? We'll talk to Everett, then we're out of here. You know, some little old lady is probably just ogling you from a window." I giggled.

The nurse and lady we'd seen earlier were no longer outside.

"The only one I want drooling over me is you." He feathered his lips over mine. "You know, we have the night to ourselves. We can do room service, a bubble bath, fuck like bunnies, and run around naked."

Flames of lust burned south to settle between my legs. "Care to tell me what you would like on the menu? The sex dungeon *is* wide open."

He whipped his head over his shoulder. "Maybe later."

I followed his line of sight, and our intimate connection vanished in a millisecond.

Kendra was pushing Everett's wheelchair down the winding concrete path.

"I hope we find something out," I mumbled, my attention on the frail eighty-year-old man who looked like he'd had a rough life.

His cheekbones poked out, his glassy brown eyes were sunk inward and rimmed with dark circles, his skin tone was yellow, and his arms seemed like they were the size of pencils. From my viewpoint, I would guess he didn't have long to live, just as Kendra had stated.

Sam wrapped an arm around me. "Now who's nervous? Your pulse shot from sixty to a hundred in a flash."

"Just anxious to hear what he has to say," I said under my breath. I was also saddened that I didn't even know him and angry at my mom for keeping her past hidden. Maybe if she hadn't, Orion and Luna wouldn't be missing.

If your mom were alive, you might not have met Sam.

I kicked my inner voice to the curb while Kendra settled Everett on the concrete between the narrow aisle of grass and the bench.

I took a seat to rest my trembling legs. Sam hovered behind me, briefly touching my shoulder as a sign he was there to help me if need be.

Kendra locked the wheels in place. "Everett, this is your great-granddaughter Layla."

Everett studied me with stunned intensity. "I don't know where to begin. I can't even believe you're here. I searched for your mother for years. Kendra tells me Meredith passed away from breast cancer," he said in a brittle tone.

I nodded. "That's right. She never shared her past with my dad until she was dying." I wasn't exactly sure how much my mom had told my dad. I'd only learned recently that my mom had vampires and witches in her bloodline.

"I can't really blame her." He regarded Sam. "Is this your vampire husband?"

I touched Sam's hand that rested on my shoulder. "This is Sam."

"You look scarier in person than on TV," Everett said, giving us a toothless smile.

Sam chuckled. "I get that a lot."

Everett rubbed the journal that was in his lap. "Thank you for coming." His voice was soaked in despair and loneliness.

I'd read the article several times on Agnes Monroe Drake, my maternal grandmother, that Cooper had found. I'd even tried to dig for more info on the Monroes and Drakes with Cooper's help. The only information we'd found was on the disappearance of Agnes and the deaths of Derrick Drake, my grandfather, and his daughter Vanessa, my aunt, who had died before Derrick.

My heart broke for Everett. "Do you have any family nearby?" Kendra hadn't mentioned if his wife was alive or if he had siblings.

"I don't. Your great-grandmother died young. I believe she was murdered, but the police didn't think so. They had no evidence to prove she had been. The autopsy indicated a heart attack. But she was healthy and in good shape with no heart issues in her family."

I glanced past him to the water. Maybe that incident was what had prompted my mom to flee her past.

"He thinks the Monroes had something to do with his wife's death," Kendra chimed in, fixing the plaid blanket on Everett.

"I swear it was some type of witchcraft," he said. "I'm sure of it because it wasn't long after Agnes's sister Maeve Monroe showed up in town when my wife was found dead in her car."

The more I was learning about my mom's family, the less I wanted to know. But we were here for my frail great-grandfather to shed some light on the prophecy and how it related to my children.

"Kendra tells me you know quite a bit about a Monroe prophecy," I said to Everett.

He reached up with a shaky hand and scratched his balding head with a long yellow nail. "At first, my daughter-in-law wasn't forthcoming about her past, except Agnes told my son that her family burned in a house fire."

I cocked my neck at an angle and gave Sam a knowing look.

Sam gently squeezed my shoulder. "A house fire? The same way your son died?"

Everett flashed glassy eyes our way. "Seems so. I wasn't naïve enough to believe my son's death was an accident. The more Agnes opened up about her family, the more I was discovering that witches like to burn stuff. Agnes's sister Maeve believed fire was purifying. A way to cleanse the earth of evil. Still, Agnes didn't exactly lie about her family perishing in a house fire. Some had, but not all of them.

Their family or coven has been targeted for generations by other witches because of the Monroe prophecy. It's a two-hundred-year-old prediction that has been etched in stone by a Monroe seer."

My stomach was churning like an epic tornado, and I knew where he was going with this story—which was causing my head to hurt and my chest to constrict.

Everett regarded Kendra, who was sitting beside me now. "When Kendra told me about your quadruplets, I was shocked. I'd always thought the Monroes were one banana peel away from the crazy house." He sighed heavily. "But I guess I was wrong. The Monroe seer had a vision of her entire coven being turned into vampires by an inhuman child born to a Monroe witch. This child is prophesied to be able to turn not only members of the Monroe coven but any witch into a vampire. According to Agnes, if this happens, witches could lose their powers and in turn could disrupt the supernatural balance. Too many of one species is never a good thing, which could affect humanity as well."

I gasped, my eyes popping out of their sockets, even though I knew this already. My mom's words were blaring in my head. *Ripple effect. Change the course of humankind. Upset the balance.* Everything Everett was detailing.

"You're referring to a child of ours?" Of course he was. That was the urgency in this meeting, but I had to ask, just the same.

Sam circled the bench and wedged his way between me and its arm. "So are you saying a Monroe witch has our two children?"

Everett lifted his small shoulders. "Maybe. Or maybe it's another coven. The witch community is very well aware of this prophecy. At least, that was what my daughter-in-law told my son and me. But Kendra informed me that two of your children are missing. I would bet the remaining months of my life that a coven definitely has them. I guess I should ask—are your children inhuman?"

Sam's jaw was rock solid. "We believe two of them are."

Bile was pouring into my throat as my breathing was all over the place. "Does this child only turn witches or humans as well?"

He extended the journal to me. "Before my daughter-in-law disappeared, she gave me this and begged me to not let this out of my sight until the time was right. I'd asked Agnes how I would know. Her response was, 'You'll just know.' Anyway, you might find the answer in there."

The worn, scratched leather book seemed to vibrate in my hands as if it was prompting me to open it. I was curious if it was a book of spells or maybe information that could lead us to Orion and Luna.

Sam rested his forearms on his knees. "Sounds to me like you don't think Agnes is dead."

"I believe she left either to protect herself and my son, Derrick, or to find Meredith, or she could very well have returned to her coven. Of course, she might not be alive. I wish I knew. She was distraught when Vanessa died and even more so when Meredith left home. Agnes was also livid with Maeve." A veil of sadness hung over him. "My daughter-in-law was a sweet woman. She loved her daughters and my son. If she saw you now, Layla, she would love you just as hard." He inhaled a deep breath. "I'm sorry, Layla. I wish I could've met you under better circumstances."

I frowned sadly. "The feeling is mutual."

He pointed at the journal. "I'm glad I'm able to pass that book along to you and share what I know. Agnes had given it to your mother not long before Meredith left. Agnes had been surprised to find that she didn't take it with her. She thought the contents could keep Meredith safe. But it seems my granddaughter did a terrific job on her own."

"My mom was a strong lady and a fighter. She loved hunting vampires too."

Kendra let out a weak laugh. "Thanks to the vampire boys she'd found attacking humans one day."

I was relieved to hear that my mom hadn't lied to me when I'd seen her in the afterlife.

Sam dug his elbows in his knees, fingers touching his mouth. "Where in all this does it say our child is involved?"

Everett clasped his hands in his lap. "It doesn't. But the prophecy says the child will be born to the Monroe witch who bears quadruplets."

Kendra put her hands together in prayerlike fashion as she brought them to her chin. "This is a lot to take in." Pity weaved through her words. "Layla, you're the first Monroe witch in their bloodline to have quadruplets." She rose elegantly then faced me. "Which one of them is that child who will grow up to turn witches into vampires? That's the mystery. My guess is, and I hate to say this, but maybe they want all four dead. By *they*, I mean any witch, not just the Monroes."

"How did they find my children? Witchcraft? Spies?" I asked.

Her grass-green eyes darted past me. "As far as I'm aware, they keep track of their bloodline. Maybe the Monroes have kept tabs on your mom all along. They didn't react or bother her because she had three daughters separately, not four children at once. Or maybe they approached her, and your mom found a way to hide again."

Sam sat up straighter. "Because we're dealing with witches and visions and seers, my guess is a witch had a vision that our four babies were born. Either way, it's becoming clear to me that a witch is behind the kidnapping."

I threw my head in my hands, wanting to scream.

Sam rubbed my back. "This is a lot to take in. But I need to know where to start looking for a Monroe witch. Everett, if your daughter-in-law is alive, any idea where she might be or where the coven might be?"

"Agnes had a good friend, Zoey, who was a powerful witch. I don't know her last name. It's been many, many years. But I do recall that Zoey teaches at a school for witches. Agnes had been thinking of enrolling Vanessa and Meredith there. But I don't remember where the school is or if it still exists."

Sam and I exchanged a knowing look. It was just a few days ago that he'd recommended to Jo a special school for Abbey. The only problem was how to find the school. I highly doubted schools for witches or vampires were publicized on the Internet, although the vampires did have their own web of information.

"We have resources to find the school," Sam said confidently.

Regardless, in one way, I was relieved to finally understand the prophecy. In another, I was ready to puke. A child of mine would change witches into vampires. Did that mean I could be turned? The possibility that I could live for eternity with Sam and my children excited me.

"Does your daughter-in-law, my grandmother, have white hair and orange eyes?" I asked. Kendra remembered her with brown hair, but that was during the time when Kendra went to high school with my mom.

Everett let out a gurgling laugh. "When witches use their powers, their eyes turn orange. Agnes, though, could have white hair by now. Her natural color was brown."

I was beginning to believe Agnes was the good witch in my vision and also in Abbey's.

"A nurse is coming," Kendra announced.

Sam and I turned in our seats.

"It's dinnertime," Everett said.

Sam yanked his ball cap as low as it would go. "We need to leave."

I gripped his arm. "Don't move yet." I was afraid if he did, the nurse would definitely recognize him. "Keep your eyes down." A hat would only go so far, and Sam had stark green eyes that sucked a person in.

"One more thing," Sam whispered. "Why are these witches trying to kill Layla?"

Kendra cleared her throat.

The short woman with clear-amber eyes joined us, pinning her gaze on Sam. "Everett, your dinner is ready."

Everett waved a hand at me. "I want my great-granddaughter to take me in."

I cocked an eyebrow as Everett gave me a pleading look. This was the only time I would see him, particularly if he only had a short time to live. I would love to hear more about my mom. Before we'd left the Catskills, Jordyn begged me to find out everything I could on our mother. When I had my children back, I might consider returning, if Everett hadn't passed away by then.

But I couldn't escort him inside. Sam was extremely nervous.

"Very well," the nurse said. "You know where the dining room is." She then wavered for a long minute, her suspicious gaze on Sam and me.

Jumping up, I clenched my teeth, shielding my husband by placing my body in front of him. I wasn't jealous but afraid she was a hot minute from recognizing him. Thank fuck I hadn't gone through with the Tim Cox interview and shown myself on national television.

"Is something wrong?" I asked the nurse.

"One of our patients who was out here earlier has been mumbling that the vampire, Sam Mason, was here."

My heart dropped to my feet. "I haven't seen him. He's hot, though. Right?"

Then out of the corner of my eye, I saw Kendra falling.

The nurse ran to her aid. "Are you okay?"

"I think so. I'm just dizzy. I think I need some water," Kendra complained with a heavy breath.

It took me a second to realize that Kendra was trying to distract the nurse.

I turned to Sam. "Go to the car. I'll meet you there."

If the nurse figured out who he was, his presence here would go viral the second she told anyone. If my grandmother had hired Claude to hunt down Sam, then it wouldn't be long before his men were on their way from Bozeman to Great Falls, which was about two hours away, if I was correct.

In vampire speed, Sam was gone.

By the time the nurse helped Kendra to her feet, she asked, "Wasn't there a man sitting there?"

"He had an urgent text to deal with." I was lying through my teeth.

"Corinne," a nurse called from the door in the distance. "We need your help."

Kendra moved hair from her face. "Go. I'm good. I'll bring Everett in."

Corinne hurried off.

Once she was out of earshot, I slapped a hand on my chest. "That was close. Thanks for acting so quickly, Kendra." Then I addressed Everett. "It was nice meeting you. I wish I could stay."

His smile was heartbreakingly sad. "Take care of yourself and your family. I wish we had more time."

I did too. I gave him a quick kiss on the forehead. "Thank you for all the information."

His toothless smile made my heart hurt. "Oh, and Layla, two things. One, the answer to Sam's question on why the witches want you dead. I don't know, but I think they're afraid you'll have another set of quadruplets."

I laughed, bringing tears to my eyes. "Quadruplets are rare. I doubt it would happen again." I wasn't taking any chances—not because of some prophecy, but because I'd died three times during childbirth, for fuck's sake. "And the other?"

Sam's voice was in my comm. "Baby doll, hurry up."

"If Agnes is alive and you find her, will you tell her I love her?"

I tamped down tears. This poor, poor soul was going to die alone in a nursing home. My soul was crying like a baby. No one should die alone.

I touched my heart. "I will."

Kendra and I said our goodbyes, agreeing we would be in contact later.

As I flew like the wind to the SUV idling with its back door open, I had another dark thought. What if Agnes was the bad witch? What if she was the mastermind leading the charge to kill my babies?

20

SAM

Conrad pulled up to a sprawling ranch located forty-five minutes south of Great Falls. The rustic log home belonged to a friend of Conrad's who was in Alaska fishing this time of year. He'd given Conrad the thumbs-up to use his place for the night.

Thank fuck. Hotels and motels weren't the place for me because of my national public notoriety, and especially since someone inside the nursing facility had seen me. I guessed the ball cap hadn't done the trick.

But we had bigger problems. Huge fucking ones. My brain felt like a knot the size of the earth, tangled into a ball of confusion and questions. I didn't even know where to begin to unpack the prophecy, the witches, and the seer who'd predicted this crazy notion that a Monroe witch would bear quadruplets and that of those four, one would turn witches into vampires. To say nothing of the fact that my wife was a witch—as in, a card-carrying woman who could perform spells. Not that I didn't believe Layla could have magical abilities. It was clear her bloodline had passed on powers to Rorie, for one. Those around us even said they could feel Layla's magic. I did as well when she was around our babies. Even our

151

physical connection when Layla held Rorie proved there was something there.

But Everett had made it sound like Layla was a powerful witch. If that was true, how could we unlock her powers? I would feel better knowing she had a formidable way to protect herself.

"I'll clear the inside and alarms," Conrad said as we climbed out of the SUV.

Layla's blue eyes held wonder as she took inventory of the property—a stark contrast to the zombie mode she'd been in since we left Great Falls. During the long silent drive, she'd bitten her nails, stared out the window, and held on to the journal Everett had given her as if it contained the code to engaging a nuclear bomb.

I was curious what was inside that book that Agnes had her father-in-law guard with his life. But we would find out soon enough. Right now, I was also absorbing the light breeze, the warm air, and the scents of nature.

Violets and blues swept the sky, providing a beautiful backdrop to a well-manicured landscape of shrubs, trees, and colorful flowers that decorated the property as far as the eye could see. In the distance, a dirt driveway led from the road to a barn with a corral next to it, and the aroma in the air was a mixture of cut grass and a hint that Conrad's friend had a horse or two.

As if I'd said the word *horse* out loud, Layla flashed her big blue eyes up at me. "I think he has horses." Her voice rose as she followed the stamped stone path around the house until it jutted out in the direction of the barn.

I was on her heels. "Hold up. We need to make sure there aren't any threats."

Conrad trusted his friend Zeke, a vampire he'd met while living in Montana. I had faith in Conrad, but that didn't mean I wouldn't be cautious. That wasn't my style even if we weren't in our current predicament. As a soldier, it was second nature to vet everyone and everything.

She twirled around, glancing in all directions. "You're right.

What was I thinking? Actually, my mind is still foggy after listening to Everett. I feel like I'm in a maze, not knowing which way is out. Can you pinch me, please? I want to make sure I'm not dreaming."

Instead, I smashed my mouth to hers. I, too, needed something to ground me in reality. I needed to feel her, smell her, and taste her—all the things about her that helped to quiet the demons inside me.

She anchored her hands on my waist, opening her mouth, giving in to the kiss. She tasted of home and freedom, of happiness and love, and I should be pinching *myself*. How did I get so lucky to have a mother, wife, partner, lover, and fighter so beautiful, so strong, and so in love with my arrogant ass? I thanked the vampire gods any chance I had that she and I had met, even if it had been under hunter-versus-vampire circumstances.

She broke the kiss, tears streaming down her face, giving off equal parts of sadness, happiness, and love.

I grabbed her hand. "After we check for threats, why don't we see if there are horses?" That would cheer her up.

As we crossed the property in the direction of the barn, I opened my senses.

"I need to have another vision," she said. "I'm pretty certain the white-haired lady who saved me the other night is Agnes. Sam, this is too much to swallow. Where do we even begin or make sense of any of this? These witches, whoever they are, supposedly want our children dead. According to the white-haired woman, Orion and Luna are alive. But that was three nights ago when I saw her in my dream. Are they still alive?" Her pulse quickened.

Mine did as well. I wished we had answers, and it was driving me insane that we didn't. Four fucking days since Orion and Luna had been taken. Ninety-six-plus hours of madness. I'd been through hell and back several times, but the hole in the pit of my stomach felt similar to when Layla had died three times during childbirth. The notion that I might never have the chance to see my son and daughter again was boring a hole into my heart.

"Who do you think can turn a witch into a vampire?" she asked. "Orion? Rorie? We don't know yet if Luna or Ellie need blood. I mean, that is a sign of a vampire, right?"

"From everything I know, yes. But our children are not the norm, baby doll. Maybe witches need blood."

"Kendra said I was a Monroe witch, which means our child can turn me?" Her voice hitched so high it was difficult to flush out if she was excited or fearful. "I would love to spend eternity with you and our family."

The possibility both thrilled me and gave me reason to pause. Vampires were born with a recessive gene, which meant that the process was seamless. What would that look like for her? Could she die during the change? Or die from the change? Not only that, but was Layla a true Monroe witch? Sure, her grandmother was a full-blooded one, but the bloodline had been watered down since Layla's grandfather and father were humans. What factor did that play in the scenario?

We weren't about to find the answers at the moment.

"Stay out here while I zip through the barn," I said. "I just want to be sure no one is hiding."

I was confident there weren't any threats around. I could only detect the horses but no other scents or heartbeats. Nevertheless, I went in and out of the barn for a few seconds before I gave her the thumbs-up.

Layla hurried over to a stall housing a brown-and-white horse. "This is a mare," she said. "The one next door to her is as well."

"If Zeke is out of town, who's taking care of them?" I asked myself more than her.

The barn was a decent-sized space. It contained four stalls, a loft packed with bales of hay, and a workstation with tools, gloves, hats, and other equipment for working in a barn.

"Come here and pet Sadie," she said.

"I'll pass. I'm not exactly an animal kind of man. How do you know her name?"

A foster family of mine had a cat who despised me. That was the gist of my animal experience.

She flicked a finger inside the stall. "It's carved into the wall."

An engine whirred and grew louder.

Layla and I exchanged a wide-eyed look before I poked my head out.

A truck came down a gravel driveway.

Layla sidled up to me. "It's probably just the pet sitter."

I didn't give a fuck who it was. "We can't take any chances. TV stations are probably converging on the nursing home. We also have to keep your grandmother in mind. That Claude Irving character probably has men all over the state."

My old man had recently dealt with Claude in an attempt to help Jack Aberdeen. After Claude learned of Ray Aberdeen's death, he'd sent his men to Jack's house to collect on his brother's gambling debt.

My father had been successful in brokering a deal with Irving on Jack's behalf. What that entailed, I hadn't asked—or rather, had never had a chance to learn more about it. But my father had compelled Claude to forget Jack and Ray Aberdeen. Too bad he hadn't added Harriet Aberdeen in the mix. Nevertheless, I made a mental note to ask Conrad if he had an update from Jonah about what Harriet was up to.

"Hide," she said. "I'll deal with him."

"You are not approaching him on your own," I said, keeping my eye on the driver as he got out of his truck. "I'll just compel him not to remember anything while he was here."

The stocky dude, wearing a cowboy hat, mud-encrusted jeans, and boots that had seen the inside of a horse stall, ambled toward us.

The man wasn't human nor vampire.

"He's a shifter," I mumbled as I met him halfway.

"Zeke just told me he had guests." He extended his pudgy hand. "I'm Jay. I take care of the horses for Zeke."

We shook, but I didn't say my name. "My wife loves horses."

He removed his hat, showing a bald head, and nodded at Layla. "Ma'am. Maybe if you're here for a few days, I'll saddle one up for you."

Layla gave him an award-winning smile. "I would love that, Jay. But we're only here for the night." She hooked her arm around mine. "Honey, we should head up to the house."

I wasn't leaving until I made him forget us, although I'd never compelled a shifter or attempted to either.

He laughed. "Don't try anything, Sam Mason. I know all about you, and as a shifter, I can give you a run for your money." His brown eyes morphed to a deep amber that almost glowed, his wolf rising to the surface.

His threat didn't rankle me at all. But I'd never fought a wolf, and I wasn't about to break my virginity by tussling with the mutt. My SEAL brother, Ben Jackson, had been bitten by one, and he hadn't fared well. Then again, he was a hybrid—half human and half vampire, and his human side had been the problem.

"We don't want any trouble," Layla said sweetly, flashing her blue eyes.

Jay tucked his wolf away. "Neither do I. Zeke is a longtime friend, and I wouldn't do anything to ruin our relationship." He swung his gaze to me. "But if you're trying to be inconspicuous, you need to do a better job. The local news is reporting that you were at a nursing home in Great Falls." His forehead wrinkled. "What the fuck were you doing there? Our supernatural community is blowing up, and you're not helping matters."

Anger, hot and sticky, had my fangs snapping into place. I wasn't pissed at him. In fact, I appreciated his candor. I was mad at the fucking world. It was one thing to blame myself for opening the door to Pandora's box, but to hear someone actually come out and accuse me drove a nail into my chest. Though he didn't exactly say I was at fault for starting anarchy with humans, but he didn't have to. I could see it in his eyes and hear it in his voice.

"If you must know," Layla said with a bite in her tone, "we were there as a matter of life and death. Our children have been kidnapped."

Conrad sprinted from the house and was standing beside Jay in seconds.

Jay took one look at Conrad and lowered his shoulders. "Zeke didn't mention you would be here. He only alerted me that some friends of yours needed to lie low. But he and I did get cut off. A cell signal in Alaska is hit or miss."

Conrad relaxed his jaw. "Zeke is probably in the middle of nowhere, trying to catch that big fish."

The two men laughed like old buddies.

"I didn't tell Zeke that Sam was the *friend* of mine," Conrad said. "The less he knows, the better. You as well. I hear the shifter community is up in arms, just like the vampire government is."

"No lie there," Jay said. "Packs all over are meeting. If we can't quell the humans, we're in for a dark and bloody future."

I officially felt like a fucking shithead.

Conrad regarded me, tipping his head in the direction of the house. "Why don't you and Layla get settled? I'll take things from here."

Conrad knew the importance of secrecy, so I trusted he would deal with Jay. Besides, it was best that he handled the shifter. I was a walking time bomb, and we didn't need any more attention on us. I also didn't need to have shifters on my ass either.

Layla exchanged pleasantries with Jay as we left. I didn't. I was too busy silently swearing at myself.

Snap the fuck out of it, dude. Stop brooding about something you can't change.

When we were halfway to the house, I pushed out the air I'd been holding and unclenched my teeth.

"Don't you dare feel like crap over what he said to you, vampire. It's not your fault that we're in this mess."

I laughed, which was the only thing I could do. Otherwise, I

might be responsible for burning down the world. That would probably happen anyway—and not by me but because of me. That one
instant at the hospital had changed the course of humanity. It wasn't
a child of ours or our children who would affect humankind. It was
fucking me, Sam Mason. Guilt was a fucking bitch as it gnawed
inside me like a school of piranhas.

Layla jerked my arm, stopping us abruptly. "Sam, snap out of it.
You can't keep blaming yourself for what's happening with
humans." She planted her hands on her hips, pursing her lips.
"Guilt doesn't look good on you either."

I briefly closed my eyes, inhaling and exhaling.

She rubbed my face. "Hey, I feel you. Literally and figuratively."

I leaned into her touch as she continued. "Regret is the one
emotion that will eat at you until there's nothing left. You never
intentionally set out to reveal the existence of vampires to humans.
You were just being you in the heat of the moment, as you should."

I loved her for trying to soothe my emotions.

"Babe, vampires have the right to be themselves," she said.
"Please don't think for a second you started a war. The war started
eons ago with prophecies, hatred, people who wanted money, power,
and control. And by people, I mean human or supernatural. Knowledge that vampires exist was meant to be. It's time." She curled her
fingers inside my jeans pockets. "Your dad believes that. I do too. It's
time we blend the melting pot of species together. It won't be easy.
But hopefully with your dad at the helm, the merger will be easier
and with less mayhem." She swallowed. "On top of that, if my
mom is correct, you and I will save humanity. How? That's a
mystery." She scrunched her nose on the last part.

I didn't believe we would save humanity. Humans had to save
themselves. In my eyes, the underlying message from her mother
was that Layla and I would be the spark to a better world where
humans and supernaturals could coexist together. Though I was
also the spark that started this mess.

I hugged her with all my strength. I would probably always feel at fault, but knowing she didn't blame me took away some of that guilt. "Thank you for all that. I am the luckiest vampire on the planet to have you as my partner."

She raised up on her toes and brushed her lips over mine. "I couldn't imagine my life without you, Sam."

21

SAM

A few minutes later, I was sitting at the marble island in the gourmet kitchen of Zeke's beautiful, eclectic home. Layla had darted off to the bathroom, and Conrad was still down at the barn, talking to Jay. My guilt wasn't as strong thanks to my wife, but I still felt like a shithead. Even more so as I watched a local news segment on my phone where a local station had converged on the nursing home. My name was plastered on the bottom of the screen. "Sam Mason Sighting," the headline began.

I growled as my phone rang with a Massachusetts area code number. It was either Jo, Webb, Tripp, or my father. Since I had a burner phone, I didn't have my contacts programmed in yet.

"Hello?" I said as I answered.

"Samuel, it's your dad. Tripp gave me your number."

"You're okay," I said with a chuckle, but deep down, I was relieved as hell. He'd warned me that if anything happened to him, I should stay the course. Although, if anything had happened to him, Conrad would've said something when he gave Layla and me an update. Or maybe not, if my dad had sworn Conrad to secrecy.

"Conrad tells me you've thrown the elders in a cell, and things are tense there."

"Nothing for you to worry about." The strain in his voice wasn't as prevalent as it had been the last time we'd spoken. "I'm calling because I just got word about the news reporting that you were at that nursing home. Are you and Layla okay?"

"Info travels fast," I fired back. "We're good. We're lying low at a friend of Conrad's place. Did you question Norman Collier? Or read his mind? Because we're pretty sure he's working with witches. They're having him do their dirty work." All assumptions on my part, but man, that was the only thing that made sense now.

I proceeded to explain everything Layla and I had learned from Everett—about Monroe witches, Agnes, the journal, Zoey, a witch school, and the prophecy.

Layla joined me halfway through bringing my dad up to speed.

After I finished, there was dead silence. I took that time to put my dad on speaker.

"Dad, Layla is here and listening."

She was on the other side of the island, leaning her elbows on the marble surface.

He cleared his throat. "Layla, I am beside myself that my grandchildren are missing. Please know I am doing everything I can from this end."

"I know you are, Steven," she said. "Thank you. So, did you happen to read Collier's mind? Or were you able to?" She knitted her eyebrows.

"The mind-blocking drug wore off, so I managed to get a few things out of him." He sounded as relieved as Layla looked.

I whisked a hand through my hair. "Please tell me he gave up the name of the person who has your grandchildren."

Layla and I could surely use a break. We had the name of Agnes's friend, although I wasn't sure how Zoey could help. As soon as I had a window to ask my dad about a witch school, I would.

"Norman Collier and Nurse Beverly are dating, and both have been feeding Roman Brown all our secrets, including the existence of my grandchildren and that they're inhuman. We've found Beverly, and Jo read her mind and extrapolated the same information as well as the additional fact that Beverly has been the one talking to Roman directly."

Beverly's phone records had raised red flags with us. Collier's involvement wasn't a surprise since he'd been caught red-handed.

Nevertheless, my ire had me gritting my teeth while anger colored Layla's face.

Layla tapped her lips. "Steven, did Collier reveal anything about my grandmother?"

"No," my dad said. "But that's not to say she doesn't have her hands dirty. Jonah is tailing her. So far, it looks like she might be behind the contract on Sam's head."

Again, no surprise there. I was dying to axe the old lady much like Lizzie Borden had supposedly done to her parents.

"Pops, Harriet is working with Claude Irving. He and his men are human. Surely, they don't stand a chance against me."

"Son, don't underestimate a human, particularly Harriet. She's been around long enough to know some immortals."

"Like witches," Layla mumbled. "Speaking of them, if Collier and Beverly have their noses up Roman's ass, he must be working with a witch or coven."

"Possibly," my dad said. "Until we can confirm witches are involved, Roman is our number one suspect in the kidnapping. Oh, and I couldn't find anything in Collier's brain about the woman who was with him. He was trying hard to keep me out of his head."

I bounced my knee. "Pops, Everett mentioned that Agnes was friends with a lady named Zoey who teaches at a school for witches. Do you know any schools like that? Zoey might know where Agnes is, if she's alive."

"I don't, son. I'll have Jo do some research. Your sister told me about Layla's and Abbey's visions. Actually, since Jo learned about dream walkers and Abbey's interest in them, she's been looking into all that."

I wasn't surprised. Jo was one of the most curious people I knew. On top of that, if there was a witch school, then that might bode well for Abbey or even my children.

A clinking noise sounded behind him. "A few more things. Webb is working hard to locate Adam's and Roman's whereabouts. Son, you mentioned that Kendra found Layla's great-grandfather. Has Kendra looked for anyone from the Monroe family, like Agnes? Or is there anything in the journal we can use to open up some doors for a lead?"

Layla nodded. "Yes, Kendra went to Regina, Saskatchewan, looking for Agnes. She said the Monroes aren't there anymore. As far as the journal, I haven't had a chance to go through it yet." She worried her bottom lip. "Steven, do you believe the prophecy that Everett told us?"

His laugh was weak. "I usually believe in prophecies. They tend to come true. But you have to keep in mind that a seer only visualizes a flash of something at that point in time. We also have to consider that when stories are passed down, small details are left out or could've changed. Honestly, it doesn't matter if you and I believe it or not. The fact that the witches do is the only thing to focus on right now to find Orion and Luna. The rest will reveal itself in time."

Layla stared at me blankly.

I reached over the island and touched her hand. "Pops, now that you've heard everything, can you try one more time to read Collier's mind? We really need the name of the woman who was with him in the nursery when Luna and Orion were kidnapped."

I was certain my dad had been thorough, but sometimes, memories were buried so deep that an expert mind reader couldn't find them. Jo had articulated that very thing when she'd read the mind of a former enemy.

"I'm sorry, son. I killed him," my father said with no remorse.

Layla gasped, and I grabbed my hair, my eyes widening.

I wasn't flabbergasted at his admission but at the timing of it. He'd been working tirelessly for many years to toe the line with obeying laws, following rules, and keeping the peace. He'd become an elder for that very reason.

"I'm confused, Dad. What happened to your diplomacy and tempering the chaos? Won't your actions look bad on what you've been trying to accomplish with the elders?"

He grunted. "Samuel, we have no room for elders or guardians sabotaging what we've worked so hard to do. We had an elder working with Edmund Rain, if you recall. Now we have two elders who've sided with our enemies to take out you, your family, me, Jo, Webb, and Abbey. The evidence is astounding. This is not a conversation I wanted to have over the phone. But today is a new day. I will not stand for anyone who fucks with me, my family, or our mission to protect our people and humanity. I have the support of every head of state in this country. I am officially in charge."

I pulled Layla into my arms and hugged her while wearing a goofy smile. If my dad were here, I would've thrown myself at him.

My dad cleared his throat. "One last thing before I go, and listen carefully." His tone brooked no argument.

Layla and I separated.

"If anyone tries to fuck with you, especially if they try to kill you, both of you have my permission to defend yourselves. Don't worry about the media or anyone. I'll handle the aftermath. Now, that being said, I do want to save lives. My message, Samuel, isn't anything different than what we do as Vampire Navy SEALs. My point is, do your job as you have always done. Are we clear?"

Layla had a deer-in-the-headlights look. "Yes."

I couldn't contain my grin. I felt like a weight had been lifted off my shoulders. "Crystal clear, Pops." Best fucking news today.

"There's more to come," he said. "Before I go, let's recap. Jo will look into witch schools to find Zoey. Webb is leading the charge on tracking Roman and Adam. Layla, if you find anything in the journal that can help, call Jo. Finally, Jonah will need help in dealing with Harriet, so in the morning, head down to Bozeman to meet him. I would like Harriet off our list and in our hands. She might know where Roman and Adam are. Lastly, Sam, have Kendra contact me. I would like to offer her a job."

After we hung up, Layla and I stared at each other as Conrad came in through the French doors.

He cocked a thick eyebrow. "Why do you two look… I can't find the right word. Happy? Ready to burst with glee? Did you find Orion and Luna?"

"It's the dawning of a new world," I said with the biggest smirk ever.

Conrad's face brightened. "So, it's official? Your father is now in charge?"

"You knew?" I asked.

"Not really, man. But I had a feeling it was coming after your father kicked the elders to the curb."

With my father at the helm, the future didn't look so dark.

22

LAYLA

I was sitting cross-legged on the plush carpet in the great room with my back to the rock-faced hearth sans the fire. Zeke had a beautiful home with high ceilings, lots of windows, a dining room fit for at least ten, an office, four bedrooms each with en suite bathrooms, and a guest bath off the gourmet kitchen.

I gazed out the wall of windows and into the darkness. Night had fallen over the twenty-acre property, and if I listened intently, I could hear the cicadas singing outside.

Sam brought a finger of bourbon over from the bar in the dining room. "This will help you relax." He set it on the weird S-shaped coffee table in front of me.

I'd been hyped up since talking to his dad two hours ago. I was as elated as Sam about Steven being in charge. I felt like someone had shot me with several doses of adrenaline. Plus, we were off to see my grandmother tomorrow. It was time to deal with her once and for all. More importantly, my intuition was telling me we were closer to a lead on Orion and Luna, maybe because Jo was researching witch schools to find Zoey. That gave me hope that Zoey might know where Agnes was. Everyone was pitching in.

The news about Norman and Beverly feeding Roman information didn't shock me. Dane Gray thought Roman had his hand in the kidnapping. Dane had even gone as far as to say that Roman could've made a deal with witches or the other way around. His comments might have some truth to them.

"I haven't had a drop of liquor since I first met you," I said. "So you might have to carry me to bed."

His cheesy grin spoke volumes as he waggled his eyebrows. "That might be fun." He had a beer, his drink of choice, in his hand as he sank into a spot on the couch near the arm, which was close to me. "But it might help you sleep."

I giggled. "While you guard the bedroom door?"

"Damn straight." He lost that goofy smile. "Conrad and I are taking shifts."

They'd been discussing who would keep watch first when I'd been on the phone with Jordyn, which was another reason I was feeling good. She'd reported that Ellie and Rorie were doing well. Jordyn was keeping busy, helping Greta in the dining hall for a couple of hours while Alia and Abbey watched Ellie and Rorie.

Still, I hated that Conrad and Sam couldn't relax. They both needed rest as much as I did. But I wasn't about to argue. I had to choose my battles, and this was one I didn't want to challenge. Besides, I wanted to dream or have a vision. I was desperate to see that white-haired woman again.

Sam swept his gaze over the coffee table. "It's cool how Zeke had the places he's traveled to etched in the wood."

The home décor was definitely unique—cowboy-country style blended with abstract modernism.

Sam leaned forward, his head slightly angled at me as he eyed the journal in my lap. "You haven't opened it yet?"

"I was waiting on you." And thinking of life and my great-grandfather. "I feel bad for Everett. I want to help him."

Sam took a swig of his beer. "When this is all over, we can talk about him." He patted the spot next to him. "Come here. We'll read the journal together."

I was curling up next to him in a flat second.

Conrad came in with a bourbon.

I picked up my glass. "Cheers. Here's to finding our children."

We toasted before I sipped the hard liquor and almost choked as the alcohol burned its way down my throat.

The guys chuckled.

Conrad got comfortable on the other couch. "So, time to learn about witches. I can't say I know any."

"Well, you do now." I pointed a finger at myself.

I was far from a witch, and the idea that I was considered one because of a family moniker was difficult to comprehend. My banshee scream and an inkling of mind control had come from my babies when I'd been pregnant.

Sam rested his arm on the back of the couch while I opened the leather-bound book that had seen better days.

The pages were stiff and yellow, and a handful were ripped or folded at the corners. I flipped through the journal to get a sense of where to start, and the darn book seemed to have a mind of its own, opening to a stained red page.

I gave Sam a sidelong glance before I read aloud so Conrad could hear. "'Striga, also known as stria and strix, are blood witches who possess the power to overthrow the natural order of things.'"

This book was Agnes's, so I was assuming she was referring to her coven. I wondered what the difference was between a blood witch and a regular one.

I took a much-needed swig of bourbon to coat the dryness in my throat. "That definition kind of aligns with the prophecy. Or am I reading too much into it?"

Sam took over reading as he leaned into me slightly. "'In addition to the Monroes, there are two other known covens that fall into the category of blood witches, the Onyx Coven and the Crane

Coven, but the Monroes are the first of the blood witches and hold more power than the other two.'"

Conrad crossed one leg over the other. "This is interesting."

I took another drink of bourbon, which seemed not to burn as much. "Listen to this. 'For a blood witch to unlock her true power, she must place three drops of blood on her tongue from a Monroe witch who came before her.'" I lifted my gaze to Sam then Conrad. "Oh my God. I unlocked Rorie's powers when she drank my blood. It was her who made the pillows float."

Sam scratched his head. "Maybe our children's need for blood is more witch-related than vampire."

"Or both," Conrad chimed in. "If the prophecy is true, one of them has to be a vampire, right?"

That called for more bourbon to temper my nerves. "That prediction didn't say anything about the child being a vampire but rather, inhuman."

"You'll need a Monroe older than you, baby doll, to unlock your magic," Sam said.

I wasn't interested in that part at the moment. I was still stuck on the prophecy. I finished off the bourbon, and my body was giving in to the alcohol as warmth loosened my muscles. Regardless of my indifference at the moment, it was interesting to discover that I had to find a Monroe older than me to unlock any latent powers I might have.

"I need another beer," Sam said, pushing upright.

I was quick to hand him my glass. I might need the bottle of bourbon if we kept reading, and he might be carrying me to bed.

I scanned through the pages and stopped to read the prophecy, which aligned with what Everett had told us.

Sam returned with drinks and resumed his seat.

My eyes were becoming heavy, and I was sure another round of bourbon would put me to sleep—until I landed on my mother's name on a page in the back of the journal. The first line started with *My Dearest Meredith*. I read the first few lines to myself but could feel Sam and Conrad waiting for me to speak.

So I started reading it aloud. "'My dearest Meredith, it breaks my heart that you have chosen to leave, but I understand more than anyone the need to shed your past and hide who you are. We are alike in so many ways. The second I was able to leave home, I did. All I wanted was a normal life. But as a Monroe witch, I was naïve to think that I could have that happily ever after.'"

A wave of depression breezed over me at the last part of Agnes's sentence. Sam and I wanted our happily ever after too. Though I knew a peaceful life wasn't in the cards for us. Not because of my supernatural background but his.

He kissed my head. "We'll get that happy life, baby doll."

I wanted to believe him. Yet if everything we were learning about my mom's family was true, and I couldn't see why it wouldn't be, we would have to work fucking hard to achieve peace.

Girl, your mom did it. She hid from her past. Maybe so. But times had changed. The Monroe family hadn't found her—or maybe they had. Then a gut-wrenching thought zapped the energy out of me. What if she hadn't died of breast cancer? Everett had mentioned that his wife had mysteriously died of heart failure. Maybe the coven had found my mom and cast a fatal spell on her.

I was ill all of a sudden.

"You don't have to read the rest," Sam said, feeling my emotions.

I handed him the book. "Why don't you?" While I drowned my sorrows in liquor.

Conrad's rapt attention was glued to us.

Sam set his bottle on the table and read. "'Because of the prophecy, my ancestors will always be on edge with any witch born into the bloodline—but as long as you don't fall for a vampire, you have nothing to worry about.'"

I almost spit out the amber liquid. I'd failed on that part, but I would do it all over again in a blink of an eye. I couldn't imagine my life without Sam. We were destined to be together. We had a purpose in this world. Maybe my mom had been onto something when she'd said Sam and I would save humanity.

Sam continued reading. "'I know you hate bloodsuckers, so I take comfort in knowing that won't happen—but please don't ignore who you are, where you've come from, or the supernatural world around you. In doing so, you put your life and your future family's at risk, especially if you have daughters. If you do, I implore you to explain who we are, our heritage, and the importance of keeping our bloodline clean of vampires.'"

I wondered if my mom had ever read this journal and the letter from her mother. She hadn't taken the journal with her when she left home.

"Do you want me to stop? Your pulse is high," Sam said.

My gaze landed on Conrad before Sam for no other reason than to inhale a few quick breaths. "Keep going." I couldn't ignore any of this. I wondered for a split second, though, if my mom had embraced who she truly was, would life be any different?

"'Our coven might've been born by the union of a vampire and a powerful witch,'" Sam continued reading, "'but after the prophecy was written in stone, the Monroe coven was banned from having any relations with a vampire. However, you might think that in modern times, the world is too big a place for anyone to keep track of you. That it's impossible to hold your feet to the fire over a two-hundred-year-old prophecy. If that's your way of thinking, then you've already failed. No one can stay hidden forever. I tried and failed, Meredith.'" Sam took a breath. "'The only way you can ensure your safety is to accept who you are and unlock your powers. If you ever need any help, and I'm not around, contact Zoey Thorn...'" Sam squinted at the text. "The last three letters are smudged, but it looks like *lan*. Thornlan."

I examined the name. "The *a* might be an *o*, I think." Some of the lines and words weren't that clear because of Agnes's curly letters running on top of each other.

"I'll take a pic of this and send it to Jo since she's trying to find the witch school," Sam said.

We'd spoken to Jo not long after we'd hung up with Steven. Sam was always singing his sister's praises about her research capabilities.

My eyes were definitely quite heavy, and I was light-headed as well.

Conrad's phone trilled, and Sam and I rounded our attention on him.

Conrad had been trying to reach Jonah since we'd spoken to Steven to let him know that we would be in Bozeman tomorrow and would meet him at his hotel.

"It's Zeke," Conrad said as he excused himself.

I yawned and shivered.

Sam extended his hand, helping me up. "We should get some rest. It's going to be a long day tomorrow. Harriet isn't about to come to us easily."

I got another blanket of chills at the mention of Granny Harriet. If Agnes was alive and we found her, I prayed she wasn't evil like Harriet.

Before I could take a step, Sam lifted me in his arms.

"I can walk, vampire. The bedroom isn't far."

He raised an eyebrow. "You let me be the judge of that."

I zipped my lips shut, hooking an arm around his neck and resting my head against his. "You know, I'm suddenly feeling horny, vampire."

He laughed. "Layla Mason, do you want to take advantage of me?"

I nibbled on his ear. "I want you to do as you please to me."

His jaw was tight. "As much as I want to, I think a good night's sleep is in order." He gently set me on the bed.

I pouted. "Sam Mason is declining sex. Oh my."

He switched on the bedside lamp. "You're a little tipsy and can barely keep your eyes open."

That was all true.

He undressed me, leaving my bra and panties on. "Beautiful," he mumbled before he peppered light and gentle kisses on my thighs, abs, and cleavage, sending sparks of heat to my core and goose bumps to blanket my body.

Giving in to the sensations, a feeling of weightlessness washed over me, and suddenly, I was dropping into a deep sleep.

23

SAM

In the quietness of the morning, I stood in front of the French doors between the kitchen and dining room, my mind a jumbled mess. I was going mad, trying to unpack the conversation with Everett and what we'd read in the journal. My sister had texted me an hour ago to let me know that she'd gotten my email, and she would call the minute she found anything on Zoey. If I knew Jo, she would not sleep until she found the witch school and Zoey.

I snagged my glass of lukewarm blood from the marble island and resumed staring out at the breaking dawn. Sparkles of dewdrops glinted on the blades of grass. A rabbit sat at the tree line on the far side of the property. Zeke's spread was off the beaten path, but it was still too exposed for my liking. Which was one reason I hadn't slept. Conrad and I had planned on taking turns guarding Layla and the house, but in the end, we'd both kept watch.

Luckily, Layla hadn't sleepwalked, and the night had been quiet, allowing Conrad and me to strategize how to deal with Harriet. Normally, it would be easy. Snag the old lady and throw her in a car trunk. But she was surrounded by Claude Irving's men, and I would bet Harriet had an arsenal of weapons to use against vampires. The other potential issue was Roman. He could have his men protecting Harriet. Though I found that hard to believe, if Adam Emery had kicked her off the genetic engineering team.

I was looking forward to dealing with the old lady. She certainly would be a distraction and a way for me to release some anger and frustration. We needed a fucking break, an opening, a lead, or something on Orion and Luna. I couldn't shake the thought that Orion needed blood or that he and Luna were hurt in some way.

I pulled my hair, tears burning my eyeballs like someone had dropped acid in them. I couldn't lose my shit. I had to stay strong and positive. It was growing harder and harder as each day passed. I'd been trying to steal moments with Layla any chance we had in order to keep us sane. To keep her from wigging out. She was doing okay as long as she was preoccupied or feeling like she was doing something to find our babies.

A heartbeat grew louder as Conrad came into the kitchen. It was easy to detect a vampire from a human since our heart rates were much slower.

"I tried Jonah again," he said in a worried tone. "It's unlike him not to check in."

I pivoted on my heel. "We should leave for Bozeman soon, then. I'll text my dad to see if he's heard from Jonah." I set my glass down, picked up my phone from the island, and texted my dad.

Conrad was freshly showered, his black hair damp and slicked back. "We'll need loads of caffeine today."

All I needed was adrenaline and a hot shower. Then I would be ready for anything.

Conrad rolled up his shirtsleeves as he prepared the coffee. "You think Layla's ready to fight? Because you know dealing with Harriet isn't going to be a cakewalk. I could go alone."

My eyebrows drew down. "No fucking way you're going alone. We talked about this last night. Why the sudden change?"

The coffee machine gurgled as the aroma of dark roast swirled in the air.

He leaned against the eight-burner stove. "I would hate for anything to happen to you and Layla. That dream walker is trying to kill her. Roman is involved in taking Orion and Luna. Harriet has a contract out on you. The media is involved. Sam, I'm worried—especially if Irving's men and Harriet made Jonah. Considering that media circus at the nursing home after we left, I got a bad feeling. Let me handle this. I owe you and Layla anyway."

While he made good points, that last statement had me twisting my face. "Owe us? For what?"

"I failed to protect Orion and Luna, so I would feel even more like shit if something happened to you or Layla."

I cocked my head so hard it almost locked in that position. "What? You're blaming yourself?"

Regret was steeped in his hazel eyes. "Fuck, Sam. My job was to protect Layla and your kids. I'm your fucking bodyguard."

I swiped a hand over my hair, my gut twisting into a knot. "I failed too. The other vampires on duty did as well. Don't you dare feel like you're the only one at fault." I appreciated his honesty and how seriously he took his job. "I've been kicking myself in the ass every time I think about that night. What did I miss? Why didn't I hear anything? Which brings up a thought. Knowing we were dealing with witches, maybe they cast a spell to block our hearing."

We felt as though we were missing some key component to how we hadn't detected a fucking thing.

He proceeded to pour a cup of coffee. "That is entirely possible. But it doesn't make me feel any better."

I'd been standing at the end of the island with my hands pressed into its rounded edge. "Conrad, the bottom line is, you're not going to Bozeman alone."

He made me a cup without asking. "You're okay with Layla joining us?"

I took the cup he handed me. "Not at all. I hate that my wife has to fight. But I'm pretty sure you know her by now. You even told me she did well in facing Rianne in the diner in Maine. She's hunted and killed our kind, man. If she can handle us and her monster sister, she can handle herself. Why don't we ask Kendra to tag along? We could use all the help we can get. Above that, don't think for one minute Layla will stay here, especially knowing that her grandmother is involved."

He smirked knowingly.

I closed the distance between us and squeezed his shoulder. "We're in this together, Conrad. From that day we met in Montana outside of Jack Aberdeen's ranch, you have been there for Layla and me. We're family now."

He set his cup down on the counter before we exchanged a bro hug. "Thanks."

I was happy we had that settled. He was turning into a great friend, and Layla adored Conrad too.

The sound of running water filtered into my ears. "I think Layla is up."

"I'll call Kendra." He strutted out onto the deck.

I went in search of my beautiful wife, who was in the shower when I entered the en suite bathroom. She was rinsing shampoo out of her hair, her voluptuous tits sticking out, her toned legs leading up to her gorgeous pussy.

I ogled her, my cock jerking in my jeans. The only thing on my mind was her and me fused together—a fucking awesome way to start a day and clear my head.

She wiped the water from her face and locked eyes with me. "Morning. Want to join me?"

"Nah," I said, shucking out of my clothes. "I want to fuck you." I stepped into the small space swirling with steam.

She pointed at my groin. "I see he's wide awake." She dragged her nails along my erect shaft, light and teasing, before she rubbed the tip of my dick.

Growling, I hauled her to me and spun us around so my back was toward the wall but under the spray. Then I bent over slightly and captured her hard nipple between my teeth.

She proceeded to stroke my dick while I sucked her other nipple into my mouth.

The sounds of light moans and soft grunts competed with the running water.

I trailed my lips up her neck, lingering on her carotid artery beating and pulsing at a rapid rate. My gums throbbed painfully before my fangs elongated, the bloodthirst getting stronger as my throat burned.

As if she knew my intent, she angled her neck, tightening her hold on my cock.

I kissed my way to her ear. "What's your pleasure?"

"For the moment, I just want to feel the sensations your mouth is giving me," she said in a breathy tone.

"What are you feeling, baby doll? Tell me." I scraped a fang over her earlobe.

She flinched and moaned at the same time. "Tingles, a strong throbbing between my legs, flutters in my stomach, and excited anticipation that you'll bite me. I want you to, Sam. I need you to."

Fuck. I could just cum off her last statement.

I nipped at her ear, then her neck with my canines. "What do you feel when I bite you?"

She levered back and regarded me through hooded lids, studying me with a lustful wonder. "At first, it stings, but the second you begin to drink and do that move with your tongue where you lick really fast, it sends me into outer space. It's euphoric and orgasmic."

I beamed at her as she pressed her forefinger to the tip of my fang until blood oozed out.

My gums hurt, my throat was bone dry, and if I didn't taste her blood in that instant, I would die.

She shoved her finger in my mouth, and I sucked like a starving baby. But it wasn't enough. I needed more. My insides were hurting as if I hadn't fed in weeks. I dropped to my knees and buried my face between her thighs as she guided me to the spot she so desired.

I lifted my gaze upward. "Are you sure?"

She nodded, breathing heavy.

The inside of her thigh, midway between her pussy and knee, was my usual sweet spot, but she wanted me to bite her farther up on her leg and super close to her clit.

I was impossibly hard. We didn't have to fuck for me to get my rocks off. Sucking her blood would do it for me and only because of the way her body reacted to me.

I struck hard and fast, sinking my fangs into that soft skin.

She cried out for a second, then began playing with herself as her breathing increased, spewing soft moans and encouraging words to keep my mouth tethered to her.

With my free hand, I started off stroking myself slow and steady, making sure my tongue was working as fast as she liked while I drank from her.

"That's it, Sam. Faster."

I was pumping my dick at warp speed. But I had to be inside her, feel her slick, tight pussy walls around me. I retracted my fangs and flicked her hand away as I took over, suckling her clit into my mouth. She gripped my head, pushing it into her as she rolled her hips forward.

"Yes. Harder. Right there." Then she yanked on my hair. "Wait."

I froze.

My little minx batted her big blue eyes with a flirty smile, crooking her finger, urging me to come with as she inched backward, steam billowing around her.

I wasn't sure I could walk.

She pivoted around, grabbed onto the towel rack, bent over, and stuck her ass in the air. "Fuck me, vampire."

I was on her in a flash, although standing up from a kneeling position, I almost faltered.

She giggled.

I rubbed my hand over her ass cheeks before dipping my finger between her folds. "Soaking wet, I see."

"Shut up and stick that humongous cock of yours inside me." Her voice was pained as if she was suffering from blue balls. I knew I was.

I wasn't about to disappoint my wife. "Spread those gorgeous legs."

She did as I commanded.

When the wide head of my dick entered her, she gulped air in.

I slid my hand over her back, coaxing her to bend forward. "Relax." I gripped her hips before slamming into her, hard and deep, then stilled.

"What's wrong?" she asked. "If you're worried about protection, the waiting period is over for the pill, so we're good."

I wasn't thinking along those lines, although I should've been. "Just enjoying the feel." Man, it was mind-blowing. Those sharp tingles that came right before I was about to explode inside her were pulsing in my lower back. "I want to stay like this all day."

She wiggled her hips. "I'm on the verge of having the best orgasm ever. So move, vampire. Now!"

Boy, did I ever. I fucked her how she liked it, hard and fast. I was lost in the movement, in us, the sounds of skin slapping skin, watching my dick slide in and out as she pushed her ass into me. I was loving the way she was clenching and unclenching around my shaft.

Motherfucker.

"Play with your clit," I ordered in a voice that didn't sound like me.

She obeyed. "I'm not going to last."

Neither was I. But I didn't want this to end. I never wanted to stop fucking her.

She stiffened, hanging her head as she whimpered her release.

I kept going, pushing in and out in a frenzy—faster, higher, deeper—and when she gripped my cock as tight as she could, my whole body shook, and I grunted out my release, gasping for air.

Layla moved, and I was the one whimpering now.

My legs were shaking as I went under the shower spray. The water was cooler now.

She joined me and pressed her body against mine. "I love you."

I held her tightly, still trembling but also feeling a huge hole in the pit of my stomach that wouldn't be going away until our family was whole again.

"Are you okay?" she asked. "You seem far away."

So much for a clear head. I was once again thinking of our children.

"I'm perfect." I wrapped my arms around her. "Did you see the white-haired lady in your dreams?" I asked, though if she had, she would've said something by now.

She laid her head on my chest. "No. It's frustrating."

I quickly changed the subject, only because she needed her wits about her when we faced Harriet today. "Are you prepared to deal with Harriet?"

She perked up. "Hell yeah. We need to be done with her once and for all."

A knock sounded on the bathroom door. "Sam," Conrad said. "You need to see this. Meet me in the great room."

Layla and I exchanged a questioning look as we got out of the shower. We toweled off and dressed as fast as we could. All we could surmise was that something big was on TV, which wouldn't surprise me.

Layla and I met Conrad where he stood in front of the TV that hung over the fireplace. I faltered at the scene on TV.

"Is that Jonah?" I asked even though I knew it was.

"He's nailed to a craps table." Layla's voice rose in pitch. "Oh my fucking word. Harriet has lost her ever-loving marbles."

She had a long time ago.

Layla read out loud the line that was glued to the bottom of the screen. "'This will all be over once Sam Mason returns my grand-daughters Jordyn, Rianne, and Layla to me.'"

A local female reporter out of Bozeman stuck a mic into Harriet's face. "Mrs. Aberdeen, what would you like to say to Sam Mason?"

Harriet glared into the camera. "Sam, I want you to bring Layla to me. I know you're in the state with her. She deserves to be home with her family. She doesn't belong with a vampire."

"She looks sickly," Layla said. "The blood cancer must be taking its toll."

The old lady had lost weight, her blue eyes were dull and hollow, and her reddish-gray hair was much shorter than it had been when I'd last seen her.

"I almost feel bad for her," Layla said, fixated on the TV.

Behind Harriet, it appeared Jonah was passed out. I pitied whoever was around if he woke up.

Conrad stabbed a finger at the TV. "It looks like those nails are cobalt. His skin is burnt."

My phone trilled from somewhere in the house, and I remembered I'd left it on the island. I crossed the room, bypassed the dining table, and picked up my cell. Tripp's name flashed on it.

I hit the speaker icon. "Hey, man. We've got the news on. Layla and Conrad are here." Though they were still watching the news.

"Seems we have an Aberdeen problem," Tripp said. "When will this end? When will these Aberdeens lock themselves in a coffin?" His voice blasted into the room. "No offense, Layla."

Whipping her gaze at me, she crossed the great room and came into the kitchen. "None taken. But don't throw my sister Jordyn into that group." She pursed her lips.

Tripp scowled, sounding like he was ready to brawl. "I understand from your father, Sam, that you are going to deal with Harriet."

"We spoke to him last night," I said. "But now the game has changed. We have more to contend with—reporters, spectators, and who knows how many of Irving's men, or dare I say Roman's men, if that fucker is involved in this."

"I've been gathering a team for you," Tripp said. "Lucien, the head vampire for Montana, will be there with his team."

"I know him," Conrad chimed in. "He's a kick-ass and take-no-prisoners kind of guy."

"I also talked to Jack Aberdeen," Tripp added. "Not sure if he can offer anything, but it is his mother we're dealing with."

Layla had gotten herself a cup of coffee and was drinking it. "He should step up and throw his mother in a psych ward. Don't worry, Tripp—Jack and I will take care of her."

My huntress was definitely ready to kick some ass. But it wasn't going to be as easy as she was making it out to be.

Tripp continued. "As you are aware, Steven is in charge of the vampire government. He's given us more leeway than the council of elders ever has. However, Sam, our mission statement still applies. We save human lives as much as we can. I'll text you the address where Lucien wants to meet you. He's in charge. So follow his orders."

"Copy that," I said.

Tripp let out a sigh. "One more thing. Layla, it might be prudent to speak to the media. Not about your children but about you. Tim Cox's recent news segment has humans interested in seeing you. The crowd outside the naval base here is asking for you. Steven, Webb, and I agree that you might be able to rally the public and soften the mess we're in."

Layla briefly regarded me with a spark in her eyes. "I can do that."

"Good," Tripp said. "Stay safe, and for all that is holy, don't let Harriet escape." Then he was gone.

"She isn't going anywhere," Layla mumbled. "Not if I can help it."

That's my girl.

I had a feeling this would be a hell of a day—hopefully, a good one.

24

LAYLA

I chewed my nails as Conrad sped down the highway toward Bozeman. Sam was in the passenger seat with his phone to his ear. Ever since we left the house, he'd been talking to Lucien, Kendra, and my uncle Jack, and he was now speaking to the reporter Tim Cox.

I'd been tuning in and out of Sam's conversations while my thoughts consumed me. Every now and then, Conrad and I locked eyes in the rearview mirror or Sam turned to check on me.

I was on my last nerve with my grandmother. She and Rianne were sharp thorns in my side. At least Rianne was locked up—one less Aberdeen to worry about. Harriet wasn't far behind her, not because we would throw her in a cell but rather due to her cancer. She'd looked so drawn on TV. Part of me didn't believe she had cancer, but it was clear she was sickly. I also wasn't surprised she was fighting to the end. Aberdeens were staunch fighters—never giving up or giving in.

I had to give her props, though. She didn't waste time once she'd figured out Sam and I were in the state. She also knew I would come to her and Sam would as well. He wouldn't allow a teammate of his to die.

I couldn't help but continue to wonder if she knew where Orion and Luna were or if she was helping Roman or a witch or both. After the conversation with my great-grandfather and what I'd read so far in the journal, I was leaning toward no. One thing was certain —by the end of the day, Harriet wouldn't be a problem anymore. I would make fucking sure of that.

The *tick, tick, tick* of the blinker shattered my thoughts as we exited the highway.

Sam lowered his phone. "Take a right at the end of the ramp. We're meeting at a scrapyard about three miles from the casino."

"Is Tim in Bozeman?" I'd caught wind of Sam asking Tim that very question. Not that I cared. I was just curious.

Sam flashed his green eyes at me. "He's not, but he has a colleague here. Her name is Violet Keller from CBC 4. She covered Emery's news conference in Chicago. She knew way too much inside information about the Vampire Navy SEALs for my liking, yet she also gave me the impression she was on our side. Tim recommends that if you do speak to the press, she should be the gal you talk to. She can help drive the narrative our way."

I was both nervous and stoked to share my story or at least counteract Rianne's lie that I was compelled by Sam to fall in love with him and have his babies. If I had the chance to talk to the media, then fine. But first and foremost, my priority was dealing with Harriet.

I spotted my uncle Jack when Conrad pulled into the scrapyard with the boarded-up office and piles of old cars and metal lying around in a lot behind the building.

I hadn't seen my uncle since he had his nervous breakdown after seeing his son Noah go from a handsome young man to a hairy beast because of genetic engineering.

Jack was listening to Kendra with his signature blank look, which meant he was carefully considering whatever she was saying. I had yet to tell Jack that Kendra hadn't killed my father, Jack's brother. I was guessing my uncle didn't believe a word Kendra was saying. Either that, or he didn't want to be here. He had to be as disgusted with his mother as I was. Tripp wasn't sure if Jack could offer any help in dealing with Harriet, and I had to agree. Jack wasn't her favorite son. Ray had been her golden boy before he'd died of a heart attack.

Conrad parked parallel to Kendra's car, Jack's truck, and the black Escalade that I assumed was Lucien's, who was on the phone and pacing but lowered his cell when he saw us.

After we got out, we went through introductions, mainly for Lucien's sake. The imposing vampire with broad shoulders, big forehead, and soulless black eyes was scary as fuck. If the plan was to look inconspicuous, then we were screwed. The man would stick out like a giant among elves.

Nevertheless, while Sam and Conrad talked to Lucien about Jonah's predicament, I regarded my uncle.

His grayish-blue eyes took me in as he gave me a warm smile, reminding me of my dad. I almost tripped over myself at the realization that he was seemingly happy to see me and even more so when he gave me a hug.

I returned the gesture. "It is good to see you."

"I wish it was under better circumstances," he said, squinting at the sunlight that was shining directly on him. "I'm also sorry to hear about your kids." My uncle seemed different—as in, less of the ogre that I'd always known him to be.

Seeing Noah as a monster would definitely change a person's outlook. I would bet that was the reason Jack came over to our side. Originally, he hadn't wanted to get in the middle of a war with vampires. But it was hard to ignore what was happening in the country or with his own family.

Once the evil Aberdeens were out of my life, I didn't intend to fight every battle alongside Sam. Frankly, I didn't want to. I had children to nurture and protect. I had a sister who needed me, and I wanted to build a good home for my family. I couldn't do any of that until I found Orion and Luna and washed my hands of Harriet and Rianne.

"How's Aunt Tab?" I asked.

I knew what it felt like to have my babies ripped from their cribs in the middle of the night. I felt her grief over her loss of Noah even though he was still alive but wasn't human anymore. However, he was a grown man who had made his own decision to give up his humanity. Still, that had to be agonizing. Not to mention, her first-born, Junior, had recently died in a car accident.

"She's not doing well. I had to tell her about Noah." His voice was soaked in misery.

I had no comment except to say, "Rianne is probably in a cell next to Noah now." That statement wasn't meant as ill will but to hopefully make him feel like I understood.

I darted my attention toward Kendra. "Did you and Jack make amends?"

Kendra was dressed entirely in black, including a bulletproof vest beneath her tank top, which showcased her toned biceps. "I told him Fred Emery killed your father. Whether he believes me or not, he hasn't said."

"It's true, Uncle Jack. That should be even more of a reason for you to fight with us. The war with Intech is just starting. Rianne is a monster like Noah. More and more humans will die if we don't stop Adam and Roman. Luckily, Fred is imprisoned at the naval base." I gritted my teeth. "We've learned that some inside vampires have been spilling our secrets and personal information to Roman Brown. We're pretty sure Roman led the charge in the kidnapping of Orion and Luna."

Kendra's mouth came unhinged. "Are you kidding me? You think he's also teamed up with witches?"

Jack paled. "Witches?"

Conrad, Lucien, and Sam were listening to me now. The six of us were in a circle, with Sam and Jack flanking me.

Lucien growled. "I want to kill that bastard Roman with my bare hands."

He would have to get in line behind me and Sam.

A muscle ticked in Sam's jaw. "My father was able to extract that information from the vampire we caught in the nursery. He was about to take Ellie. Look, I would like to free Jonah and capture Harriet as soon as possible. Whatever you do, Harriet needs to be taken alive. We think she might know where Roman is."

My husband, the vampire soldier, was wound tight and ready to bash in heads. Unlike Lucien, who was dressed in a police uniform with weapons clinging to his waist, Sam was in casual attire. He wanted to fly under the radar and not call attention to himself with the media and all.

"Then let's proceed," Lucien said. "First the bad news. I just learned a few minutes ago that Harriet Aberdeen isn't anywhere in the casino or in the mob outside. I have men searching the grounds."

"Unbelievable," I said. "She makes this big production on TV to lure us out and then disappears. No way. She's nearby." I was sure of it.

"I agree with Layla," Jack said.

"Have your men been in the casino?" Sam asked.

Lucien's fangs lowered as his nostrils flared. "Yes. But the door to the main gambling room where Jonah is being held is rigged with C-4. My team hasn't had any luck clearing the media and spectators from the immediate area. The humans are more fascinated with vampires than saving their own lives. Some don't even believe we're telling the truth about the bomb."

Sam chuckled. "Harriet thinks I'm going to run in and save Jonah. Then she'll blow me to smithereens."

It took a lot to kill a vampire, but while Sam had survived a C-4 explosion at a house I'd rented in Massachusetts, he'd gotten lucky. If he'd been in there any longer, the fire would've taken his life.

My uncle Jack was scowling. "I hate to say this, but I want to murder my mother."

Lucien's long fingers danced through his ebony-colored hair. "We're working with the human police, and they're bringing in their bomb squad. I have no idea yet if it's on a timer or just rigged to blow when you open the door. To prevent a disaster and save the stupid humans, I would like Layla to address the media. Tripp tells me you might be able to get through to them."

Sam's green eyes melted to liquid steel. "That will depend on where the media is," he said. "No fucking way she's standing in front of the casino. We don't know how much C-4 is involved. That building could blow sky-high."

"What if we find a safe distance away from the building," Lucien offered. "We can snag a reporter to do a one-on-one with Layla so she can encourage people to get the fuck out of here."

"Violet Keller," Sam said, warming up to the idea. "She's a reporter that Tim Cox recommended."

I was ready to walk away. I didn't have time for this crap. But I wanted Harriet in my grasp, and I also wanted to help save lives. One of the reasons my sister Jordyn was so insistent on teaming up with Vampire Navy SEALs was because they protected humanity. Even if I hadn't fallen in love with Sam, my career would've been in law enforcement.

Sam plucked his phone from his jeans pocket. "I'll talk to the press with Layla."

Lucien had his bulky arms crossed over his chest. "That could go one of two ways. Either they'll love you and listen, or they'll throw stones at you, Sam."

Conrad scratched his chin. "It's too volatile at the moment for you to be showing yourself to the nation."

Sam snarled at no one, shoving his hands through his hair.

I grabbed Sam's hand. "Can I speak to you alone?"

I had to calm him down before we did anything. I needed him focused and not worrying about me.

We walked away from the group as they started talking amongst themselves.

Once Sam and I were out of earshot or, rather, far enough away that the vampires would really have to listen intently to hear us, I craned my neck up at him. "I hate this as much as you do. I am tempted to leave right now. I am so fucking tired of Harriet. But if we are not thinking straight because of our concern for each other, we'll miss the opportunity to find Harriet. You and I know she's around here, watching, or she might've changed her appearance to blend in with the crowd. Find her. Disguise yourself—hat and sunglasses. You'll fit in since you're not in uniform. You call Violet Keller, and I'll talk to her while Lucien's men figure out the bomb. Conrad will guard me. Take Jack with you. He can recognize his mother faster than you."

A slight breeze ruffled the wispy strands of my hair, and he moved them off my face. "You know, if I could lock you up to keep you safe, I would." His tone was serious even though he had that lopsided grin on his face.

"I know, but you can't. Believe me, if we weren't dealing with my family or trying to find our children, I would be back at the shifter compound with Ellie and Rorie. I'll be fine, and I'm not leaving here until we deal with Harriet. I feel responsible, and I need to carry my weight when it comes to her and Rianne."

He tipped up my chin. "Your family's actions aren't your fault. But I understand where you're coming from. Let's do this." He pecked a kiss on my forehead.

I wished upon a star that we would find Harriet. If we did, she was leaving in a straitjacket.

25

LAYLA

Gray clouds skated across the sky and intermittently blocked the early afternoon sun, casting dark shadows over the throng of people gathered outside the casino.

I'd been inhaling and exhaling as Conrad drove from the scrapyard to a location close enough to get a glimpse of the crowd but still far enough away from the Pacific Dome—aptly named after the shape of the casino—for safety.

I'd never been drawn to gambling my money away. I couldn't help but think of my uncle Ray.

"My uncle Ray is probably laughing from his grave at how the landscape of America has changed," I mumbled. If I knew my uncle, he would have been in the thick of it with Harriet, Rianne, and Noah, if he were alive.

Conrad pulled into an empty lot next to a fenced-in area full of brand-new cars that belonged to a local dealership. "Are you ready?"

I snorted. "Hell no. I just want to find my babies, Conrad."

He placed a gentle hand on my arm. "I know, and we will. I still haven't heard from my contact on the darts. I'm hoping that when I do, it will give us the location of the person who purchased them."

"You're a good man, Conrad."

He cut the engine. "Come on. Let's make this quick."

Everyone had their roles to play. Kendra, Jack, and Sam were scouring the crowd for Harriet. Lucien and his men were helping while the bomb squad had arrived to deal with the rigged door. When I was finished speaking with the reporter, Conrad and I were to head to our rendezvous point—a warehouse that was located five miles from the casino. Lucien used the warehouse for storage and other vampire business.

I hoped I could convince the humans to leave the area. I didn't want innocent people to die. But I could only do so much.

A cold chill tiptoed down my spine, feeling like sharp claws made of steel as we exited the vehicle. I wasn't a public speaker. I'd failed that class miserably in high school. I swallowed the dryness in my throat as I adjusted my bulletproof vest, felt for my trusty dagger inside my boot, and touched the comm in my ear. I doubted I needed any protection to speak with Violet, but we were covering all bases just in case Harriet came out of nowhere or any of our other enemies did, for that matter.

Conrad was one step behind as we walked up to Violet, who was standing outside her CBC 4 news truck.

The brunette reporter with a short bob and wide brown eyes extended her hand to me. "I'm Violet Keller. Thanks so much for this opportunity. I'm actually a fan of the Vampire Navy SEALs. I grew up not far from the naval base. In fact, my older brother, Diego, helped Webb London out of a jam about five years ago." She was talking fast and breathing heavily. "I'm sorry. I sound like a crazy fan. Don't I?"

"Kind of," I teased. "It's cute." Her excitement about the Vampire Navy SEALs and her job as a reporter could certainly help us drive the narrative. "Layla Mason. Nice to meet you."

After a quick handshake, I asked, "How will the crowd hear me?"

"I have a colleague in front of the casino who will pick up the feed. He'll project your speech so everyone down there will hear you, and, of course, whoever's watching on TV or streaming the feed will be able to as well. Once we are live, other reporters might converge here, along with spectators."

I checked on Conrad, who was looking behind Violet in the direction of the casino. "If that happens, we jump in the car. Again, let's make this quick."

"The goal here is nothing more than people's safety," I said. "We stay on topic, please. And why isn't everyone leaving, including the media? There's a bomb in the casino."

She shrugged. "I know this might sound ignorant, but with all the hype about vampires, we're not sure what to believe anymore." She smoothed a hand down her CBC 4 golf shirt. "Recently, we've been told so many lies that it's hard to discern fact from fiction. Not to mention, people love an intriguing story, and the images of that vampire staked to a craps table has gone viral." Her nose wrinkled. "I hope you're successful, or if there truly is a bomb, that it doesn't go off."

She didn't even believe there was a bomb. Incredible.

Violet acknowledged her lanky cameraman with a dip of her chin. "All right, Ash, it's go time. Layla, stand beside me."

I moved into position with my back to the casino and crowd.

Violet held her mic, lifted her chest, and smiled. "Today, we're coming to you live from a safe spot near the Pacific Dome casino where the hostage situation is taking place. With us today is Layla Aberdeen Mason. You may remember that her sister Rianne spoke at a press conference in Chicago a month ago. During that segment, Rianne led us to believe that Layla had been swept up against her will by Sam Mason—compelled to fall in love and have his baby. If there's time, we'll talk a little about Layla. But first, she has an important message to share with you." Violet angled the microphone toward me. "Layla, tell us. Is there really a bomb inside the casino?"

I was laughing inside at the craziness of what was happening with humans. Those nerves I thought I would have over speaking to a camera weren't there.

I placed a hand on my chest. "If you are standing outside the Pacific Dome casino, leave now!" I raised my voice. "The main room of the casino is rigged with C-4. Harriet Aberdeen, who you heard from this morning, is the one responsible for endangering your lives in an effort to kill Sam Mason."

"Harriet is your grandmother, right?" Violet asked. "She's doing this to kill Sam?"

"That's right." I glared into the camera. "I'm here to bring my grandmother in. If you're listening, Granny, give yourself up. Your son Jack and I are here to take you home." I was lying through my teeth. "We want you to live out your final days in the comfort of your home and among your family."

"Keep talking, baby doll," Sam said in my ear. "The bomb squad is still working. No sign yet of Harriet. Sadly, no one is moving either."

I smiled, knowing my hunky vampire was listening to me.

"Is Harriet sick?" Violet asked.

"She's suffering from a rare form of blood cancer. She believes that genetic engineering will save her life."

Violet's jaw dropped. "But we've seen the before-and-after images of Rianne recently. Adam Emery's prototype program isn't working as intended. Surely, Harriet knows this."

"People will go to great lengths to survive," I said. "Once again, I implore the people outside the Pacific Dome casino to leave now. Go home to your loved ones."

Violet said a few last words before Ash lifted the camera off his shoulder.

I turned around, as did Violet. People were leaving. Thank God.

"Thank you, Layla," Violet said. "At some point, would you

consider sitting down with me and discussing yourself? My viewers would love to know more about you. I've gotten many emails and calls asking about you. The public is hungry to learn who Layla really is."

I half smiled. "Or do they only want to know about Sam?"

"To be honest, both. You two are becoming celebrities," she said.

I imagined we were.

Conrad called my name. "Time to go."

News trucks were coming our way.

Just as I was about to say goodbye to Violet, an explosion rent the air.

I jumped a freaking mile.

Conrad grabbed my arm and rushed me into the SUV.

Violet and her cameraman stared out at the casino, where a plume of dust was dispersing into the air.

"Sam," I said into my comm. "Are you okay?" He should be. He wasn't inside the casino.

Dead silence.

My heart punched my ribs. "Sam!"

As Conrad sped toward the casino, my pulse flipped out.

26

SAM

"Motherfucker," I mumbled to myself as my ears rang like a bitch. It didn't help that car alarms were going off left and right.

I pushed off the ground as people frantically ran in all directions. Someone had knocked me on my ass.

Idiots.

Even when Layla's voice had been projecting from the news-truck speakers, not many humans left the area. Now they were scattering like rats, falling and tripping over those on the ground.

I guessed the bomb squad fucked up.

I scanned the immediate area, looking for Jack. I'd spotted him chasing a woman just before the explosion. I felt for my comm and came up empty. I must've lost it when I fell.

I whipped out my phone, and I was stalking past a row of cars when a driver backed out and rammed into me. My cell flew out of my hand in one direction while I was knocked to the ground.

I growled loudly as my fangs shot out.

The driver didn't seem to care that he'd hit someone or something because he kept going.

196

I climbed to my feet, grabbed the bumper, and lifted the beat-up old clunker. The middle-aged, balding man behind the wheel looked over his shoulder and froze.

I was about to toss the fucking car in the air when I caught a glimpse of a person's head bobbing up and down in the four-door sedan next to me. Probably another scared human.

"Sam," Kendra shouted from somewhere nearby.

I let go of the bumper, glaring at the driver before he scrambled out of the car and took off like the wind.

Kendra slowed to a walk as humans continued to run by, oblivious to either of us. "I saw Jack with someone, but I lost him after the explosion."

"I did as well," I said, searching for my phone. "I lost my comm, and then my cell fell and went that way." I stabbed a finger at the area near the four-door sedan.

Normally, I wouldn't give a shit, but I needed a way to communicate. Layla was probably freaking out right about now.

Kendra and I began checking around the sedan. As I skirted the trunk, a heartbeat inside the car was pumping quite fast. I was about to ignore the human until I caught sight of a gun in a woman's hands aimed in Kendra's direction.

I tore the door off its hinges at the same time that another explosion rocked the fucking ground. I stumbled backward into the open parking space as the woman in the vehicle scrambled out, dropping her gun in the process. She bent over to pick it up, and as she straightened, her beady blue eyes made me do a double take.

"Harriet," I said. I had to really look at her because she'd lost weight and appeared sickly.

She snarled, raising the gun at my chest. "You're supposed to be in the casino, saving your vampire."

"I came here for you," I said in an excited tone. "But go ahead —take your shot. You know bullets can't do permanent damage." I was sure she had cobalt bullets, which could slow me down, and enough of them could burn my heart to a crisp, as in dead as a doornail.

I closed the short distance between us and yanked the gun from her shaky hand. Dare I say I felt a modicum of pity? She looked sicklier in person than she had on TV earlier that morning.

I grabbed her arm. "Let's go. Layla wants to see you. Oh, and your son Jack does too."

She stiffened in my grasp. "Jack?"

As I forced her to walk with me, I asked, "You don't remember your son?"

"Sam, is this your phone?" Kendra asked, rushing up on the other side of Harriet.

"Yeah." I took it from her and pocketed it for the time being as we meandered through what looked like a dystopian landscape.

The air was laden with dust and smoke, flames spewed out of the dome of the casino, and people were walking around us like zombies. I was sure their ears were ringing like mine.

"Where's your car?" I asked Kendra. I'd ridden with Lucien, who had parked behind the four-level garage on the other side of the casino.

She pointed to the road alongside the parking lot.

We beelined it in that direction.

"Kendra, do you still have your comm?"

Kendra shook her head. "Negative. It fell out during the first explosion."

"Can you call Layla for me?" I asked her.

She attempted to, but then she said, "No signal."

Motherfucker.

Harriet laughed.

I tightened my grip on her arm. "Careful, old lady. I might feed you to Rianne and Noah. You remember them? Your grandchildren. They just might eat you alive. Or you tell me where Roman and Adam are, and I'll go easy on you." I knew that wasn't a good threat. She was dying, so she probably didn't care.

"The question you should be asking me is where are your children?" she said in a sweet tone.

I yanked her to a stop just as we reached Kendra's silver Toyota Camry. "Where are they?" I clutched her throat, pinning her against the vehicle.

Kendra inserted her arm between Harriet and me. "Sam, if you want answers, back off. You won't get any if she's not breathing."

Harriet took that opportunity to sink her teeth into Kendra's bare forearm.

The blond vampire snarled, her fangs gleaming from her upper gums. "Woman, I am so tired of having an Aberdeen fucking with me. Do that again, and *I'll* end you right here and right now."

I shoved Harriet into the back seat, then climbed in after her. "Rendezvous point," I said to Kendra as she slid behind the wheel, fuming.

Kendra opened the glove compartment, pulled out zip ties, and tossed them to me. "You'll need these. Too bad I don't have a muzzle." She growled at Harriet.

Once Grandma Aberdeen's wrists were secured, Kendra sped down the road, away from the emergency vehicles converging on the casino.

Harriet sat quietly. It was shocking that she wasn't running her mouth or bragging.

I would ask her again where my children were, but I would be wasting my energy. I could kill her, but we needed answers. It was best to wait until we were with Layla. Though my wife was itching to strangle Harriet.

I checked my phone for a signal. I had one bar, which should suffice, and called Layla.

"Sam?" she asked in a hurried tone as she answered. "Thank goodness."

A rush of air punched from my lungs. I figured she was okay, but just hearing her voice loosened more of that tightness in my chest. "Are you at the rendezvous point?"

"Yes. Conrad and I have been trying to call you."

"I lost my comm, and I didn't have a cell signal. But I have a surprise for you."

"You got Harriet?" she asked, her tone dripping with excitement.

Harriet glowered at me.

"Get ready to interrogate her," I said to Layla. "We should be there in five minutes." Then I disconnected. "Harriet, if I were you, I would say all your prayers now."

She let out a sinister laugh. "You think you've won. You're such an arrogant asshole. You are so blinded by dealing with me that you aren't prepared for what's coming."

"Do you think you hold the last card?"

"I don't think, Sam Mason. I know." Her tone was resolute.

I had to hand it to her. She was a fighter, and she wasn't going down easily.

27

LAYLA

I was on the roof of the warehouse with Conrad as we glanced in the direction of the casino, where smoke billowed into the air in the distance. The second I'd heard Sam's voice, my pulse had slowed. For a hot minute, I hadn't been able to shake the feeling that he was hurt or Harriet had captured him.

I shivered. "He's got my grandmother. Let the games begin." My stomach fluttered with excitement that I was finally about to confront her once and for all. This was it. After today, I didn't want to see her or deal with her ever again.

"Doesn't look good for Jonah." Despair colored Conrad's tone.

I'd never met Jonah but felt bad just the same. "He might be okay. Sam survived a house explosion."

Conrad stabbed a finger in the air. "Did it look anything like that? I can tell you the casino is probably leveled and in flames. Claude Irving and Harriet weren't fooling around."

"Why would Claude blow up his casino?" Granted, the man was rich as fuck. Maybe he didn't care.

"Money, I suspect," Conrad said. "My guess? Harriet or Roman paid him a hefty sum."

A silver car sped down the road toward the gate leading into the warehouse that was home to crates of weapons designed to combat other vampires. Lucien had a large security team guarding the facility.

"That looks like Kendra's car."

Sam hadn't mentioned who he was with other than my grandmother, but he had to be with Kendra. I hurried down to the main floor with Conrad on my heels. I'd just reached the first level when dizziness made me sway.

Conrad grabbed my arm. "What is it?"

"It's nothing." I blinked several times as that tingling sensation radiated in my legs.

It was the same feeling that warned me something bad was about to happen or another vision of the white-haired lady loomed. Lately, I couldn't tell what those feelings meant anymore.

As quick as the sensation struck, it was gone in an instant. I didn't move for a beat, taking inventory of my mind and body. No more dizziness or that weird prickle in my thighs.

Tires screeched and echoed as Kendra drove into the warehouse. The space was large enough for vehicles to drive through from one bay door to the other.

My stomach pitched and rolled at the notion that Harriet was finally in our grasp. My boots scuffed along the concrete floor, and my attention fixated on the car as I marched in that direction.

"This should be interesting," Conrad mumbled at my side.

Words escaped me when Sam dragged Harriet out of the back seat. I had to question why we were even wasting our time. She wouldn't tell us squat. The best thing for us was to ship her off to Steven and Jo for them to read her mind. Yet a large part of me had to give it the old college try to see if we could extract anything from her about our children.

Sam shoved Harriet onto one of many crates lining the perimeter of the warehouse on both sides.

My grandmother feigned a smile, tracking my movements with

disgust in her blue eyes. I returned the expression, gritting my teeth. Harriet Aberdeen, the matriarch of my father's family, had always been composed—dressed in expensive clothes, makeup always in place, and hair perfectly styled. Yet despite the heavy coat of foundation and the bright-red lipstick, her cancer was taking its toll on her. Up close, my grandmother looked awful. She'd lost weight, which was evident in her face.

She held her head high. "Layla," she said in that sugary tone I hated. "Are you ready to come home?"

I choked on my saliva, crossing my arms over my chest. "What imaginary world are you living in? Don't answer that. I already know. Where are my children?"

She wiggled her hands that were secured with zip ties in her lap as she pinned a look on Sam, who was a few feet to my right.

Kendra and Conrad stood to my left.

She returned her attention to me. "Why don't you ask Roman?"

I fisted my hands at my sides. "You know where they are, don't you?"

Harriet gave me a smug grin, lifting her chin, not afraid that she had three vampires near her and a group guarding the warehouse. "What I can tell you is that their DNA will cure my blood cancer."

I had my fingers around her throat before she could blink. "If you don't start talking, I'll have Sam rip out your insides with his fangs."

Sam came over. "Layla, let her speak."

Why? I wanted to ask. Anything that came out of her mouth would only enrage me further.

Nevertheless, I eased up, shaking. "Granny, are you really that diabolical to abuse your great-grandbabies?"

"I'm not doing anything of the sort," she said as though she was pure and innocent. "You can do whatever you want to me, but I can't tell you where they are, because I don't know. Where's Rianne?"

"Dead." I bit out the lie easily. "Like your grandson Noah. You are responsible for their deaths. I hope you rot in hell too."

Harriet lost her smirk when a car's engine filtered in my ears before Jack's truck wheeled into the warehouse behind Kendra's car.

All of us, including Harriet, turned our attention to Jack and the woman in the passenger seat. Her face didn't register until Jack ushered her out of the truck.

"Look who I found," Jack said, pushing a thin-as-a-rail woman who I knew all too well.

I lost the ability to speak as Ray Aberdeen's wife bared her teeth at Jack. "Do that again, and I'll knee you in the balls."

"That's the woman you were chasing," Kendra said.

I swallowed thickly, ungluing my tongue from the roof of my mouth. "Aunt Deb? What are you doing here?"

"Aunt?" Sam asked. "Another Aberdeen has joined the fray?"

It appeared that way. I was trying to figure out why, but shock had shut down my brain, and then my aunt narrowed her brown eyes and sneered at me.

"Tell her why you're here." Jack's tone was deadly as he snarled, keeping a tight grip on Deb's arm.

"You've decided to join your crazy mother-in-law in her quest to what? Kill Sam?" I asked.

Like Harriet, Deb had lost a ton of weight. For a split second, I wondered if she, too, had an incurable disease. The last I'd seen her was two years ago at my father's funeral.

Deb's face brightened, and she shrugged out of Jack's hold. "I'm here to kill both you and Sam." Her tone dripped with hatred. "I'm the one forking over the bounty on your beloved bloodsucker's head." She lifted her chest as if proud to announce that revelation. "I took the life insurance money from Ray's death and decided to enlist Harriet's help and Claude Irving's. I figured if I could lure Sam out, you would be right there with him. How lucky were we when we found out you were in the state? You murdered my husband, Layla. You took Ray from me and our kids. So did that bloodsucker."

Sam mumbled "Bitch," under his breath.

I marched up to her. "You hate me enough to take my life?"

She couldn't hurt a fly. In fact, she had never hunted with the family, although in all fairness to her, she had small children to take care of, and Ray didn't want her near vampires.

"You're my number one target," Deb spat.

My eyes bugged out. "You're not experienced enough to fight vampires let alone me. You couldn't hurt a mouse, Deb."

She shrugged. "Maybe not. But I do have men who can hurt your children."

Harriet let out a wild laugh.

Before my brain could catch up with my hands, my fingers were clamping her neck. "Are you the one who kidnapped my children?" Stars danced in my vision as anger, blazing hot, seared my insides.

The tall glass windows high above rattled. The ground seemed to shake as well.

"Layla," Jack snapped. "You're choking her."

"Shut the fuck up," I said to my uncle. "Talk, Deb."

She grasped my wrists, her brown eyes showing no fear.

As Jack tried to pry my hands from Deb, Sam was in his face. "Step off, Jack."

"Mason, I agreed to talk to my mother not kill my sister-in-law," Jack said. "She has kids, for fuck's sake."

I shoved Deb so hard the woman flew toward the stack of crates across the wide aisle and landed on her ass.

She scrambled to her feet, brushed off her jeans, then studied me as her hand disappeared behind her. The closer she got to me, the wider her lips spread into a cunning smile.

I wasn't about to go down without a fight. Just as I grabbed my dagger out of my boot, Deb charged forward with a syringe pointed at me.

No fucking way! I was not becoming another victim to the serum.

Then hell broke loose.

I lunged at her and drove the blade into her stomach. "No one will use that fucking serum on me." I yanked out my dagger.

Deb screeched as the syringe fell from her hand.

Jack tried to catch Deb as she stumbled, blood soaking her yellow shirt.

I picked up the syringe that was at my feet and examined the yellowish liquid inside. Memories of that day I'd been held prisoner at Intech's West Virginia facility narrowed to sharp pinpoints. That was the day Rianne injected the serum into me, but luckily, not enough had gotten into my system to do any damage.

Deb held her stomach. "You deserve to be like your bloodsucker."

Clearly, she was delusional. "Maybe I should use it on you." Now, there was an idea. "After all, it was your husband who started this mess when he teamed up with Intech." Truth.

Ray had been more desperate for money than he had been to kill any vampires, including Sam.

As I stared at Deb, pity wormed its way into my psyche. She was only trying to avenge her husband's death, and in a way, I couldn't blame her. I would do the exact thing if the tables were turned.

"I feel sorry for you, Deb," I said. "Go home and be with your kids." She wouldn't die from the stab wound, though she would need medical attention.

Jack sighed at her side.

I had other plans for the syringe. With my dagger in one hand and the syringe in the other, I spun on my heel and walked over to Harriet.

"What do you think, Granny? How about you take it? You're dying anyway. You can join Rianne." I shoved the needle in her face.

She turned white as a ghost. "Get that away from me."

Sam came over and took my dagger. "I'll hold this, baby doll," he said with a boatload of excitement in his voice.

Conrad and Kendra watched from the sidelines with rapt

attention.

I was sure the Aberdeen family dynamic was interesting to witness. Hell, if I were on the outside looking in, I would be anxious to see what happened next too.

I angled my head. I hadn't decided what my next move would be. "You're afraid of this needle?" I asked Harriet. "Why? You want to live, right? This is your ticket to immortality." I pointed the syringe at her neck. "This should prolong your life."

"No, it won't," Harriet shrieked.

Sam sidled up to me. "Start talking, Harriet. If my wife doesn't jam that needle into you, I will."

Granny's body jerked. "You two are married?" She swallowed. "I knew you had kids, but no one told me you were married. What a sacrilege. Disgusting. Your father would gut you for marrying a vampire, Layla."

I pricked her skin with the tip of the needle, and blood oozed out. "Actually, he would do that to you for what you've done to Noah and Rianne. Now tell me where our babies are."

Oh, I wanted Granny to suffer for everything she'd put me through.

Jack flanked me on the other side. "Layla, think about what you're doing. Killing vampires is quite different from taking a human life, especially a blood relative's."

I whipped my angry gaze at Jack. "Seriously? Look what she did to Rianne and Noah. She might not be responsible for Junior's car accident, but in a way, she is. She threatened Jordyn to exchange her life for mine. Which was why Jordyn and Junior were on their way to Harriet when the accident happened. Wake up, Jack."

Harriet trembled. "Listen to your uncle."

"I will when you give me a location on my children." I wasn't leaving until she talked.

"Tell her, Mom," Jack ordered in a tone that permitted no argument.

"Son, you know I love you. Please," Harriet begged. "Layla

needs to be locked up. Not me."

I snorted while Sam's growled laugh echoed through the warehouse.

Jack stared at his mother. "No. Layla is right about you. *You* are responsible for Noah. I'll never forgive you."

I was shocked at Jack's change in demeanor.

"You've put Tabitha and me through hell," Jack said, spitting fire all of a sudden. "You should be ashamed of yourself. If you tell Layla where her children are, I'll take you home and make you comfortable until the cancer claims your life—because there will never be a serum to cure your disease." His voice blared in the vast space.

Harriet shook, her face turning tomato red. "There is one. It's Layla's children!"

Electricity arced through my body as blind rage consumed me. I plunged the needle into Granny's neck without blinking an eye. "That's the last time you refer to my children." Then I pushed the serum into her until the syringe was empty.

Deb screamed. "No!"

Harriet glowered at me. "You'll go to hell for this, Layla."

I got in her face. "Me? I don't think so. You know what's a sacrilege? You are. Now you can join Rianne and Noah."

Inching backward, I darted my gaze around the warehouse. Jack, Conrad, Kendra, and Sam were fixated on Harriet.

Granny began to convulse and foam at the mouth. Her face turned blue. Blood dribbled out of her tear ducts and nose.

"Her heart is racing extremely fast," Sam mumbled.

A second later, her body went limp.

My eyebrows drew down. "She was supposed to change into a monster like Rianne."

"Remember what Rianne told us about Carly's test subjects dying instantly?" Sam asked. "The serum speeds up the disease's processes."

I'd forgotten about that part. Then something else made the

blood pool to my feet. "Fuck. I should've waited until she told us where our babies were." I began pacing as a war raged in my head.

Part of me was relieved she would no longer be a problem in our lives. The other part of me was angry as hell that I'd acted without thinking.

Sam wrapped me in his warm embrace. "Don't beat yourself up. Harriet didn't know squat about where Orion and Luna are. I thought she did. But I realized Roman wouldn't have shared their whereabouts with her."

While he was probably right, it didn't make me feel any better. Above that, I'd just killed my grandmother—the woman who had given birth to Jack.

I shrugged out of Sam's hold and regarded my uncle. He stared at his mother with equal parts sorrow and relief.

I closed the distance between Jack and me. "Uncle Jack." I touched his arm. "Are you okay?" I was beginning to feel like a terrible person. I'd just taken his mother away from him.

He swung his gray-blue gaze to me. "I will be. I was just thinking of all the times she screwed this family. I believe you did the right thing."

I tilted my head. "Really?" I was expecting a speech on how horrible and selfish I was. Something he'd told me a few times over the years.

"She needed to be stopped," Jack said. "She wasn't giving up until she got what she wanted, no matter who she hurt in the process. She's at peace now. But I'm worried that what you've done will haunt you."

His words surprised me. Jack Aberdeen had only cared about his wife and kids.

"Maybe," I said. "But what is haunting me right now is not knowing where Orion and Luna are or if they're hurt." *Or worse, dead.*

Something had to give. We were five days into the kidnapping, and my emotional well-being was tanking hard and fast.

28

LAYLA

After a harrowing day where I'd almost turned into a monster, learned there was another crazy Aberdeen gunning for me, and taken a mostly silent car ride from Bozeman to Zeke's house, I stood in the en suite bathroom, staring at myself in the mirror. Sam was concerned about me. I'd reassured him I was fine and that I just needed some quiet time to process what had happened.

The emotions coursing through me were all over the place—sorrow, anger, shock, despair, and relief. We didn't have Harriet to deal with anymore. Yet my aunt Deb might be a problem.

I shivered, my heart punching my ribs in a steady *boom, boom, boom.* Jack was right. Harriet wouldn't have stopped until she got what she wanted. My uncle also assured me Deb wouldn't bother me again. He had made it his mission to take care of her and find her the help she needed to heal physically and emotionally.

"Layla," Sam called as he knocked on the bathroom door. "Can I come in?"

"It's open." I pivoted on my heel and leaned against the sink.

He sauntered in, hair tied in a low ponytail, jeans slung low on his hips, and love pouring off him. He held out his phone. "Jordyn wants to talk to you." He kissed me on the forehead. "I'll be in the kitchen with Conrad." Then he left.

I lifted his cell to my ear. "Sis."

"Oh, Layla." Jordyn sounded panicked. "I've been so freaking worried about you since I saw the news."

Just hearing her voice made me cry. "I'm okay. Granny is dead." Saying that line out loud felt freeing.

"What? How?"

I closed the lid of the toilet and sat down. "I injected her with the serum. But there's more. Aunt Deb was the one who had the syringe of serum and intended to use it on me."

"What the fuck," Jordyn shouted. "Has the entire Aberdeen clan, except you and me, gone completely insane?" She lowered the volume of her voice. "I'm guessing Aunt Deb is mad at you because of Ray's death."

Bingo. "Yep. Deb was the one footing the bill for the bounty on Sam. She teamed up with Granny."

"Unbelievable," she said in horror. "Did Granny have anything to do with Orion and Luna missing? Or did Deb, for that matter?"

"I never got an answer out of Granny. Roman knows where they are, though."

I counted the tiles on the floor as silence stretched over the line.

"I'm sitting here flabbergasted about Aunt Deb," Jordyn said in a low tone. "She was always the quiet one. Any more Aberdeens lining up to make our lives miserable?"

Between Jack's kids and Ray's kids, we had a baseball team of cousins. I wasn't worried about Jack's kids. Ray's were another matter. They could grow up to seek revenge for their father's death.

"Where's Aunt Deb now?" Jordyn asked.

"I stabbed Aunt Deb. But she's going to be fine. Uncle Jack is taking care of her. Before he left, he mentioned something about finding help for her."

"I'm sorry you're dealing with our family alone," she said. "I want to be there with you. But on a good note, Ellie and Rorie are doing well. They're here with me in the communication room."

I couldn't stop the tears as they slid down my face. "I miss them terribly."

She sniffled. "Stop. You're making me cry."

I ripped toilet paper from the roll and blew my nose.

"Any word from Jo on that lady Zoey?" Jordyn asked. "Or have you had a vision of the white-haired witch?"

I threw the soiled toilet paper in the trash. "I think I was about to have a vision at the warehouse just before we interrogated Granny. But it didn't happen. I'm wound so tight."

"Layla, I know all this is taking its toll on you. Try to relax. Have a glass of wine or your favorite bourbon. Push Granny out of your head. To be honest, I can't say I'm sad she's gone."

I couldn't either. "I love you, Jordyn. I don't know what I would do without you." I felt as though I was sucking the life out of her. "You deserve a medal and your own happiness."

"Pffft," she said. "I am happy. I have beautiful nieces and a nephew. I have a sister who I would die for, and I am right where I want to be. Now stop your brooding, eat, fuel up, relax, and maybe that vision will happen."

"Kiss my daughters for me and Sam."

"For sure. I'm relieved you're okay. I have to run to feed Ellie and Rorie. Call me when something big happens. Love you."

After we hung up, I splashed water on my face, collected myself, fixed my hair, and then went in search of Sam.

He and Conrad were lounging in the great room. Sam was on one couch, absorbed in his phone, and Conrad was on his laptop.

A fire crackled in the stone hearth. Any other day, I would've thought it was a warm and inviting atmosphere, but I could feel the tension as if I were an empath like Sam.

He glanced up from his phone, and as I crossed from the hall into the great room, my legs prickled, then dizziness ensued until blackness encroached on my peripheral vision.

In a blink, I was standing beneath a blanket of stars with the moon's rays spraying down over the cornstalks that I was sure traveled for a mile or more, but I could only see so far.

"Hello," I called.

I glanced in front of me and behind me but didn't see anyone.

"Agnes," I called. "Are you trying to contact me?"

A breeze blew over the tips of the cornstalks before the white-haired lady appeared directly ahead of me as if she'd teleported.

I froze. For all I knew, she could be the dream walker who wanted me dead. But I didn't think so. How could she kill me in a maze of corn?

Confident the woman wasn't evil, I started in her direction.

"Layla, my child." Her orange gaze sized me up. "We have so much to discuss. But right now, I don't have much time. My sister, Maeve, is keeping tabs on me."

"Agnes?" I asked.

"That's right. I'm your grandmother."

"Not evil, I hope," I said.

She gave me a warm smile. "Maeve is the evil one."

I touched her arm. "Why do you feel real? Am I dreaming, or am I actually somewhere other than Montana?"

"It's just a vision," she said. "I tried to contact you earlier, but my connection broke."

"My babies?"

"They're fine. Maeve has them. But we need to get them away from her as soon as possible. Find Zoey Thornton. She's a powerful witch at the Sacred Flame Academy. She'll explain a lot, but more importantly, she has something that will help you in your efforts to rescue your babies. Ask her for the infinity bracelets too. She'll know you're legitimate." She glanced over her shoulder. "I have to go."

"Wait. Where are my babies?"

"A farm in North Dakota." Then she vanished into thin air.

I jolted upright, my eyes wide as my surroundings materialized, as did Sam. He was pacing in front of the fireplace.

He came to an abrupt halt. "Did you have a vision? I didn't want to disturb you in case you were having one."

Conrad slid a glass of bourbon from one side of the coffee table to the other. "This might help. You look like you could use it."

No shit. I took a sip, then explained to them what happened. "The white-haired witch is Agnes. The one who tried to kill me, I'm pretty sure, is Maeve. Agnes didn't confirm that. However, she did say that Maeve has our babies. They're fine, according to Agnes, and they're at a farm in North Dakota."

Sam bobbed his head. "We know."

I leaned back against the couch, my eyebrows almost to my hairline. "Since when?"

"We were about to tell you when you came in," Sam said.

Conrad eyed his laptop. "My buddy finally tracked those darts to a UPS store in Bismarck, North Dakota."

At least Agnes hadn't been lying to me. "Have you heard from Jo, Sam? Agnes told me Zoey's last name is Thornton, and she teaches at Sacred Flame Academy. Apparently, she has something we need to rescue Orion and Luna, and we also need to ask her for infinity bracelets."

Creases dented Sam's forehead. "I don't understand."

I didn't exactly either. Witchcraft was foreign to me.

"I'll call Jo," Sam said.

I was curious how she would find anything on Sacred Flame Academy. I didn't think a witch school would be publicized on the Internet. It didn't matter. If anyone could locate it, Jo was the person, or Sawyer was.

My stomach was fluttering like crazy. Orion and Luna were alive. We kind of knew where they were. We just needed to work out the logistics.

The day had started out with phenomenal sex, tanked severely when I murdered Granny Aberdeen, and now it was on the upswing.

29

SAM

It was late afternoon with gray skies and a chill in the air as Layla and I walked across the campus of Sacred Flame Academy—a pristine manicured landscape with trees and shrubs perfectly placed throughout the expansive property.

We were meeting Zoey Thornton in the main building. Its structure reminded me of old-world architecture with high peaks and stained-glass windows.

"Pretty area," Layla said as we climbed up the stone steps to the entrance. "Maybe one day our kids can go to this school."

"Let's not get ahead of ourselves." We had a long way to go before we made any decisions on schools for them.

Jo wanted to join us more out of curiosity and to learn if a school like this would fit Abbey. I'd said no. We didn't have time for tours and information gathering other than our strict purpose to talk with Zoey about Agnes and leave with whatever it was that we needed to rescue Orion and Luna.

Frankly, I wanted to storm into the farm in North Dakota. Unfortunately, we hadn't yet located which farm Orion and Luna were at, and Tripp was pulling together a team to send to North Dakota.

Conrad was already in Bismarck at a satellite office that my father had set up for us. The heads of state, who were now working under my father, were very accommodating. I appreciated Lucien's help in Bozeman. Thankfully, because of him, Jonah was alive, even though the craps table had been rigged too. That was the reason for the second explosion. Luckily, both of them had gotten out before the building went up in flames. Still, Harriet and Deb Aberdeen weren't completely stupid. They had covered all bases in their quest to take me out. What they'd failed to understand was—I wasn't an idiot.

Layla and I wound our way through the school, following the signs above to the administrative offices.

"We need to thank Greta when we return to the Gray compound," Layla said.

For the last three days, we'd been working around the clock on strategies, gathering personnel, and locating the school and Zoey. We'd gone through Agnes's journal from front to back a few times to ensure we hadn't missed any hidden messages that Agnes might have written about Zoey and her whereabouts. It wasn't until Greta called me that I remembered the conversation she and I had on her porch not long after we'd arrived on the shifter compound that first night.

"Do you know a witch I can talk to?" I asked.

"It's been a long time. But the witch community is tight. I'll see what I can do," Greta said.

She had actually called me to pass along the name of the witch she'd finally gotten a hold of. One phone call later, and Greta's witch friend had told me where Sacred Flame Academy was.

When Layla and I reached the check-in office, a female voice behind me in the hallway asked, "Sam and Layla?"

Layla and I turned around and met a short lady in her forties, I would guess, gliding toward us.

"I'm Zoey Thornton." The witch with gray-blue eyes and salt-and-pepper hair waved her hand toward a room that had the words "Teacher's Lounge" tacked to the door.

"Thank you for meeting us," Layla said, taking in her surroundings.

Windows lined the far wall that overlooked part of the campus. Tables, couches, a kitchen, and lockers completed the roomy space.

Zoey led us to a four-chair table by the window. "Would you like a beverage before we start?"

"No, thank you," Layla said.

I held out a chair for Layla. "I'm good for now."

Zoey grabbed a soda from the fridge and emptied the contents into a glass.

"When do students return for the fall semester?" Layla asked.

I slid into a chair next to Layla, looking out at the groundskeeper in the distance as he trimmed hedges while his partner zipped around on a riding lawn mower.

Zoey joined us, taking a drink of her soda. "In another month, the campus will be crawling with students. It's the best time of year. I love the first-year students. They're like sponges, excited to learn how to use their powers and study everything about our kind."

Layla flicked her head at me. "Sam and his sister went to a vampire high school. Although with their elemental abilities, I would think they'd have done better here."

I doubted that. "I'm not a witch."

"That, you're not," Zoey said. "You are what I call an elemental vampire. A powerful one. It's common knowledge in our community who the Masons are. But your notoriety of late doesn't bode well for supernaturals. No offense."

"None taken," I said, even though that guilt I carried around was waking up. "We're here to talk about Agnes, and supposedly, you have something that can help us rescue our children."

She dipped her chin. "We have much to discuss before we get to that. It's important you understand what you're up against." She examined Layla for a beat. "You look nothing like your mom, Meredith."

Layla had spoken to Zoey on the phone and explained who she was. Zoey had only agreed to meet with us after Layla had mentioned two key words—infinity bracelets. According to Agnes, the bracelets signaled to Zoey that Layla wasn't just human or a reporter or maybe even an enemy of Zoey's. Outside of that, we hadn't shared any more details on the phone.

"You knew her?" Layla asked.

"I've only seen pictures of your mom as a teenager. Agnes wanted to send her daughters to the academy. She thought this would be a good school for them to learn and practice their powers. That's how I met Agnes. She'd taken a tour of the school many years ago. Since then, we've kept in contact on and off, especially when I found out she was a Monroe witch."

I studied her intently. She didn't look old enough to have known Agnes for many years. Layla's mom would've been at least in her late forties if she'd lived.

Zoey laughed. "I see, Sam, that you're trying to figure out how old I am. For now, I'll just say vampires aren't the only ones who don't age."

I hooked my arm on the back of Layla's chair. "Fair enough. What are we up against?"

"Layla, fill me in on what Agnes relayed to you in your vision," Zoey said.

Layla shrugged. "Not much to tell. She brought up her sister Maeve, who's keeping tabs on her. She confirmed she was my grandmother and told me that Maeve has our two babies."

"Twins?" Zoey asked.

"Quadruplets," I said. "Three girls and a boy."

Her rosy cheeks lost their color as soupy silence dangled over us.

Layla and I looked at each other while Zoey seemed to be frozen.

Layla slid her hand across the table and tapped it a couple of times. "Zoey, we know about the prophecy, if that's what has you spooked."

"We're well aware that one of our kids is prophesied to turn witches into vampires." My guess was that as a witch herself, Zoey was freaking out about the idea that she could be turned into a vampire. Supposedly, if that happened, she could lose her powers.

"Now I understand why Agnes sent you to me." Zoey's voice hitched. "There's a second part to that prophecy that only surfaced about six years ago. Right before Agnes disappeared, she showed up at the school. She was beside herself with fear. She'd found out that Maeve had a vision much like the seer had two hundred years ago." She sipped her soda.

Fucking great. Another prophecy, and this one had to be a doozie with the fear emanating from her.

Layla rested her hand on my thigh. "It's bad, isn't it?"

"It's not good," Zoey said. "You see, each coven is led by a head witch or Magistra, as she is called. This Magistra is only as strong as her coven. Some witches, though not all, are always seeking more power and control."

I remembered Greta mentioning that very thing. "And Maeve wants that."

Zoey gave me a nod. "Which is where the second half of the Monroe prophecy comes in. It states that the Monroe witch who bears the quadruplets will become the Mystic—the one true witch who will have ultimate power. Meaning, the Mystic doesn't need a coven." She laced her fingers together, resting her forearms on the table. "I teach a class on prophecies, and I have my students research them. They go as far as interviewing older witches, if they can, to find facts. Our goal at this school is to record all prophecies and predictions along with details like loopholes, whether a prophecy actually happened, and such. Since Maeve had this vision, I've been studying Mystics, and they date back to the seventeenth century. Only two have been recorded in history, but the details of how the two witches became a Mystic are different in each case."

Layla leaned back in her chair, her pulse beating rapidly. "There aren't any Mystics today?"

"No," Zoey said emphatically. "Those in my community who know about Mystics fear them simply because out of the two witches I'd mentioned, one was not destined to take on that role. She'd killed to become the Mystic, and she succeeded. In doing so, this witch abused her powers. Think black magic. If Maeve's vision has substance, then she'll need to be stopped at all costs. Otherwise, the world is in for darker times."

I felt her fear as if it were my own.

I covered Layla's hand that was still on my leg. "We're already there."

Zoey shuddered. "No, we're not. If Maeve succeeds, she'll wreak havoc. Witch wars will break out. Humans will suffer. Vampires, even. The world isn't ready for Maeve to rise to power."

Layla pressed her hand into my thigh, tensing up. "If I'm understanding all this, are you saying I should be the Mystic?"

"Again, if Maeve's vision is true, then yes," Zoey said. "Keep in mind that prophecies are predictions. Not all of them come true. Yet witches take them very seriously. In this case, Maeve certainly has, which leads me to believe she's figured out how to make herself become the Mystic."

"I didn't have a chance to ask Agnes, but I'm pretty sure Maeve was the dream walker who almost succeeded in having me plummet to my death," Layla said. "Yet how can I be the Mystic? My only magical ability is a banshee scream."

"The how is a longer story for another time," Zoey said. "We need to deal with Maeve. She isn't going to stop until she gets what she wants."

"Wait a second," Layla said. "Her success is predicated on killing me. Is it that easy? I'm dead, and she rises to power?"

Zoey placed her hands around her glass on the table. "That's the first part. She needs to sever the connection between you and your children. Since Monroes are blood witches, I'm guessing there will be some ceremonial blood ritual that will more than likely include your children, meaning she needs all four of them present."

I growled under my breath at the thought of anyone using my children for their benefit.

"Agnes said our children are special but also feared because together, they're the perfect storm," Layla said.

"If the first and second parts of the prophecy prove to be true, your quadruplets are a curse and a blessing," Zoey said.

I rose and helped myself to a glass of water. I would prefer blood, which not only took away my bloodthirst but helped to lower my pulse.

Zoey pushed her chair back, the legs creaking along the floor. "Why don't we get some air? I know this is a lot to take in. But it is necessary for you to understand before you face Maeve."

I couldn't imagine what Zoey had that would help us rescue Orion and Luna. Whatever it was, it sure as fuck better be a special weapon to kill Maeve. If not, I was prepared to use my bare hands.

30

LAYLA

Sam trailed behind Zoey and me as we traveled the halls of the school, passing classrooms, a theater, an auditorium, a witch lab, and other rooms that had no signs on them.

I had a ton of questions as I went through everything Zoey had told us so far. I was sure there was a ton more to learn, but like Sam, I just wanted to rescue Orion and Luna.

Here I'd thought Harriet was a force to be reckoned with. Granny paled in comparison to Maeve. Witches weren't people to fuck with. In my book, we had no armor, so to speak, to fight off witchcraft.

"Can Sam's elemental powers stop Maeve?" I asked.

Zoey came to a halt outside a door with no knob or handle. "He could give her a run for her money, but neither you nor he should be presumptuous to think air, water, earth, or fire can stop her." She regarded Sam and me. "I caution you. Her husband is ex-military. He has his own small army around Maeve."

I didn't want to brag, but we had an impressive military team of our own.

"Is her husband a vampire or shifter or even a witch?" Sam asked.

"The Monroe coven doesn't have relations with vampires," she said. "But no, he's human from what Agnes told me years ago."

"We think she's working with a team of vampires, though," I added.

Zoey didn't react to my comment. Instead, she faced the door and held her palms up and drew an imaginary circle over the wood structure as she mumbled what sounded to me like gibberish. Within seconds, the door clicked open.

That was cool. I'd never witnessed a witch casting a spell.

"Follow me." She led us down a set of winding stone steps.

The air was musty, with a scary vibe to the atmosphere.

She flipped a switch at the bottom, and the room was bathed in soft-yellow lights that dangled from the ceiling.

I walked around, examining shelves packed with history and reference books, closed cabinets, and a glass-enclosed case containing relics of amulets, crystals, and talismans. I didn't see anything that might be the infinity bracelets that Agnes had spoken of.

Sam was doing the same as me while Zoey was muttering a spell to open a cabinet.

"Zoey, why do you think Agnes disappeared?" I asked. One of the many questions pinging my brain.

Zoey carried what must be the infinity bracelets over to a table. "To protect her husband but mostly to regain her powers. Agnes felt she needed to be able to stop Maeve one day, especially after Agnes learned of the second part of the prophecy. Of course, your children weren't born yet, but if Maeve had that vision, I wouldn't be surprised if she also had another one that showed her your babies being born."

Sam was super quiet. I imagined he was thinking through everything as well.

Zoey held up a leather bracelet that was connected on two ends with a silver infinity symbol. "Once you put this on, a witch can't use her powers on you. So Maeve can't cast any spells against you."

Sam picked up the second bracelet. "But I can use my elemental powers on her?"

Zoey shook her head. "It works both ways."

"When Layla and I face off with Maeve, we're basically humans. Is that what you're saying?" Sam asked.

Zoey's gray-blue eyes lit up. "That's a good analogy. You'll still have your normal vampire abilities but no elemental powers. No witch will be able to use spells against you as long as you're wearing the bracelet."

A thought hit me. "Do you have any for my children? Can we use something like this to stop the blood ritual? Or cloak them so no witch can find them?" Holy crap. That would be fantastic. That way, we wouldn't have to worry so much as they grew up.

Sam was bobbing his head. "Great idea."

Zoey adjusted the watch on her wrist. "We can talk about that later. First, let's focus on the task at hand. The second and most important element is unlocking Layla's powers."

I knitted my eyebrows. "If the bracelet prevents the use of magical powers, why is it important to unlock mine?"

"As a backup in case something happens to the bracelets. You don't want to be dead in the water. Also, it's time you become the Monroe witch you were destined to be."

"A Mystic," I said with a laugh. I was still having a hard time with that one.

"If that is your destiny, then yes." Her features hardened as if she was mad at me. "Don't take any of this lightly, Layla. I understand it can be daunting, but you might be the one to save all of us."

Her comment reminded me of my mom's message about Sam and me saving humanity.

I blew out a long-suffering sigh.

Zoey went over to a cabinet that was actually a refrigerator. It took me a beat to realize that to unlock my powers, I needed the blood from a Monroe witch who had come before me as Agnes's journal had stated. When Zoey opened the door, bright lights came on inside, illuminating six shelves of blood vials.

"You keep blood from other witches?" I asked.

Sam inched closer to the fridge. "Those vials can't be fresh."

Zoey tossed a look over her shoulder at Sam. "They don't have to be. The intended purpose isn't to nourish or transfuse into another but to unlock a witch's powers."

Sam closed the distance between us, standing beside me near the table. "How are you doing with all this?"

I leaned my head on his chest as he wrapped me in his arms. "Not sure yet. Too much to handle. But if any of this works to help us get Orion and Luna, I'll do just about anything."

"It can't be," Zoey said in a tone that made the hackles on my neck stand at attention.

Sam and I glanced at her backside. She was bent over, reaching into the bottom shelf.

"Is there a problem?" Sam asked.

"Agnes's blood isn't here," she said, sounding horrified. "I check this fridge at least twice a month. Mainly to be sure the unit is working. I did inventory two weeks ago, and it was here." She still had her head inside, seemingly looking again.

Sam's nostrils flared. "Who else has access to the fridge? And are there any other vials missing?"

"No one but me," she said, straightening as she closed the refrigerator. "Only Agnes's blood is gone. I hate to say this, but Maeve must've found out that Agnes kept her blood here."

I found the timing too coincidental since my recent vision with Agnes.

"You might be right," I said. "Agnes did tell me that Maeve has been keeping tabs on her. I think that was the reason Agnes was ambiguous in her instructions because she never outright said you had her blood. Her exact words were 'She has something that will help you rescue your babies. Ask her for the infinity bracelets too. She'll know you're legitimate.'"

"Unless you're working with Maeve," Sam said, scrutinizing Zoey.

If anyone could detect a liar, it was a vampire. On top of that, Sam's strong suit was his empath ability.

Tension, quick and thick, hurtled around the room.

Zoey's features hardened. "I'm trying to help, not start a war."

It was possible that Zoey was on team Maeve. My gut was saying otherwise only because when she'd been explaining the Mystic earlier, she'd visibly shuddered, particularly at the part about how if Maeve succeeded, witch wars would break out. Plus, it was clear to me how dumbfounded she was over the blood vial missing.

I grabbed Sam's arm. "She's on our side. Plus, the bracelets are important for our goal." At least, I thought so. We were up against witches. None of us were experienced in dealing with them.

Sam's jaw looked like it was set in stone. "What if you lose the bracelet? I would be comfortable knowing you had magical abilities to protect you. After all, Maeve is gunning for you."

Zoey took a seat. "At this point, the only way for Layla to unlock her powers is Agnes herself. I'm so sorry." Her tone was riddled with sorrow.

I sat in the chair next to her. "It's not your fault. You've been a great help. I can't be sure, but I think Agnes is with her sister, Maeve. In both of my visions with Agnes, she glanced over her shoulder before she said she had to go. That could mean she was being followed, although my gut is telling me otherwise. Still, is there a way for me to talk to Agnes on the phone instead of in a vision? And why the dream walking, anyway? Why not track me down in reality?"

Zoey combed her fingers through her short salt-and-pepper hair. "In instances where we're dealing with life and death, dream walking and entering another's visions is the safest way, and you did just mention that Maeve is keeping tabs on Agnes."

"So you don't have a phone number to contact Agnes?" Sam asked as he loomed over us with his arms folded over his chest and a frustrated look on his face.

"The fact that Agnes's blood vial is missing tells me she's been compromised. Maeve is onto her," Zoey said.

"Which might mean Maeve knows we're coming," I added.

Sam's fangs shot out. "I don't care. Once we have a location, I'm storming the damn farm."

"In North Dakota, right?" Zoey asked.

The excited butterflies stirred. "Do you have a specific address?"

Zoey sighed. "The last Agnes told me was that the coven lived two miles north of Bismarck. That was six years ago."

They were still there, according to Agnes.

"Again, I'm sorry." Zoey rose. "If I learn who stole the blood, I'll be sure to let you know."

I pushed to my feet. "I'm not an expert in witchcraft. Seems to me whoever stole the blood did know your spell to open the fridge."

"I'm well aware. I'm assuming the culprit found my personal grimoire only because that's where I kept the spell," she said.

Sam checked his watch, then shoved the bracelets into his pocket. "We need to head to the airport."

Several hallways later, we were standing outside the school. As we were saying our goodbyes, a question popped into my brain.

"Zoey, we talked a lot about the Mystic. You seem more worried about that than a child of ours turning witches into vampires. Aren't you afraid of becoming a vampire and losing your powers?" I had a feeling I knew the answer, but I wanted to hear her thoughts.

"That pales in comparison to what we could face if Maeve succeeds in becoming the Mystic," she said.

Sam shoved a hand through his hair, clearly disgruntled and pissed. "Can witches detect a vampire or shifter in the immediate area around the farm?"

"A witch can feel another witch's magic close by, or they could have visions of anyone coming." She slipped her hands into the pockets of her black slacks. "No matter how you slice it, you have a challenge ahead of you." She frowned. "I will leave you with one final thought. I explained a lot of information today. So just remember that prophecies are predictions. There are loopholes to most of them, not all of them come true, and some can change. Yet perception is reality, and Maeve believes in her vision. Stop her at all costs."

We planned to do just that.

31

LAYLA

I'd never thought the day would arrive when we could possibly be bringing Orion and Luna home. I was humbled, grateful, and amazed at the outpouring of help we had—the Vampire Navy SEALs, Dane Gray, Rebekah, and half her Special Forces unit were ready to rescue my children. Plus, her remaining team was due in tomorrow, but we were praying like crazy that Orion and Luna would already be safe in our arms by then.

We had to change the plan at the last minute when we learned from the local news the day before that Maeve and her husband were attending a charity event in downtown Bismarck that night. Actually, they were the honored guests. But the gala had started an hour ago, and the couple had yet to leave.

I was ready to pull out my hair and unleash a banshee scream if we didn't do something soon. Knowing Orion and Luna were literally a football field in distance from Sam and me had me gnawing every nail on my fingers in the back seat of the SUV.

My husband, who was next to me, wanted to bash some heads in. The military vampire was itching to exercise every weapon he had strapped to him.

Leading up to this point, there had been six days of sleepless nights since we'd returned from Sacred Flame Academy. Everyone had been working nonstop, gathering intel. Based on Zoey's knowledge that the farm was located two miles north of Bismarck, Tripp had a military drone fly over the area to pinpoint farms and take pictures. Once we had two farms narrowed down within that radius, Dane had shifted under the cover of darkness to sniff out Orion's and Luna's scents. Thankfully, Jordyn had given Dane items of Orion and Luna's, so he had what he needed to execute his mission. I'd bawled when he returned and told us our babies were in one of two houses on a farm exactly two point five miles from downtown Bismarck.

"Do you think they're not going to the event?" I asked, bouncing my knee.

Conrad eyed me in the rearview mirror. "Do we have the wrong date?"

We didn't. I'd triple-checked. I'd jumped up and down when we learned that this was a perfect opening for us.

Tripp looked at his phone from the passenger seat. "No. The gala is this evening."

"We do this tonight, regardless," Sam said, tense and lethal. "Our plans were set even before we knew about this gala. So we stick with them. If the witch does leave, it would, of course, make it easier for us. But right now, I don't give a fuck. I'm getting my kids out tonight." Sam reached over the armrest between us, his palm facing up. "Right?"

I grabbed his hand. "Right," I parroted.

We would've preferred to have more boots on the ground as backup, just in case. As it stood, there were fourteen of us. But with Sam and me concentrating on our kids, we wouldn't be able to fight like we wanted to, especially not while carrying them out.

From the drone pictures, we'd counted ten people on-site, not including Orion and Luna. If Maeve and her husband were leaving for the gala, that would reduce our opponents' head count to eight and even fewer if guards accompanied them.

Not only that, but none of us were exactly comfortable that we were dealing with witches—a new enemy that the SEALs weren't experienced with, nor were the shifters, for that matter. Sam and I were wearing the infinity bracelets, and part of me was skeptical that they would even work. Maybe because I was having a hard time believing in witchcraft or Zoey, for that matter. We'd only met her once, and while my gut believed she was on our side, I was still waffling back and forth. What if the bracelets were designed to hurt us in some way rather than help us?

"I wish you had another vision with Agnes," Sam said. "That would've given us some much-needed insight."

Considering her blood had been stolen from Zoey Thornton's fridge on school property, I was betting Maeve knew what Agnes was up to, which was probably why Agnes hadn't contacted me. Regardless, we were assuming Agnes was on the farm. If so, I was wishing upon a thousand stars that she was on our side and not luring me in to kill me. If I needed my witch powers in our efforts to rescue Orion and Luna, then I might have to slit her wrists unless she was on our side.

Tripp's radio crackled, drawing me back to hell.

"We have movement." Petty Officer Olivia Brock's voice was loud and clear. "Couple is leaving with two guards."

I sighed loudly as Sam squeezed my hand, bobbing his head, his fangs elongating, his green eyes melting to liquid silver. He was definitely bursting at the seams.

"Kendra, the targets are on the move," Tripp said into his radio.

"Copy that. They just announced to the guests that the couple is on their way," she returned.

She was at the event to keep an eye on Maeve and her husband. The couple had been instrumental in leading the charge and raising money for the new children's hospital that had been built in Bismarck.

"I'm in position on the north side of the property," Petty Officer Olivia Brock continued. "We have two men carrying weapons and guarding the main house facing the cornfield and another two outside the two-story home closest to the barn. No occupants in the main house."

"Kraft, check in," Tripp ordered.

"Ben and I are in position in the barn. From our vantage point, we count four bodies in the two-story home—one upstairs and three downstairs. It appears there is one adult body in what looks to be the main living area and two who are smaller in size in a separate room."

I sucked in air. "Do you think that's Orion and Luna?"

"That's the building where Dane picked up their scent," Sam said.

I blinked away tears. This wasn't the time for a meltdown or a celebration. But for fuck's sake, we were so close to holding our babies again.

"Shifters are ready," Dane said into the radio. "I won't shift unless it's necessary."

"All right, everyone," Tripp said into his radio. "It's 9:15 p.m. Layla and Sam are heading in." He swiveled in his seat and regarded Sam and me. "Ready?"

Yes. Excitement coursed through me that I would have Orion and Luna in my arms shortly.

No. Nerves were a bitch and made me want to vomit.

Just the same, I nodded, moistening my dry lips with my tongue. It had been fourteen days of suffering since Orion and Luna had been kidnapped from their cribs. Sam was right. Whether or not Maeve and her husband had left, we had to execute the plan. I couldn't go a minute more, let alone another day, without seeing our son and daughter.

Sam, on the other hand, said, "Fuck yeah." To say he was wound tight was an understatement. But he lived for the battles, that adrenaline rush, and he used his fear as well as other people's to keep his wits about him.

Conrad laughed as he shook his head. "Only you, man, would get your rocks off in tense situations."

"The only way to stay alive," Sam fired back.

"Truth," Tripp chimed in.

My dad always said that fear was good and kept a person on their toes. It certainly had when I'd hunted vampires. This shouldn't be any different, except we were up against witches. That was the issue making me apprehensive.

Nevertheless, I grabbed my backpack that had a bulletproof blanket and other amenities for one of the babies in case of an emergency. Sam had one as well.

Once the four of us were outside the SUV, a shifter trotted up out of the tall brush that lined the side of the road. I recognized Rebekah immediately with her tan coat, red-tipped ears, and glowing amber eyes. She dipped her head at us before she pushed her snout into my hand as if to say good luck. Then she turned her head slightly, causing me to follow her line of sight. In the distance, several shimmering pairs of different-colored eyes cut through the darkness. Yet again, I thought she was trying to tell me that she and her team had my back.

I petted her muzzle, nodding. Then she darted off. I owed her a huge apology when the time was right for suspecting that she might've been the woman who had been talking on the phone with Roman when Rianne overheard Roman's conversation.

Sam hiked his backpack higher on his shoulders, ensuring it was secure. Then he checked his watch. "I would like to be in and out in thirty minutes."

"Conrad and I will be waiting right here," Tripp said, looking as badass as Sam. "If you two get separated, there's a second vehicle a mile away on the north side of the farm. Olivia will be there. Any questions?"

"Sam, do you think you should wear that infinity bracelet?" I asked. "I think you shouldn't. Maeve isn't there, and you need your elemental powers."

"I've been thinking about that, but there could be more witches. I can always rip it off if I have to," he said. "You need to keep yours on. I want you to leave there alive." His green eyes morphed into burnished steel.

"Move, you two," Tripp ordered.

"Good luck," Conrad said.

Luck, lots of it, would be fantastic, yet somehow, my intuition was poking me in the gut, saying that all this seemed too easy. I was assuming my children were important to Maeve's plan to become the Mystic. If so, why would she leave only four men to guard the property?

I'd voiced that concern to Sam and Tripp. While they knew it could be a trap, we had to take the chance. I wasn't complaining. If it came down to it, I would give myself up to save Orion and Luna.

32

LAYLA

S am and I were running across the field. Thank God the moon was out and providing a smidge of light for me to see. The closer we got to the barn, the tighter the knot gripped my stomach.

Just before we cleared the field, Sam stopped short, holding a fist in the air.

The blood rushed out of me. "What is it?"

"A woman is on the move," Kraft said into our comms. "Hold tight."

Sam grabbed my wrists and pulled me to a crouching position.

"It appears she's heading from the home closest to the barn to the main one." Olivia's voice came over the comms.

The air was deathly silent, and the only sound was my pulse in my ears, just like when I'd hunted vampires. The first time I had, I peed my pants. It had been quite some time since then, but with the way my nerves were going wild, I wouldn't be surprised if I did that again.

"She's inside. You're clear to continue," Olivia said.

Sam and I took off.

Once we were in the barn, I released a huge amount of air.

Phase one was a success. Now on to phase two.

Kraft stepped out of the shadows. The tattooed petty officer was massive, with the whites of his eyes standing out amid his black clothing and vampire-black orbs.

If Ben was in the loft, he didn't show himself. Instead, he said in our ears, "All quiet. We have a heat signature upstairs, and two in the first-floor room on the south side."

Kraft stabbed a gloved finger to the right of the barn. "Your kids should be in that room. There's ten yards between here and there. So stay low and move. I'll give the signal to have Dane cut the power once you leave this barn, then he'll join you inside. At that point, you have five minutes at most to get in and get out. We'll deal with the guards and the woman who is in the main house."

Sam and I adjusted the headlamps from around our necks to our heads, then we checked ourselves one more time before grabbing our guns.

"Follow behind me, baby doll."

I had my weapon angled downward, staying close to him with my heart in my throat.

When we reached the opposite end of the barn at the other exit, Sam gave Kraft the nod. In turn, Kraft radioed Dane.

"It's a go," Dane said into our ears.

As if that were a switch that flipped my focus from cloudy to clear, I jumped into action, running behind Sam. He kicked the door in and moved to go inside but seemed like he couldn't.

"What's wrong?" I whispered.

"I'm hitting an invisible wall. You try."

I stepped over the threshold and had no problem entering. "They must've put a spell on the house to ward off vampires." That had to be it.

"Motherfucker," he said through clenched teeth.

I didn't even think. We had come this far. We couldn't quit now. I bolted inside, following the hallways to the room on the far side while Sam radioed Dane.

Footsteps pounded somewhere nearby.

I tuned out everything but my own breathing until I reached the room where Orion and Luna were supposed to be. The second I opened the door and laid eyes on my babies sleeping in cribs, I gulped in air as tears shot out. It took me several deep breaths to calm my pulse and a few rapid blinks to clear my vision before I rushed in—only to slam into an invisible wall.

What the fuck? I guessed I now understood why Maeve had only left four guards to patrol the property.

"I can't get into the room," I said into my comm. "There's a spell on this one too."

"Abort, Layla," Sam said.

I tried again. No luck. Then a thought sideswiped me. I removed my infinity bracelet and shoved it into my pocket. Maybe that was blocking me. After all, it was designed to protect me from witchcraft. I tried again and failed. I was beginning to hate witches.

"Layla, talk to me," Sam said in my comm.

I am so fucking close. I am not leaving without them.

Sam was talking frantically in my ear, telling me to abort.

I couldn't. This was our only chance. Otherwise, I feared we would never see our son and daughter again.

Rage kick-started that familiar tingling in my stomach. The one right before my banshee scream took over.

Think, Layla.

I needed a witch or Agnes. Maybe she was the person upstairs. I darted down the hall, gun at the ready, and into a cluttered room containing empty twin beds, ammunition, guns, tranquilizer darts, and empty beer cans everywhere.

I banked right when I spied the stairs and started in that direction when I saw Dane escorting a white-haired woman down the steps.

Her brown eyes took me in. "Layla? You came? You must've gotten my blood." She glanced at my wrist. "I don't see the infinity bracelet."

"Agnes?" I asked, not lowering my gun. I didn't one hundred percent trust her, even though she'd given me key information in a vision and had calmed me down when she told me Orion and Luna were alive. For all I knew, she'd done all that to lure me here to kill me.

"Put the gun away," she said.

"No. How come I can't get into the room where my children are?"

Dane nudged her to move, his red wolf eyes glistening.

She inched around the clutter. "Were you able to find Zoey Thornton?"

"Someone stole your blood from her."

Her mouth fell open. "You need to leave now."

"I'm not going anywhere without my babies," I bit out.

"If Zoey doesn't have my blood, Maeve is onto me."

My arms were beginning to shake holding the gun. "Are you saying I've walked into a trap?"

"I don't know. Maeve doesn't tell me anything. When she learned I was dream walking the last time I spoke to you in a vision, she took my powers away."

Dane glanced out the open front door at a prone body of a man. "Hurry up, Layla. We don't have much time."

Agnes glanced up at him over her shoulder. "You brought a shifter with you? Smart."

Dane was in human form, except his canines were on display.

"Where's Maeve's daughter?" she asked.

I had no clue who she was talking about. "Not important."

"Yes, it is," Agnes said. "Patricia is as powerful as her mother. She probably alerted Maeve the second the lights went out."

I lifted my eyebrows. "Then she can remove the spell on that room. Someone find Maeve's daughter, Patricia," I said into my comm.

"You won't find her. Plus, the only one who can remove the spell on that room is Maeve."

I lowered my arms, seething, nostrils flaring.

Sam was shouting in my ear. "Talk to me, Layla."

I threw my head back and unleashed my inner banshee that was louder and higher than it had ever been.

The comm popped out of my ear, glass shattered, pictures on the wall fell to the floor, and the house shook on its foundation. When I finally righted my head, Agnes was holding her ears, and Dane was snarling at me. Good to know that my one magical ability didn't make them pass out like it did humans.

The aftermath of my Hollywood scream had the wolves howling and my babies wailing, and Sam was jumping over the body on the porch.

"What's going on?" he asked, taking one step over the threshold then another. "The spell broke."

I dashed back the way I came until I was rushing inside the babies' room. No barrier. Holy shit! Had my scream broken the spell?

I froze for a second as I stared at Orion and Luna for the first time in two weeks. Tears poured down my face as I lifted Luna. The minute she was against me, she stopped crying.

Sam blew in, and his eyes bugged out. "Thank fuck." He dove into action and grabbed Orion.

We made quick work of wrapping our babies into the bullet-proof blankets.

Agnes came in, seemingly astounded. "How did you learn to do that? A vampire shouldn't be inside, and you couldn't have broken Maeve's spell."

"But I did," I said without looking at her.

Sam touched his comm. "Olivia just radioed that the woman in the main house is gone."

"There's an escape route in the basement," Agnes said. "I have no doubt Patricia called her mother. This place will soon be crawling with men. So you need to hurry."

After we had our babies secured to us and ready to leave, Sam froze as he touched his comm again. "Seems Agnes is right. We have three vehicles turning down the road along the farm."

Sam and I hurried out.

"Wait," Agnes said, following us. "If you're to leave here in one piece, you'll need my blood." She held her finger up to Sam. "I don't know how long it will take before you have your magic. It all depends on you, Layla."

Holding his son to his chest, Sam punctured her skin with a fang.

"Open your mouth, Layla," she ordered.

I did as she commanded.

When her blood hit my tongue, a wave of dizziness knocked me back a step, warmth zipped through me, and my vision sharpened. If I didn't know better, I would've thought she'd given me a triple shot of bourbon.

"If all of us make it out alive, I want to see you again, Layla," she said. "If not, I wish you the best." She kissed me on the head. "Go."

Sam and I ran for our lives through the house and out the back door. The engines grew louder, gunfire ensued, and just as we were about to enter the barn, headlights blinded us from the opposite end before the car sped toward us.

I darted right. Sam went left.

The barn collapsed as the SUV screeched to a halt.

Holding Luna tightly, I bolted away from the car, running as fast as I could when another vehicle blocked me.

A man jumped out of the back seat.

My pulse was so high I was sure I was a second from blacking out. Instead, I lost my breath when I laid eyes on the blond vampire standing before me.

Roman opened his arms, wearing a sinister grin. "Layla, I've missed you."

If we had our doubts about Roman's involvement with the

witches, we didn't anymore. Now I just had to figure a way out, because I was not becoming his prisoner or anyone else's ever again.

To be continued…

———

Sam & Layla's story continues in ***The Rebirth*** and will release on 8/15/2023. You can preorder your copy HERE.

ABOUT THE AUTHOR

Bestselling author **S.B. Alexander** is an independent author with over 30 titles to date. She writes paranormal, new adult, and sweet romances that feature hot heroes stealing hearts.

S.B. or Susan as she likes to be called is a navy veteran, former high school teacher, and former corporate sales executive. She's a lover of sports, especially baseball, although nowadays you can find her on the golf course, swinging for that hole-in-one.

Her motto: "Life is too short to waste. So live every moment like it's your last."

You can connect with S.B. Alexander in the following ways:
Reader Group: http://sbalexander.com/sbareaderroom
Author Website: https://sbalexander.com
Newsletter: https://sbalexander.com/newsletter
Email: susan@sbalexander.com

facebook.com/sbalexander.authorpage

twitter.com/sbalex_author

instagram.com/sbalexanderauthor

amazon.com/author/sbalexander

bookbub.com/authors/s-b-alexander

pinterest.com/sbalexander0046

GLOSSARY OF TERMS

Natural-born vampire: A human born with the vampire gene that, when activated, will turn them into a vampire.

Activation process: Those who carry the vampire gene can only turn by drinking the blood of their vampire father at the age of sixteen years or older.

Council of Elders – A group of five vampires who set the laws.

Genetic engineering: Turning humans into vampires through a process of restructuring their DNA.

Cobalt – A vampire's kryptonite. The metal will kill a vampire if staked through the heart. It will also burn a vampire's skin if they come in contact with it.

Reproduction: A natural-born vampire is born by a male vampire and a human female with a rare blood type of Vel negative.

Council of Eternal Affairs: The legal department of the vampire government.

Vampire characteristics: Sunlight doesn't burn them. Their hearts beat at <5 bpm. Skin temperature is ten degrees cooler than a human. Eye color changes to black except for a few chosen ones.

Steven Mason: Vampire and father to twins Jo and Sam Mason. He's dubbed the most powerful of all vampires because of his many powers, including his mind-reading abilities. He can only read minds when touching someone except when it comes to his children. His normal eye color is green. His vampire eye color is silver.

Jo Mason: Turned at sixteen. Powers include seeing the future through her dreams, mind-reading without touching a person, telekinesis, and she's an elemental with the ability to manipulate water, air, earth, and fire. Her normal eye color is silver. Her vampire eye color is violet.

Sam Mason: Turned at sixteen. Powers include feeling what others feel (Empath), telekinesis, and he can compel a person using a series of numbers woven into a magical spell. He's also an elemental with the ability to manipulate water, air, earth, and fire. His normal eye color is green. His vampire eye color is silver.

Guardians: Vampires who are equivalent to the human police.